ANGEL AND THE FRENCH WIDOW

If Agnes Turner had not gone back to the hairdressers to collect a hairspray the whole weird, tragic, stupid affair would never have happened. Louise Le Mesurier, occupant of the ground floor flat where Agnes lived, would still be alive and Agnes would not have rescued the dog and set off a flare of hatred. But the hairspray was fetched and Agnes arrived back at her flat ten minutes later than she would have and saw and heard what was to start the snowball rolling downhill, getting bigger and bigger as it rolled and more and more dangerous.

ANGEL AND
THE FRENCH WIDOW

Angel And The French Widow

by

Anthea Cohen

Magna Large Print Books
Long Preston, North Yorkshire,
BD23 4ND, England.

British Library Cataloguing in Publication Data.

Cohen, Anthea
    Angel and the French widow.

    A catalogue record of this book is
    available from the British Library

    ISBN   0-7505-1806-5

First published in Great Britain in 2000
by Constable, an imprint of Constable & Robinson Ltd.

Cover illustration © Adam Swaine by arrangement with
Swift Imagery International Photo Library

The right of Anthea Cohen to be identified as the author of this
work has been asserted by her in accordance with the
Copyright, Designs and Patents Act, 1988

Published in Large Print 2002 by arrangement with
Constable & Robinson Ltd.

Magna Large Print is an imprint of Library Magna Books Ltd.

Printed and bound in Great Britain by
T.J. (International) Ltd., Cornwall, PL28 8RW

PROLOGUE

It is strange when you look back, how a small, seemingly unimportant incident can trigger off a series of events leading to something that shatters peace of mind and alters many people's lives.

In this case, if Agnes Turner had not gone back to her hairdresser's to collect a hairspray she had paid for and forgotten to put into her bag, if she had decided to leave it till her next visit, if she had said to herself, 'Never mind, I will collect it next week, I've got enough to last till then...' If she had said that, thought that, the whole weird, tragic, stupid affair would not have happened. No one would have died and Louise Le Mesurier, occupant of the ground-floor flat in the block where Agnes now lived, who at that moment, the moment of Agnes's decision, was sitting in front of her dressing-table mirror, outlining her lips with a pink lipstick pencil, would still be alive.

Agnes would not have rescued the dog and set off a flare of hatred that would eventually lead to...

But the hairspray was fetched and so Agnes arrived back at her flat about ten minutes later than she would have, and so saw and heard what was to start the snowball rolling downhill, getting bigger and bigger as it rolled, and more and more dangerous.

1

A week before her visit to the hairdresser, Agnes had decided to give a small drinks party, just for the other occupants of the flats, six in all. She had slipped a note through each door, omitting one ground-floor flat as they were away in Australia visiting their daughter and son-in-law.

She had suggested six o'clock and the first to arrive were her nearest neighbours on the top floor, number 5. Agnes's flat was number 6. Major and Mrs Warburton. Mrs Warburton was a small white-haired woman with a low breathy voice. Every remark she made sounded as if she was telling a secret. Indeed she cast her eyes from left to right as she spoke, emphasising the impression. The Major was typical of the breed.

Agnes had moved into her new flat six weeks ago now, and it was Mrs Warburton who had acquainted her with the lives and doings of the other residents. Mr Leeming had lost his wife two years ago and had sold his big house in Devon, had no children and drank rather a lot. Miss Horrocks was said to have been a hospital matron but had to retire early due to ill health. The French lady in Flat 2, according to Mrs Warburton, 'keeps herself to herself, but is always very smart and has a lovely car.' Agnes had taken all this in with some boredom, but now, as they were to be her guests for a brief period, was rather glad of the information.

Mr Leeming was the next to arrive and Agnes noticed he already smelt of whisky, so she offered him that.

'Arthur, Arthur's my name. Don't call me Mr Leeming, for God's sake,' he said as he accepted his drink and sat down with a bump beside Mrs Warburton on the settee. He downed half the drink in one swallow. The front door bell rang. It was Miss Horrocks. She smiled generously, showing very false teeth.

'So nice of you,' she said, looking curiously round Agnes's flat. She took a seat slightly away from the rest, a straight-backed chair.

'Oh, wouldn't you prefer something more comfortable, the armchair?' Agnes said.

Miss Horrocks shook her head apologetically.

'My back,' she said, and accepted the small glass of sweet sherry she had requested.

The French lady from Flat 2 did not put in an appearance. Agnes felt slightly put out. She could have telephoned, said she already had an engagement, at least thanked Agnes for the invitation.

The little party was to Agnes incredibly boring. Most of the talk was about television programmes, then the conversation turned to the flats.

'The lift acted most peculiarly last week, half stopped between floors.'

Miss Horrocks put her sherry glass down on the table beside her and refused another. Agnes wondered why she didn't just walk up the one flight, then remembered the woman's comment about her back and excused her.

'This cleaner's not as good as Mrs Jenvy, pity she left.' Major Warburton threw this into the conversation and was greeted by a small storm of agreement, especially and unexpectedly from Arthur Leeming.

'Someone trod some dog muck in – well, I suppose it was dog muck. Anyway, it was there for three days.'

This remark caused even Miss Horrocks to vibrate a little.

'Yes, I saw it, and she doesn't hoover properly. She should have used 1001 on that mark, that works well on stained carpets.'

Her guests grew increasingly animated. Agnes learned a lot about the flats. Someone banged the door when they came in and out. The front door needed oiling. The paper boy was using the lift, the milkman was unreliable.

Agnes heaved a sigh of relief when they at

11

last departed, but she told herself she had done her bit and she saw no reason to ask them again. As she shut the door on them, she felt a little pang, a little longing for Rose Cottage, her last home, and her dog Mac, and the grassy wild garden.

Rose Cottage, when she had bought it, had been surrounded by fields. Now these fields had been sold by the farmers who owned them to developers. Soon the fields were transformed into estates, bungalows and houses which had sprung up like mushrooms. The leafy lanes had turned into roads with council-cut lawns and faultless flowering cherry trees at regular intervals. Not a scene Agnes had liked at all. But Rose Cottage had fetched a good price and the fields were not so important when Mac died at the ripe old age of seventeen.

Because she loved Sussex, Agnes had determined to stay there. The flat in Hove had been for her the beginning of a new lifestyle, but without her dog, her garden and the few friends she had made, who had also sold up because of the building of the estate, she wasn't quite sure just what this new life would entail.

Agnes was not a great reader, she didn't play golf or paint or belong to any institutes or lunch clubs. Now she was settled in her flat and had made the few alterations necessary to her taste, she was bored. As always she needed a purpose in life and at the moment there wasn't one.

The small drinks party had done nothing to make her feel more lively, more comfortable. She was still a little annoyed about the French woman completely ignoring her invitation. If she was not free that evening, surely it would have been more polite to telephone and say so? Or maybe leave a note.

Agnes had seen the woman a few times on her way into or out of the flats, once arriving in a taxi. Agnes had had the time to admire the well-tailored black suit, the small fashionable hat perched on her short fair hair, the high, high heeled shoes, wellshaped legs and sheer black stockings. Even then though, on the few occasions she passed Agnes, her smile had been brief and rather cold. She had never spoken.

Agnes shrugged her shoulders as she thought of her. Louise Le Mesurier. Perhaps she liked to keep herself to herself. To be fair she hardly fitted with any of the others. In fact Agnes thought her clothes and general appearance were more like her own. Agnes felt if the woman would stop and speak they might find they had perhaps something in common.

A week after the little drinks party, Agnes had an appointment with the hairdresser, her third since she had moved. The first

13

appointment with a salon in Hove had been a near disaster. Agnes was very particular about her hair. Fine and soft, it had to be very carefully cut, so she had only trusted the first hairdresser to a shampoo and set. The girl, in spite of instructions, had used rollers that had made curls and waves rather than the straight hair that fell back into place if it was blown about by the wind or brushed and combed.

The next hairdresser, called rather unfortunately Pretty Heads, was in Brighton. Agnes had visited it once already and she had decided to return and risk a trim. Parking was difficult, but that was a universal problem in Brighton. Luckily, after a little driving around, she found a place a short walk from Pretty Heads. The day was fine, cold and with a slight chilly breeze. Agnes tied on a headscarf after she had locked the car, just in case her trim was a disaster when she left and the light breeze blew it into disarray.

However, the result after the girl had cut the hair a very tiny bit shorter was exactly as Agnes wanted it. She turned her head from side to side, viewed it in the back mirror and was pleased.

'Very nice. Can I book an appointment for next week, Valerie, just a shampoo and set, and may I have a large Elnet spray?'

Valerie looked pleased, put the spray on

the table beside Agnes and went to the desk to make out the bill. Agnes paid and it was not until she reached her car that she realised she had left the hairspray behind. Should she go back and fetch it, or leave it till next week? She hesitated, then made up her mind. She relocked the car and walked back to Pretty Heads. She thought she had enough of the spray at home to last a week, but she wasn't quite sure.

Valerie had not noticed the Elnet when Agnes walked back into the salon. Agnes picked it up and waved it at the girl, who was just starting another client. She smiled.

'Oh, I didn't see it, Mrs Turner, or I would have run after you.'

'Never mind, it was my fault for being so forgetful.' Agnes smiled back at her and unhurriedly left. Before she went through the front door, she took the headscarf out of her handbag and put it on, tying the ends under her chin.

'A little breezy out there,' she said.

Valerie nodded in reply. Agnes returned to her car and this time started for home.

She parked her Porsche expertly into her reserved parking space outside the large white-painted block of flats. The reserved parking place was an expensive luxury, but every time she drove into it, she felt it was money well spent. The yellow-coated wardens kept a close eye on the parking spaces and, in the seven weeks since Agnes had moved in, only once had she found her space occupied, and the eagle-eyed warden had soon sent that car on its way.

The front at Hove was almost deserted. This was partly because it was lunch-time and partly because the chilly February breeze had now blown in a slight misty rain.

Agnes opened her locking device and heard the reassuring 'clunk' of the remote controlled locks. She was about to turn and walk up the four steps to the front door of the flats when she stopped. A high shrill scream had shattered the air.

2

It came from across the road opposite where Agnes was standing. She caught a brief glimpse of three youths and two girls. One of the youths was swinging something round, waist high on what looked like a piece of rope. At that moment a large white removal van passed and blotted out her view. Then the girl screamed again. The big van passed and Agnes was able to get a clear and uninterrupted view of what was happening on the other side of the road.

The two other youths were egging their

companion on, laughing and staggering about in a way that made Agnes suspect they were drunk, but what was on the end of what she had taken for a length of rope was a small black and white dog.

That was enough for Agnes. Any animal in distress and she was there, to rescue, to help. Hardly looking to right or left, she crossed the road, narrowly avoiding being hit by a red car.

'Want to die early, love?' the driver yelled at her.

She hardly heard what he said, but put up a hand in a hasty apology and dashed on. The girl was still screaming. This time Agnes could distinguish the words in between the screams.

'Give her back to me, you'll hurt her. Don't do it, don't do it, please!'

Agnes took in the close-up of the scene with horror. The little dog was hanging from its collar on the end of a leash which the boy was swinging round. Even as she saw the dog twirl, it hit the thick green-painted balustrade that separated the promenade from the six-foot or more drop down to the sand. She grabbed the boy's outstretched arm, pulled the loop of the lead from his hand and pushed him with her free hand.

She saw his face for a second. It was white and thin. A livid purple birthmark covered one side, stretching back to his ear and a

17

little way down his neck towards the dirty blue collar of his shirt. His eyes were wide, round and wild. The purple mark made his skin look whiter.

'Bugger off, who do you think you are?' His voice was thick, slurred.

Agnes thought again, drink or drugs.

The other two boys were leaning against the railings and making howling noises, like dogs, at the two girls. One girl, the one screaming, rushed forward to where Agnes was holding the puppy. The other girl suddenly turned and ran, her short dark hair blowing back. She did not look round.

The boy made as if to snatch the dog out of Agnes's arms, but as he came forward so did she; she freed one hand with difficulty, and pushed him with all her might. The attack was unexpected, and the boy stumbled backward a few steps. Behind him was a gap, an opening in the green-painted railings, to give access to ten concrete steps leading down to the beach. As he fell backward, Agnes was propelled forward. She saw him go backward down the steps, yelling, 'You bitch, you bitch, I'll get you for this!'

His two companions leaned over the railing and looked at him, still letting out their maniacal howls. Then, as Agnes moved away carrying the dog, the girl following her, they started down the steps to join their mate. One nearly fell – he was unsteady, still yelling. One or two passers-by looked their way but did nothing.

Agnes and the girl waited for a break in the traffic then crossed over the road to the Porsche. Agnes gently handed the dog over while she unlocked the car and motioned the girl to get into the passenger seat.

'Get in, do you know your way to the vet's?'

The car glided away from the kerb. The girl nodded, cradling the puppy in her arms. It was moving more now.

'Yes, she had her injection there only last week. She didn't like it.'

She was still crying but was more controlled, the tears running down her cheeks. The puppy moved a little, raised its head and coughed.

'I thought he'd killed her, I really did!'

As they stopped at a red traffic light, Agnes turned and looked at the girl. Fair frizzy hair, good skin, no make-up. Clothes – typical teenager – denim jacket and jeans, hideous shoes. The jacket and jeans were not the cheap variety, so designer clothes. Well-modulated voice.

'What happened to your friend?' Agnes asked.

The lights flashed green and the car started forward. The girl sniffed.

'There's some tissues in the glove compartment. I said, what happened to your friend?' Agnes repeated the question.

'She was frightened, she ran away.'

Agnes made no comment. They drove a little further into Brighton. There were a few more people about now, and the rain had stopped.

'This is the road. Turn left, the surgery is about four buildings up on the right. It says "Veterinary surgery". Look, there it is.'

Agnes drove in through the open gate and parked the car, nose to the surgery wall.

'Stay there,' she said and went round to the passenger side of the car, opened the door, and gently took the dog from the girl's arms.

As they entered the waiting room, Agnes was relieved to see it was empty. A white-coated girl was sitting at the desk eating a sandwich but she got up immediately.

'Run over?' she said. Agnes shook her head. 'No, half choked to death. Is the vet here?' She was afraid the girl would say he had gone to lunch.

'Yes, he is. Hold on a moment.' She knocked and then opened the door behind her desk.

'Mr Singer, emergency.' The vet, still in his white coat, lunchtime or not, turned immediately from the white-fronted cupboard. 'What happened? Lay the dog on the table.'

He pointed to a table with a light above it. Agnes gently put the puppy down. It tried to

20

get to its feet but then plopped down again, still coughing.

As Agnes explained what had happened, the vet began gently to examine the little creature which seemed to be recovering more and more as the minutes went by.

The smells of disinfectant, hospital smells, brought back memories to Agnes. Memories of her past as a nurse and also sadder ones of Mac. She stood back a little and placed her hand on the girl's arm, smiled at her. The receptionist put her head round the surgery door.

'Could you give me your name and—'

'You go and give her your name and address and the puppy's particulars. You said you had been here before.'

The girl reluctantly left the room and the receptionist pulled the door nearly shut behind them. Agnes turned to the vet.

'What do you think, Mr Singer?'

'I'd like to give the moron who did this a damned good hiding, but luckily he doesn't seem to have done as much harm as one would have thought, probably because of your quick intervention.'

The puppy stood up, coughed again and began to wag her tail.

'She came to you for her injection about a week ago, Mr Singer.'

'I thought I recognised the young lady. Are you...?'

21

Agnes shook her head. 'No, I don't know her name even. I was just parking my car when I... My name is Turner, by the way. May she have her collar on again?' The vet nodded. 'I'm so glad you were here.' Agnes fastened on the puppy's collar loosely.

'Lucky I was – I usually go home to lunch – but it's equally lucky you were there to rescue her. The pup could easily have been choked to death.'

An hour later, Agnes was driving the girl home. Her name was Pamela Roberts. The dog's name was Polly. The girl who had run away was called Tina. Agnes learned all this as she drove, and her own assessment of the girl's appearance was confirmed as Pamela directed her into the drive of a very up-market house in the suburbs of Brighton.

'Do come in, Mrs Turner, please,' Pamela said.

As she parked outside the front door it opened and a tall, good-looking man came out, followed by an especially tall woman.

'What's happened, darling? Are you all right?'

Explanations all round. Agnes was asked in, given tea. They were very pleasant people and grateful to Agnes to an almost embarrassing degree, wanting to compensate her for the vet's fee. It took some time to convince them that the vet had not charged anything.

Agnes left after a cascade of thanks, even from Polly, who was now completely recovered, frisking around the floor after a toy.

Three days after her visit to the hairdresser, Mr Leeming – or Arthur, as he liked to be called – telephoned to ask Agnes to drinks on the following day.

'Round about twelve. Just a repeat of your little party, Agnes.'

Agnes thanked him and said she would be delighted, but she sighed as she put the receiver back. Hardly an exciting invitation if it were to be a mirror of her own party.

However, one thought did cheer her up a little.

Perhaps this time the French woman in number 2 might decide to grace them with her presence? That would at least make the party a little more interesting. Somehow, Agnes could not quite imagine Madame Le Mesurier talking about the milkman or the paper boy's behaviour. Perhaps, though, she would ignore Arthur's invitation, as she had her own.

Arthur Leeming's flat was not at all as Agnes had imagined. Perhaps the most characteristic piece of furniture was a large bar cart, filled, on quick inspection, with every kind of drink imaginable. An attractive ice bucket stood on the top shelf with the array of bottles, full of glistening cubes of ice.

Otherwise the room was furnished with taste. Beautifully draped curtains at the window, a charming Queen Anne kneehole desk – walnut, and beautifully polished. Its smallness was perhaps incongruous given Arthur Leeming's bulk. A tapestry sofa, several wing chairs and small round-topped tripod coffee tables, and a charming sofa table.

It was a surprising room and Agnes suspected the taste may have been his wife's rather than his, until his casual remark that he had been in the antique trade for years. Clearly he had a good eye for furniture of merit.

The Warburtons were already there when Agnes arrived. Mrs Warburton greeted Agnes with her usual breathy voice and stealthy manner, her husband with his usual banal remarks. He had a habit of repeating himself.

'Nice to see you again, Mrs, er... Nice to see you again!'

There was a light tap on the door, hardly audible, but Arthur Leeming heard it.

'Why the hell don't people ring the bell?'

He heaved himself up and went to let in Miss Horrocks.

'I rang the bell, but it didn't work – I think...'

Arthur Leeming put his hand round the door and pressed. The bell, loud and strident, seemed to be in working order.

'Well, it didn't work when I pressed it, Mr Leeming.'

Miss Horrocks walked in with her nose in the air, greeted Mr and Mrs Warburton and sat down in one of the wing chairs without further comment. Agnes was expecting a long discussion on door bells that worked and door bells that didn't, so broke in.

'That's a very pretty little Queen Anne desk, Mr Leeming. I hope you won't think me rude to mention it, but it's so charming.'

Arthur Leeming looked pleased and glanced over almost with affection at the little piece.

'Oh, I'm glad you like it, Agnes! It's a favourite of mine. Of course, its two foot six measurement doesn't exactly fit my delicate outline. Indeed I don't think I could get my knees under it, but my wife used it.'

When her host asked her what she would like to drink, Agnes, who had already seen the large display of bottles, said, 'May I have a brandy and ginger ale, Arthur?'

Leeming replied with a broad smile, 'Certainly you may. I'll join you in the same. Won't you try one, Miss Horrocks?'

But that lady refused and continued to sip her sweet sherry, with what appeared to be little enjoyment. She was not at all like most of the hospital matrons Agnes had known in her nursing days, and it was not until the conversation had proceeded a little – and under rather, Agnes thought, impudent questioning by Major Warburton – that it was revealed that Miss Horrocks had been a matron of a residential home for the elderly, twenty beds, which she had owned and run herself with, she confessed, some untrained staff.

'We had a very good name in the area,' she said, taking a rather bigger sip of her sherry.

Agnes felt a dislike of the Major and his persistent questioning and a sympathy for the rather prim Miss Horrocks, who may or may not have let the 'hospital matron' deception take over.

'I think the residential home is one of our most important institutions these days. You or I may land up in one, Major Warburton.'

Agnes had a mild reproach in her voice at which the Major shrugged.

'I certainly hope I don't,' he said.

'Perhaps the residential home has the same hope, Major Warburton.'

Agnes could not resist the rather waspish remark. Luckily her reply was almost masked by a sharp metallic rap on the front door, so loud and sharp that it was easily heard by everyone in the room.

Agnes looked with interest as Arthur Leeming left the room. The only guest not

26

yet there was Louise Le Mesurier. She guessed it must be her. She was correct.

'I'm so sorry, I'm late for your little party. It's too bad of me, but truly I couldn't help it, truly, truly. By the way, your bell is not working.'

The French accent was there but almost not, just enough to make the words attractive. As she walked into the room her perfume preceded her.

'A little too strong, a trace vulgar,' Agnes almost said out loud, making Miss Horrocks lean forward as if to answer her.

Arthur Leeming, smiling broadly, led his guest into the room as if he had caught her himself.

'You all know Louise Le Mesurier?'

Everyone nodded and smiled and made the appropriate remarks. Louise Le Mesurier walked gracefully across the room and seated herself in a wing chair with equal grace, crossing one slender leg over the other and revealing a fair amount of thigh.

'How nice of you to ask me, Mr Leeming!'

There was a trace of French accent there again, but only the merest trace. Agnes noticed her nails, the pale violet varnish. She was wearing a very lightweight tweed suit, beautifully cut, the predominating colours a mixture of soft beige and violet. Agnes wondered whether she changed her nail varnish daily, or with each outfit she wore. The nails looked natural, not false. Her shoes, with slightly lower heels this time, were a matching beige.

'Tonight, I go to the clothes exhibition at Mandells. Is anyone else going?'

Agnes replied that she had not heard about it.

'Oh, it is by invitation. I have one. It is for two persons. Would you care to come with me? It is not at all pleasant to be alone, I think.'

Not usually impulsive, Agnes saw her evening flash in front of her. Television and a meal she would have to cook for herself.

'Yes, I would love to come. I love clothes. May I call you Louise?'

'But of course. It is at eight. Wine and canapés. I will drive, no?'

Agnes agreed, and for the moment she did not regret her decision although she wondered if she would by the evening.

'I know you like clothes. I always admire what you wear.'

Agnes was pleased at that remark. Louise put a violet fingernail up to her hair and pushed it back. Her blonde hair was short, very blonde, like Agnes's, and cut in a certain way, again very like her own cut. The similarity made Agnes wonder if they went to the same hairdresser in Brighton.

They all left at about the same time. Agnes wondered if Louise would mention the

28

unanswered invitation that Agnes had put through her letter box. She did not. She went down the stairs, ignoring the lift.

'See you tonight, we'd better leave here about seven thirty.'

At seven thirty Agnes rang the door bell of the ground-floor flat. She had changed into a grey trouser suit with a gold lamé collar and matching gold edges to the breast and coat pockets.

'Do come in. I'm almost ready.'

Louise Le Mesurier disappeared into the bedroom, leaving Agnes time to look round her sitting-room. There were no antiques here. The room was sharp white – walls, ceiling, doors. Two black and white abstracts, one on the wall opposite the windows, one on the wall leading from the hall. They were similar subjects and looked as if they had been painted by the same artist. Lonely and sparse, and rather sad.

A black settee was curiously contradicted by a white settee, both leather. One stood near the fireplace, which was electric, imitation flames surprisingly real. The room was warm, minimalistic and clinical. The curtains on the large windows were silver, tied back with wide belts of the same material.

The only colour in the room was what looked like a Chinese rearing horse, bright pink with a red saddle, about a foot high, on a shelf between the two windows. These looked out on to the front. The sea was just visible over the green railings and the people and cars passing gave the room movement.

'Right, ready? I like your suit.'

Louise came out of the bedroom wearing a dark mauve dress under a warm-looking lavender coat, a headscarf over her hair, tied under her chin.

'My hair's impossible. A breath of wind and I look like a dancing dervish.' She laughed, showing even white teeth.

'Mine, too. I've found a hairdresser, with an awful name. Pretty Heads.'

Louise looked at her in some surprise.

'Really? That's where I go. They are quite good, don't you think? Never put enough lacquer on though.'

Louise drove a Renault. Very clean and polished. She drove well. There was quite a bit of traffic. The flashing headlights, sometimes not dipped, appeared not to worry her in the least. Neither did she comment or complain about other people's driving, a habit Agnes found very annoying when driving with some of her friends.

At the dress show Louise was conducted to a front seat by the catwalk, and immediately a girl walked along to them with two glasses of wine, smiling and calling her Madame Le Mesurier.

'I buy some clothes here, not often. I normally go up to London. I don't buy quite as much as I used to.'

She turned to Agnes. 'How old are you, Agnes? I'm fifty-six.'

Agnes was taken aback by the directness of the question. Louise lit a cigarette. Several people looked on disapprovingly, some coughed meaningfully. Louise completely ignored them and flicked her ash on the floor. There were no ashtrays. She continued to look at Agnes, obviously expecting an answer.

'I'm sixty-one.' Agnes felt a little shock as she said it.

The dress show was a mixture of the wearable and the bizarre. Different designers. Agnes bought a dress, or rather a two-piece: a straight skirt and rather unusual top with a high fitted collar, in a shade of blue she knew suited her. Louise bought a suit and made an appointment to come in the following morning. The sleeves were a shade too long and she wanted the small gold chain removed from the collar.

The drive home was just as smooth as the journey there. Agnes had been a little worried: Louise had downed three and a half glasses of wine. Agnes never drank more than one when she was driving, but Louise drew into her parking place outside the flats smoothly. They got out and Louise clicked the lock.

'Which is your car, Agnes?'

Agnes pointed to the Porsche about six yards away, gleaming under the brilliant lights on the front.

'Oh, a Porsche!'

Louise walked up to it and then peered inside.

'I would love a Porsche.'

She went round to the other side of the car, then her eyes opened wide, her voice and expression completely changed.

'Agnes, look at this! How awful, your lovely car. Who could have done such a thing?'

Agnes ran to join her. Scratched deeply along the entire length of the car were the words YOU BITCH.

'Let's go into my flat and ring the police.'

'No, I'd rather not. I'll deal with this myself, thank you, Louise.'

Her companion looked as if she could hardly believe her ears.

'Do you know who did this, Agnes?' she asked.

Agnes did not answer; she walked up the steps and unlocked the front door. In the hall, she turned to Louise, who was still talking, advising.

'Thank you for a very enjoyable evening, Louise. We must have lunch together one day, if you would care to.'

Agnes moved across the hall, into the lift. As the doors shut in front of her she saw Louise, still standing looking at her in amazement.

When Agnes got up to her flat, the full enormity of what had been done to her beloved car hit her like a personal blow.

Her first thought was that the word had been scratched by the white-faced boy with the birthmark. 'Bitch' was the very word he had called her as he toppled backward down the stone steps. But, as she cooled down a little, she realised it could have been someone else. Not the boy with the purple-marked face at all – just a passing vandal.

Agnes had hated Louise being with her, witnessing the hurt the Porsche had received. Her suggestions about the police... Police!

She had never dealt with the police when solving her problems. She had her own ways of sorting out justice. This was difficult, though – how would she find the boy? If it *was* him... His treatment of the little dog would have to be added to the damage to her car. If he was guilty of both, then she must find him. How to begin?

Brighton and Hove seemed to have many young hooligans – out of work or layabouts, some of them, with nothing to do but wilful damage... Agnes realised she had been standing, still with her outdoor things on,

33

and thinking for ten minutes at least.

She moved towards her bedroom, then knew that sleep would be impossible. She looked at her watch. Ten to eleven.

She went back into the sitting-room, crossed over to the corner cupboard and took out the brandy bottle. Ginger ale she knew was in the refrigerator in the kitchen. Brandy and ginger ale – always her drink in an emotional crisis!

In the kitchen she sat down at the table, sipping at her drink and thinking again of what she would do.

Get the garage to repair the car, that of course!

As she raised her glass to her lips, she saw that she was trembling a little. The dog, and now this – it had been rather an emotional upset!

She finished her drink and began to think more clearly. It had been about lunch-time when those boys had been strolling along the front, looking for someone to irritate or even hurt. Perhaps she would watch? She could see the spot where the two girls and three youths had stood from her sitting-room window.

She could watch for them, then follow them. She might not see them for days, perhaps not at all, but it would be a start! Tomorrow she would take her car to the Porsche garage. It might take some time to get the scratched words removed and the car resprayed, but they would lend her another car meanwhile.

Feeling a little more reassured as to her ability to do something, she went through to her bedroom to get ready for bed.

3

The next morning Agnes drove the Porsche to the garage. The mechanic who usually looked after her car was appalled.

'Oh, Mrs Turner. How awful. You keep your car so beautifully, too!'

He went off to fetch the head car salesman. An urbane, good-looking man, he had sold her the new model when she lived near Lewes, just before she had left Rose Cottage. He and the mechanic studied the marks, the mechanic smoothing his fingers over the area.

'Fairly big job, Mrs Turner.' He looked up, almost apologetically. 'It's deep. Done with a knife, or scissors, really hard.'

'Insurance?' Agnes asked.

He nodded. 'But I'm afraid you'll lose your no claims bonus, Mrs Turner.'

He stopped, and looked at Mr Harris, the salesman.

Agnes was getting tired of them. At this moment, she hated the sight of the car. She didn't want to go into any details.

That beastly boy had done this – she was almost sure in her mind it was he. After all, the use of the same words surely proved a link, and he had threatened to get his revenge.

Well, time might tell. If it was that lout, she would see to it, as she always did. He would receive what she considered a just punishment.

Not just the slap on the wrist that he would probably get if she went to the police and left it to them.

It was not only the damaged car – though that was bad enough. But the picture of that puppy, swinging round and round, choking to death – if she had not been there to intervene...

She left in a red Porsche, lent to her by the garage. They expected the repair to her car would take at least two weeks. She did not like a red car, preferring her own more conservative colour, but it could not be helped.

Agnes did some shopping, then drove back to her flat. She had no sooner closed her flat door, when the phone rang.

'It's Louise. I saw you come in. They have lent you a car. I do think you should go to the police, Agnes, I really do!'

Agnes did not answer for a second or two, then she quelled her irritation.

'Thank you for ringing, Louise. Yes, the garage supplied a courtesy car. It's almost three years older than mine and I hate red!'

She purposely ignored the advice to consult the police, but Louise persisted.

'They might catch the vandal. He really deserves to be punished, Agnes, no?'

'No, Louise. I'll do it my way. So, could we lunch one day next week?'

Louise agreed with quite a degree of enthusiasm. Agnes put the telephone down, went to the kitchen and made coffee. It was rather early yet, quarter to eleven, to start her watching. Nevertheless she seated herself in her window with her coffee and started her vigil. Coincidences had frequently helped her in her life. Maybe she would be lucky again.

Quite a lot of people walked along the front, getting fewer as lunch-time approached. One or two young mothers, some with prams, some with pushchairs, some leading protesting toddlers. Many old people leaning heavily on their walking sticks, mostly women. The females looked stalwart, determined. A few pushed shopping trolleys or dragged them behind them. The men looked frail, trembling, ashamed perhaps of their disability. Four young men, rather noisy, raised Agnes's hopes. But no, it was not them, not the same three who had tortured the dog and made the howling noises.

Disappointed, Agnes went to the kitchen to prepare her lunch. As she made herself a salad, she reasoned with herself. Perhaps they were just day visitors. No, that couldn't be true, of course. The damage to the car had been done later. Maybe he lived near here, up one of the side streets. Brighton perhaps. Nothing to do, bored, drinking, doping. They would come along again, she was sure. After all, surely the boy with the birthmark would want to see the result of his work on the Porsche. That was a point. Because of that thought she took her lunch back to the sitting-room and watched while she ate it. No luck though. Perhaps tomorrow? By two o'clock, she gave up.

The next day she had an appointment with the dentist. He kept her waiting for half an hour before seeing her, with profuse apologies. Then she had a small session with the hygienist so it was nearly lunch-time when she arrived back in the flats. She parked in her space and got out.

Immediately, a young police constable came up to the Porsche.

'Do you live here, madam?' he asked.

'Yes, I'm Mrs Turner. Flat 6 – at the top.' Agnes pointed up towards her window. 'What's happened?'

Then she noticed the large star-shaped hole in the window of Flat 2. Louise's flat. Louise came out, and greeted Agnes on the steps of the flat.

'Oh Agnes! I was so frightened, so frightened. I was just bringing a drink for myself and my friend. She has gone home now.'

Louise sounded more French. She was hatless and her fair hair was ruffled by the breeze.

'When this stone – you call it pebble? – came through the window. The glass – small pieces went all over. It was horrible!'

'Who would do such a thing!'

Agnes turned to the older policeman who was just coming out of the front door.

'Don't know, madam. Some young yob, I suppose. The lady didn't see much of him, only that his arm was in a sling.'

Louise nodded vigorously. 'Yes, yes, in a bandage thing, like so.' She put her hand up to her chest.

'Still managed a hefty throw, though. That's a double-glazed window.' The policeman motioned towards the star-shaped break in the glass.

Agnes hoped Louise would not mention the damage done to the Porsche but that was too much to ask, of course.

'This lady, my friend, had a rude word scratched on her car yesterday.'

The policeman looked concerned, but

nevertheless he merely shrugged his shoulders.

'Terrible! There is so much of this behaviour about. If you don't catch the vandal actually doing the damage, it's difficult to prove.

Agnes nodded, rather coldly.

'That's why I didn't report the incident. This, though, is rather more serious.'

She looked at the window. Was it that boy again? Did he think she lived in the ground-floor flat? Could be, but then it might not be he at all. Just a passing wilful yob, picking up a pebble from the beach and pitching it at the window.

But the sling? Had the wretched 'dog boy' injured his wrist or arm when she had given him a push and he had fallen backwards down the concrete steps?

Not that Agnes regretted it in the least. Serve the despicable creature right. She hoped he had broken a bone at least. Agnes was not a forgiving person, especially where an animal was concerned.

'I must go,' she said. 'I'm expecting a telephone call. I'm sorry you had this horrid thing happen, Louise. Do ring me.'

Agnes crossed determinedly to the lift and was glad when the doors noiselessly drew together and shut out the chattering crowd in the hall.

She was pleased the policeman had said

no more about the damage to the Porsche. He had not appeared to be particularly interested. Good, because Agnes wanted to sort this out herself. This was a cause and a cause was just what she had been seeking.

4

In a way Agnes was pleased at the way events were shaping. The two incidents, the near killing of the puppy and the damage to her car, would both have to be paid for by that young thug with the disfigured face. How he would pay, she would have to decide later. That was the way she always did things.

One thing upset Agnes. When she closed her eyes, she could still see the scratched word on her Porsche. Would she always see it? No matter how beautifully the word was erased and the car resprayed, would the fact that the perfect surface had been so defiled stay with her and make the car repugnant to her? She hoped not. Perhaps she was being over-anxious and she would not have any such feeling, but she was not sure.

The telephone rang. It was Louise, asking Agnes if she would come down for a coffee. It was twenty to three. Agnes guessed

Louise would not have lunched. She had heard banging downstairs. Probably they were boarding up the window as a temporary measure.

'No, Louise. Thank you for the invitation, but please, you come up to me. I will get a little lunch.'

Louise agreed and said she would come up in half an hour.

Agnes put a bottle of white wine in the refrigerator, made a substantial plateful of ham sandwiches and put coffee cups out. It would have to be instant, she decided. The late lunch would give her the opportunity to question Louise more closely, try to get her to remember any further particulars about the boy, youth or young man she had, apparently, only caught a glimpse of running away.

Louise rang Agnes's bell exactly half an hour later. She had changed her clothes and was now dressed in a loose-fitting caftan.

'Forgive me. I was going to rest on my bed, have a little sleep, then I thought, after this, I won't sleep. I will ask Agnes down.'

She looked at the sandwiches and wine glasses being laid out on the large coffee table which stood in front of Agnes's comfortable three-seater couch. The flat was warm. Agnes had turned the heating up a little.

'This is so sweet, so nice of you, Agnes.'

Louise sounded appreciative of the little spread.

'Do sit down. Will you have a glass of wine with your sandwiches?'

'Thank you. I had no break after all that fuss. It was such a big bang, Agnes. For a moment I thought I had been shot, it sounded like that! Elise, my friend, thought so too.'

Agnes filled Louise's glass three times. She drank the wine with obvious enjoyment and attacked the sandwiches. Drinking, eating and drinking, she chatted. Mostly about her past. Two divorces, one in France and one in Britain, several lovers, now a widow. She laughed a rather tinkling laugh as she talked. Agnes, as she listened, began to think her guest was a rather silly, air-headed woman. She had given her age as fifty-six and, Agnes had to admit, she looked far younger. Her figure was slim, her face almost unlined.

'Of course, I've had a facelift, for my neck mostly. It's there where you go first, don't you think?'

Agnes nodded vaguely and volunteered no revelations about her own past, which seemed not to worry Louise in the least. At last she stood up to leave, looked round the sitting-room, the first time she had appeared to do so.

'Nice up here, your view is so much better

than mine. I wanted a top one, but they had all gone. Perhaps the Warburtons will move, or get too decrepit to stay on looking after themselves.'

'They hardly look approaching that yet.'

Agnes tried to keep the reproach from her reply. She thought the words in poor taste. Louise laughed and shrugged her shoulders.

'Perhaps you will be lucky and I will be run over by a lorry.'

Louise gave her tinkling laugh, but did not venture any reply to this remark. She looked at Agnes, then came over and kissed her on the cheek, which Agnes hated.

'Thanks again for feeding me and making me feel better.'

Agnes thought she would press her a little more now.

'Did you remember any more about the boy you saw running away, his clothes, or appearance?'

'No, I said he was dressed like all the young ones dress these days – scruffy you call it, no?'

'Nothing more about his jacket or face?'

Louise shook her head and pressed her lips together.

'Had he a leather jacket on?'

Agnes took a chance. She felt Louise was not making much of an effort to remember the stone thrower.

Louise looked suddenly surprised, put one

long-nailed hand up and smoothed her short fair hair. She squinted her eyes at the window.

'Yes, now you mention that, Agnes, he did have a shiny jacket on, leather, plastic per-haps, and his hair was light, untidy, and of course the sling bandage. I remembered that – well, one would, I think.'

Agnes agreed and tried to think of another question to ask her. She was beginning to feel it was the same man she had pushed down the steps, but she wanted to be more certain.

'You didn't see his face at all, Louise?' she asked.

Louise shook her head. 'No, how could I? He was running away from the flat, across the road. I do remember his jacket though. I didn't tell the policeman that, Agnes. Do you think I should ring him up and tell him?'

Agnes was quite definite in her reply. She didn't want the police to arrest the boy, then just slap his wrists and deal out no suitable punishment.

That was her job, not theirs.

She saw in her mind's eye the little dog swinging on the end of the lead. Heard again the maniacal howls of the two boys egging him on, probably to make him continue his cruelty, until the puppy was dead. No, not a job at all for the police. A task of retribution for her to deliver and make no mistake she would do so. She always did.

Louise thanked her again, crossed the hall and pressed the lift button. The doors slid open at once. She stepped in, turned and raised a hand and smiled at Agnes. The lift doors swished to and she was gone.

Agnes felt that, while she had not learned a lot, she was a little further forward. Now she must resume her watching and wait for the boys to come back.

Agnes's casual suggestion that they lunch together was taken up by Louise.

'How about next Tuesday, Agnes?' Louise asked her one morning as they met in the hallway.

Agnes was just going out, Louise coming in.

Rather taken by surprise, Agnes agreed that next week would be nice, but added that she would have to look in her diary as she had appointments. Indeed she had. Not social ones, but with her dentist and, of course, with Pretty Heads.

'I don't have to look in my diary. I'm free all the time,' Louise volunteered. This ended with a laugh. As she laughed, Agnes smelt alcohol on her breath. It was just before eleven in the morning and Agnes had the fleeting thought that it was perhaps a bit early.

Then she dismissed it with her usual conclusion in these matters: Well, it's nothing to do with me.

When she got back from her trip to the shops, Agnes telephoned and said next Tuesday would be fine. She suggested a restaurant called Cartello's. She had lunched there once or twice by herself. It was a small, expensive place, but the food was good, or had been the times she had been there.

Louise was enthusiastic.

'Oh yes! I've seen that place. It looks cosy. Tuesday then. What time?'

'We'll take my car. It will, I hope, be back by then. It's quite a short distance. Say, half-past twelve?'

Louise sounded as if a little more alcohol might have been added to that she had obviously taken earlier. Agnes noted the fact and was pleased she had said they would go in her Porsche: Louise could drink as much wine as she wanted at their lunch.

5

Two days later, when she had almost given up hope of seeing the three boys, she spotted them!

They were standing in exactly the same place as they had been when the dog incident occurred. The boy with the birthmark had on the plastic or leather coat that Louise had described, and he was wearing the same blue shirt poking out of the collar of the coat.

Agnes reached for her binoculars and focused on him. His face jumped out at her, the purple mark showing more clearly.

Seen through the glasses, he did not look so much of a boy as a young man. Twenty-five, or maybe more.

He put a hand up to smooth back his light-coloured, almost blond hair and she saw the wrist was bandaged. Her heart quickened.

The other two were lunging against the railings, pushing and pulling against each other now and again, shouting at the same time.

The boy – a man, Agnes preferred to call him now – was standing there more quietly.

He appeared to be watching the flats, perhaps looking for the car he had vandalised? Well, he would not recognise the red Porsche. Then as she moved the binoculars a little she saw near them, leaning against the railings, a green-painted bicycle.

Agnes knew suddenly what she had to do. She went quickly into her bedroom, selected a warm camel-haired coat she scarcely ever wore, changed into flat brown shoes and tied a brown headscarf well over her head, hiding her hair. A pair of dark glasses helped her disguise.

One more look out of the window to see if they were still there. Yes. She waited until they began to move, then she got into the lift. She was taking a chance, but she hoped the bike belonged to the man with the birthmark.

She was in luck. As she walked down the steps of the flats, he took the bike on to the road and made a farewell gesture to the others. Another youth had joined them now. Younger, thinner. Agnes had not seen him before.

The black coat glistened in the dulling sunlight as the man took off.

Agnes was now in her car. She waited till the bike was some way up the road. It was twenty past three. She eased the Porsche out, waited for a couple of cars to pass her, then set off after him.

He was a long way ahead now, perhaps going home. Or, perhaps, on some new destructive prank or other – she would see. He did not go far. He suddenly turned up a side road and parked the bike by some tall black railings. There was a large board, black with gold letters: 'Ernest Williams School'.

Agnes parked the red car a little way up the road then walked slowly towards the school gates, keeping well out of his sight. Was he a parent, calling for a son or a daughter? It could be. She waited and watched.

Several mothers appeared, some on foot, a few in cars. One little boy of about eight appeared to have no one to collect him, but he came quite confidently out of the gates. On the path he paused and looked up and down the road to check it was safe to cross. It was. One step forward, and a voice called.

'Benny, hang on a minute!'

The boy stepped back on to the pavement, looked to his right to where the man with the birthmark was standing against the railings.

'OK, Andy? Got something?' The boy's voice was clear and young in the afternoon air.

Andy, Andy! Agnes could put a name to the vandal at last.

He approached the boy with three long strides and turned him round to face him, quite roughly.

'Shut your mouth, you stupid little lump of nothing!' He hissed the words.

But Agnes, who had drawn a bit closer, could hear what he said.

The youngster only laughed, clearly not frightened.

'Act like I'm your father, dimwit!'

The boy laughed again, took hold of Andy's sleeve, his face full of mischief and mockery.

'Hello, Dad. How's tricks then?'

Agnes had to draw back a little as Andy pulled the child towards the railings. He drew something from his pocket. A little white bag. Stiff, like a crisp bag.

'Six in there, six only. Six pounds. Have you got it?'

'I got it. The loot, booty.' The child handed something to the man. 'Sis will be chuffed. She's going to a disco tonight. Six isn't many though!'

Andy was drawing away, going towards the railings on the other side of the open gates.

Children were still coming through.

His parting shot to the boy, now getting ready to cross the road again, was clear.

'Tell her to take plenty of water with it.'

The boy called back, not turning towards

51

Andy, 'Will do, though water costs, she says, at them places.'

He disappeared, running in and out of the traffic.

Another girl came out, looked round rather fearfully. Perhaps her mother was coming for her. She went straight up to Andy, opened her lunch box, took something out. Money?

Agnes could not see from where she was standing and she did not go nearer in case he recognised her. The man's back was towards her.

He handed something to the girl and she hurried away. At that moment, a rather old mud-splattered car drew up. The girl ran across the path to get in.

'Hello, Mum. You're a bit late.'

'Well, don't go on about it. I've had a lot to do,' a rather whining voice answered and the car drew off, a large puff of smoke coming out of the exhaust.

The children were dwindling down to one or two now and Andy began to lose interest. Clearly he knew his clients here.

Agnes was appalled at what she had seen.

This beastly creature was selling drugs to these children, adding to his other horrors. Agnes realised this was the greatest of all.

What were the drugs? Ecstasy, by the sound of the advice to take water.

As Andy moved off on his bike, she

followed him.

It was difficult, Agnes found, for a car to follow a bike. A motor bike, yes, but an ordinary push bike was another matter. She managed it, however, and this time he started back to the town centre, up a side street, another, then out into a square. In the middle of the square, another square, with well-tended shrubs and trees. One side was all houses, another was taken up entirely by a single large building. Outside was a notice: 'Westwood School for Girls'. Agnes had almost expected it.

And there was Andy's bicycle, leaning against the low wall surrounding the small front garden of the school. No cars drawing up to collect little children. Agnes looked at her watch. Four twenty. Older girls perhaps – able to find their own way home. She parked round the corner away from the school, went to the corner and watched.

At half-past four the doors opened and a few girls strolled out, talking and laughing, girls of fifteen, sixteen.

Two in particular interested Agnes. They paused at the bottom of the steps leading to the front door of the school, looked to the right then to the left where Andy was perched on the low wall. He was watching the two girls, a slight smile on his lips. As they approached him he took a pack of cigarettes from his pocket, flashed a lighter

53

and drew the smoke in deeply. The girls looked at each other. They seemed slightly frightened.

Agnes approached a little closer and stood behind an overhanging evergreen shrub. She could hear Andy's loud voice.

'Oh, looking for more, are we? Daddy coughed up. Remember you owe already. What do you want?' His voice was mocking.

The girls looked at each other, then back at the school steps. Two more girls were looking towards Andy. He waved a hand at them.

He took some money and handed the two girls near to him a small packet. There was nothing secret or furtive. The two girls moved off. The other two came up to him. Agnes was amazed at the openness.

What to do? She backed towards her car. She needed to think out what to do about Andy. Somehow he must be stopped, this trade exposed.

6

When Agnes arrived home the Warburtons were standing in the hall by the lift. The Major was looking furious, punching the lift button with his forefinger, muttering. He turned to Agnes as she came through the door.

'Bloody thing's stuck again. Nothing happening. I'm not supposed to do stairs. My heart.' He looked at Agnes as if she had personally done something to cause his heart condition and was also in all probability responsible for the lift not working.

She turned aside, went through the hall doors and walked up the forty-two stairs to her floor. She felt she really could not cope with the Warburtons after this afternoon's adventure.

In her flat she determinedly kept herself from thinking about Andy yet, or what was to be her campaign against him. This afternoon had sealed his fate as far as she was concerned.

Cruelty to the puppy was bad enough, but the damage to her car, the window, all paled to insignificance when she remembered that child outside the primary school. A mere child, handing that beastly man money for some noxious substance to give, or maybe sell on, to perhaps his slightly older sister. The girls, at what looked like a private school, she did not feel quite so appalled about. They looked older, more sophisticated and probably used Ecstasy to take to raves to give them a buzz. But a girl could die with that drug, just one tablet. Then again, maybe Ecstasy wasn't all he was selling. Could they be into harder stuff? Coke, heroin? Tomorrow, or the next day, she would follow Andy again. This time it would take longer, as what she wanted to know now was where he lived, what the other two meant to him – friends, brothers? Did they perhaps live in a squat? He certainly looked ill fed, pale, thin. Emaciated almost.

The next day Agnes's garage telephoned to say the repair to her car would take longer than they had estimated. The door would have to be replaced rather than just resprayed as the cut into the metal was deeper than they had first thought. They did assure her, though, that the insurance would cover the whole cost. They also asked if she was quite happy with the car they had loaned her. She replied that the colour of the car was not to her taste, but otherwise she would put up with it. Agnes thought this latter remark might make them hurry a little with her repair job.

Three days went by and Agnes saw nothing of the young men on the other side of the road. Again the garage rang her to apologise about the delay in the repairing of her car, putting the fault firmly at the door of the firm that was to supply the door. Agnes was slightly irritated by this, but not quite so irritated as she might have been. The bright red car was so different to her own that she felt confident the vandals would not connect it with the Porsche they had desecrated.

This afternoon Agnes was driving home, having been to lunch with Violet Greenham, a sister of one of her erstwhile neighbours from when she lived in Rose Cottage. It had been a rather nostalgic lunch with naturally a lot of talk about their life before the developers took over. This chat, bringing back memories, had made Agnes slightly depressed and, as she drove back towards her flat, now her home, she felt it would never quite make her as happy as she had been in Rose Cottage. Had she done wrong to pick such a smart and urban place?

When she arrived home, the sun, spring sun yet and not very warm, streaming into her sitting-room, and the sea sparkling and blue, did a little to cheer her up. She took off her coat and headscarf and checked her telephone for calls as she always did, not expecting much. But, this time, a number had rung which she did not recognise at all.

She returned the call and the person who answered gave her name as Julia Roberts, which for a moment did nothing to jog Agnes's memory.

'Julia Roberts, Pamela's mother, the little dog, you very kindly—'

Agnes interrupted her. 'Oh, of course, Mrs Roberts. How is Pamela and the puppy —

Polly, wasn't it?'

'Yes, Polly. Mrs Turner, I am telephoning you to ask if you would come and have dinner with us one evening. Perhaps this week, if you could manage it?'

Agnes was a little surprised. She had not expected to hear from the Robertses again. Indeed, their name had almost slipped from her memory.

'How kind of you. Yes, I would be delighted to come. What evening do you suggest?'

There was a slight rustle at the other end of the telephone, and an aside whisper as if Julia Roberts was consulting someone else. It must have been her husband, because his voice was the next to speak.

'Would Thursday be convenient to you, Mrs Turner? We want you to do us a little favour which we will explain while you are here.'

Agnes for a moment thought they were contemplating asking her to adopt Polly, but almost smiled to herself at the thought. They would hardly go to such lengths, just for that reason, she decided.

'Yes, Thursday's convenient, Mr Roberts. About seven? How is Pamela? Quite got over that horrid experience, I hope, and the little dog?'

Mr Roberts avoided the question in the same way that his wife had. He did not reply to it at all.

'Six thirty, if you could manage it, Mrs Turner. That will give us more time for a leisurely drink before dinner. Is that–?'

'Yes, perfectly, Mr Roberts. Six thirty at your house, Thursday next. I shall look forward to that.'

'We will too, Mrs Turner. Goodbye until then.'

He replaced the receiver. Agnes stood for a moment, still holding the telephone, wondering what possible favour they would want to ask of her. She put the phone down. Well, her social life was certainly improving a little. Louise, Violet, and now the Robertses. But what on earth could they want of her, that they should ask an almost complete stranger to dinner?

While she was getting herself a cup of tea a little later she went over the route she had taken to the house. She was glad that her sense of direction had always been good; she had only visited the place once but she felt she would be able to find the house fairly easily, although she could not at that moment remember the name on the gate. She decided to look it up in the telephone directory, and found it. 'R. Roberts, Holmewood, Caister Road.' As she saw the name, she remembered it, printed on a wooden sign by the gate.

Thursday evening arrived and as usual

Agnes debated with herself what to wear. Long ago, when Agnes was Agnes Carmichael and not Agnes Turner, when social engagements were as scarce as the clothes she had to choose from, she had been just as careful to try to make the clothes fit the occasion as she was now.

She decided on the same grey trouser suit she had worn when she went to the clothes show with Louise Le Mesurier. Whether there were other guests at the Robertses' dinner party or just herself, it would be suitable. Not too dressy.

Agnes found the road and the house quite easily and arrived on the dot of half-past six. She noticed more this time. Her last visit had been a rather preoccupied one, with the upset Pamela and the recovering puppy dog. The front garden was wonderfully neat, the small lawn manicured into perfection and the semicircle of shrubs all tidily pruned and ready for their spring flowering. The house itself was equally well cared for, the glass of the white-painted windows shining clean. Double garage to the left of the building. A very prosperous-looking home, Agnes thought as she rang the door bell, having parked her car in the obvious place for visitors, leaving enough room for anyone who wished to back out of either of the garages during the evening.

Mr Roberts opened the door. He looked

60

sidewards at the car, red and shining in the street lamp. Smiled a pleasant, slightly tense smile.

'Good evening, Mrs Turner. A new car?'

Agnes shook her head and explained that she had had a slight accident and this was only on loan while the repair was being done.

The house was pleasantly warm, as pleasant as its owner's smile, Agnes thought, but intensely tidy. It looked like a show house, a point she had hardly noticed on her first visit.

After one or two exchanges of 'Mrs Turner and Mrs Roberts' it was agreed that Christian names were more relaxed.

'What will you drink, Agnes?'

His name was Robert, but everyone called him Bob, he said. Agnes plumped for a soft drink as she was driving. Julia looked disappointed.

'Oh, I do hope you will have a little wine at dinner with us, Agnes?'

Agnes agreed and then asked would their daughter be joining them, and how was the little dog. At this the tension in the room mounted. Both were silent for a moment, then Julia spoke.

'Agnes, please don't think we asked you to a meal just because of this problem we spoke of on the telephone. It is nice to meet you again ... but if you could help us...?'

Agnes, completely mystified, said that of course she would help them if she could, but that she could not imagine any problem in which her help would be of use to them. For the moment they did not proceed.

Bob Roberts handed her the mineral water she had asked for, then, Agnes noticed, poured two fairly generous gin and tonics for himself and his wife. She attributed this to a need for Dutch courage and, putting her drink down beside her after taking a sip, prepared to listen.

Julia and Bob Roberts sat beside each other on the sofa. Agnes could hear movements in what she guessed to be the kitchen, either a cook or some other person keeping an eye on the cooking arrangements for the meal.

'You start, Julia, because you found the tablet in Pamela's pocket.'

Then the story began. Julia took a dainty handkerchief from her pocket and proceeded to screw it into a tight ball.

What she recounted was disturbing, Agnes had to admit. She had rather expected to be bored, although having no idea what the 'problem' was, she found herself very interested, wondering too how they would ask for help.

Julia Roberts started off in the way Agnes suspected she would recount any incident, detail by detail. The story ran like this.

She had gone into Pamela's room and found it much as usual, clothes anywhere but in the wardrobe, thrown over chairs, on the floor. The dressing-table littered with make-up, nail varnish leaking out of the bottle, face powder. On the dressing-table mirror, a date for Saturday night, scrawled in lipstick. Pamela was allowed out a little later on Saturday nights, her mother explained, half-past ten. She was usually later and was always reprimanded for it, but apparently the reprimand did little good.

Mrs Roberts, Julia, had given a big sigh as she reached this part of the story and Bob poured two more drinks for them. Agnes refused another mineral water. Julia would not continue the story until he sat down beside her and Agnes felt she could easily drop off to sleep as the story went on in such detail.

There had been a safari suit that Pamela was very fond of wearing hanging on the knob of the wardrobe door. Julia noticed there was a red stain on the front pocket. She had smelled it, red wine. This had disturbed her as their daughter was discouraged from drinking wine especially when out with her young friends. Indeed, she was not allowed alcohol at all.

Anyway she had taken the stained safari top downstairs to pop it in the washer-drier. Before she had put it in, she had automatically gone through the pockets. There she had found a small plastic bag. It contained two white tablets. Agnes could guess the rest, and broke in, rudely she thought.

'Ecstasy, Julia?' She just had to stop the flow.

'Yes, yes. How did you know, Agnes? I didn't guess at first, I didn't think Pamela–'

'Many of the young ones do take this stuff, you know. It was unfortunate when that girl died recently – is that why you are so worried? Where is she getting the stuff? Do you have any suspicions?'

At that moment, there was a knock on the open door of the sitting-room.

'Everything's ready, Mrs Roberts.'

Julia Roberts got to her feet and followed the woman, presumably into the kitchen. Bob Roberts got up too. He drained the last of his gin and tonic and they went through to the dining-room.

The meal was excellent and, true to his promise, Bob did not mention the subject of his daughter while they were enjoying it. Agnes was pleased about this, for the food merited her whole attention. She hated the task of cooking for one and this was a home-cooked meal she would not forget in a hurry.

After the sweet, which was Bombe Surprise, she complimented Julia on the meal with real sincerity. So much care and effort had been taken.

'Oh, Agnes, I believe I am a good cook but this evening I only prepared what we were to eat and my helper Mrs Webster really is responsible for its cooking. I thought as you were coming and we wanted to talk, to ask your advice, I would leave it in Mrs Webster's capable hands.'

They all got up and moved from the dining-room out into the hall. As they were crossing to the sitting-room, Agnes asked, 'Where is Polly? Is she quite recovered?'

There was a silence; the question appeared to be ignored. Then, when they had at last sat down and the coffee had been put on the table between them, Julia answered. Her voice had taken on a much harder note and she looked at her husband before she spoke. He nodded as if giving her permission to tell.

'Polly was given to a friend of ours who lives some distance away. She has two more Jack Russells and is very fond of the breed.'

'But wasn't Pamela upset to lose Polly? She seemed so fond of the little dog.'

Agnes remembered how upset the girl had been and how tenderly she had held the little thing in the car, how anxious she had been at vet's, and on the way home, so loving and caring.

'She was indeed, but we had to think of

some punishment after what she had done.'

Bob Roberts spoke this time, but Julia nodded in agreement. Agnes could hardly believe her ears. Such a punishment! Pamela, poor girl, surely what she had done did not deserve this?

'Let us tell you why we feel we have done right – I must add that we would not have done anything to hurt the puppy or make Polly at all miserable. Pamela was already getting bored with her chores regarding Polly, walks and feeding were getting left to my wife. It was Pamela's dog.'

'But what did she do that was so awful, apart from having the tablets?'

Bob reached out for his wife's hand. The distress was obviously building up between them.

'The day you came back, brought Pamela back with Polly, were so kind to Pamela – after you had left she would say very little about what had happened. We felt she knew the identity of the lout who had hurt her dog, but would not tell us.'

'It didn't seem to me that she knew anything about the man! Her friend Tina ran away as fast as she could.'

Agnes, for some reason about which she was not sure, felt she must stick up for Pamela, perhaps because they had taken Polly away from her.

'Well, it's possible,' Bob admitted reluctantly. 'But it didn't excuse her behaviour. She went out that night and did not come in until two in the morning. Meanwhile we had found out that she had stolen all the money from her mother's handbag, about eighty-five pounds.'

Julia Roberts had tears running down her face.

'She did know, I think, who did that to Polly. I think she owed him money, or wanted more drugs.'

Agnes was beginning to see a tiny gleam of light at the end of the tunnel, so she asked abruptly, 'Did Pamela have a boyfriend?'

Both parents shook their heads positively. 'No, she isn't like that. Not at fifteen.'

Agnes pressed the point more strongly. 'Oh, come now, Julia, Bob. Didn't you ever hear her mention a name on the telephone, someone ringing her up? You must have!'

They looked at each other again, still holding hands. Agnes felt sorry for them but didn't think they would deserve a gold star as parents.

'Pamela started to talk a lot on the telephone. She always said it was Tina or Bella, but one day I came into the hall where the phone was and I heard her say, "I can't, not today, Andy, but I will, I do promise faithfully, I will get it!" She was crying and she sounded frightened.'

Mrs Roberts broke down completely and

had to wipe the tears from her cheeks. Agnes tried to feel sorry for her.

'It was awful that she had to steal money from me, but it wasn't the money, it was this Andy. I don't believe Pamela is just taking these rave pills. She's so cold sometimes – supposing it's heroin or crack, is it called?'

Agnes had to break in. She was mystified by their thinking she could help. 'So what do you want me to do?'

'You've seen Andy, we believe, when he was tormenting Polly. You could identify him.'

'But we don't know the man ill-treating Polly *was* Andy, do we? It could have been just a vandal, just someone getting a thrill out of hurting something or someone.' Agnes was determined to give nothing away.

'No, but you could describe him to the police, help identify him, get him locked up.'

Agnes shook her head positively. She knew only too well how difficult it would be to connect this man with Pamela and, if he was arrested, what would they do? He would probably get away with having only enough drugs for personal use, or even get rid of it all. No, if anyone was going to deal with him it would be her, and only her.

'Could you describe him, Agnes? You must have had quite a good look at him.'

She shook her head. She felt they were perhaps being too hard on their daughter and couldn't forgive them for passing the puppy to a new home after its nasty experience. She felt suddenly she must leave. She would have liked to have seen Pamela, talked to her, and had said so, but the answer she got was, 'Oh, Pamela's spending the evening with a friend.'

'Oh, I'm sorry, Julia, Bob, but I hardly caught a glimpse of his face. I was too busy getting the lead away from him and pushing him away, grabbing Polly back.'

Agnes was glad she had not revealed what the damage to her car really entailed, and she had no intention of mentioning the broken window, nor the scenes at the two schools. As always, Agnes liked to possess knowledge which others didn't. She would deal with this her way. What that way was she did not yet know, but it would come to her.

A little later she took her leave, sensing the disappointment her hosts were feeling. They had no idea that the punishment would probably not fit the crime unless she dealt with it herself. In her way.

It was a relief to get in her car, wave to the two people at the door of the house and drive away, taking with her her own secret knowledge.

Agnes would have loved to have asked them where Polly's new home was, and driven there to see that the little dog was all right, but she had not dared to go quite that far. Pamela too, she would have liked to have a word with, but she realised as she drove back to her flat that a word with Pamela was not an impossibility. After all, she knew which school she went to, she could go there and meet her coming out. She had seen Andy there and the other four girls leaving about four thirty. Yes, the thought satisfied her. She could do that.

Agnes parked the red car and locked it.

As she went up the steps to the front door of the flats she felt much more like her old self. Something was going on. She had a new purpose and one that could turn out to be quite exciting. Secret knowledge.

Her memory suddenly flashed back to her youth. How old had she been? Twelve? The orphanage had been on a trip to the Isle of Wight, a great treat. On the ferry, no hovercraft in those days. A big liner had passed them, beautifully graceful. One of the nuns had exclaimed, 'Oh, look. The *Queen Mary!*'

They had all gawped at the great ship. Apparently, she, Agnes, had been the only one in the group who had known they were wrong. It wasn't the *Queen Mary*, it was the *Queen Elizabeth*. She remembered hugging the knowledge to herself, glorying in the fact that she was the only one who knew, the only one, to her a lovely feeling. Here was that feeling again. Wonderful, like a secret power. The feeling banished her depression.

But what next? Should she wait for Andy to appear again, follow him again? Should she seek out Pamela, ask her what his bag was, what he was selling to these small children and to the older girls at her school? She must think about it.

7

Agnes sat in her borrowed red car almost opposite Westwood School. She looked at her watch. It was ten past four. So far the double front doors of the school had not opened to let anyone out.

As yet there was no sign of Andy.

She had decided quite suddenly at lunchtime to do this surveillance. This morning she had not been out. No reason to do so. This always made her feel vaguely depressed, a whole day in, more so. Usually she took a walk along the front, but as she had sat eating her solitary lunch, she had suddenly decided that today was as good as any other. Also, it was a Wednesday. Last time she had seen him had been a Wednesday. Perhaps that was the day he called at Westwood School with his beastly merchandise.

Well, she had decided to take a chance and here she was.

Agnes sat in the driver's seat. She had pushed her fair hair well out of sight under a red headscarf. It had been raining when she had started out and the fine spring rain was still misting down. She was trusting to the disguise of the red car, her well-covered hair and the high turned-up collar of her black French macintosh. If he came, he came. If he didn't, she had other plans.

She wanted, if possible, to have a word with Pamela. Most of all she wanted to find out where Andy lived and ask Pamela an even more unlikely to be answered question – where did he get the drugs from? Though she thought it unlikely that Pamela Roberts, or any of the other girls, would know that, and even if they had some idea they would not give the fact away, in case it dried up their supply.

There was plenty to find out, plenty!

Another, perhaps more vital question, was, did he supply any hard drugs to any of the girls – heroin, crack, LSD?

Andy or no Andy, she felt her trip to the school would be well worth the waiting.

Two cars drew up near the school entrance. A girl came out to each car. They threw in their bags and got into the

72

passenger seat. One car was driven by a woman, the other by a man.

Suddenly, in the distance, Agnes saw a man on a push bike approaching the school, but he pedalled by.

Not Andy.

At twenty to five Agnes decided he was not coming today. Now Pamela was the person to wait for.

The doors opened more frequently now and girls dawdled down the steps in two and threes, some drawing hoods over their heads.

It was still raining, a fine, misty rain. She hoped to find out where the man lived and what the relationship was between them. The incident with the puppy seemed to indicate that he was demanding payment for drugs. Pamela must have found out what he would do next if she did not pay him – indeed been so fearful that she had even resorted to taking her mother's money. Or could it be that the girl was so badly addicted that she had needed further supplies?

Things did not turn out at all as Agnes had visualised or indeed hoped.

The door of the school opened. There was Pamela.

Agnes was about to open the Porsche door and cross the road to speak to Pamela when an ancient rusty-looking Metro drew up between her car and the school. Andy was at the wheel. He did not even glance towards Agnes. He moved a hand towards Pamela; she moved back and came quickly down the steps, walked round the car and got in. She had to slam the door twice before it would latch properly.

Agnes was thankful that neither had even looked at her car. He had never seen her in the red car and unless Pamela's parents had mentioned the change of colour, which Agnes doubted, the girl wouldn't know either. One thing she did notice, however, was that when Pamela greeted Andy and got into the car, she did not smile. She looked almost scared. Agnes watched the car drive away.

At the end of the road, which was not far from the school, the traffic light glowed red. The rusty car stopped. Agnes started her engine, waited for a moment until the light showed green. She drove out and started to follow the Metro. It was done on an impulse, unlike her usual cautious methods, but because she had started she decided to go on. She was very curious. Were they going to his home to get more – more what? A car moved in front of Agnes which made her feel more comfortable. The headscarf framed her face, but Pamela if she got a good look, would recognise her.

They drove on quite a long way. Agnes

began to feel nervous that they might become suspicious of the red car so persistently behind them. The Metro turned into a tree-lined street. The homes had once been family houses of some standing. Not any more. Some had windows boarded up, the front doors were scuffed and most needed a coat of paint. Most of the tiny front gardens had been turned into tips for children's broken toys, old pushchairs, takeaway cartons, newspapers and other garbage. Outside one of these the rusty car stopped. Agnes drove quickly by, noting the number on the door: 35. She turned a corner to the right into a slightly better-kept street, locked the car and walked back down the path to number 35.

She walked past the house and turned into the one next door, which was obviously empty and showed black evidence of extensive fire damage. The front door was half off its hinges and hung drunkenly sidewards. The street was almost empty except for five or six young children kicking a football and shouting. They took no notice of her at all, if indeed they saw her, they were so intent on their game.

Agnes felt rather at a loss. She had no way of finding out what was going on in number 35. Was Andy Pamela's boyfriend? Surely not. She waited, and, rather to her surprise, her wait was short. Pamela and Andy suddenly appeared at the door. She could hear quite clearly what they said.

'I don't want to do this, Andy, I'm frightened.'

Pamela sounded close to tears. Andy turned the palms of his hands upwards and shrugged.

'Up to you, sweetheart. You want the shit, you work for it, or pay for it.'

He disappeared into the house. Pamela pushed the half-closed door open. She shouted out, Agnes could hear her clearly.

'Andy, aren't you going to run me home?'

Andy came back to the door. He was holding a beer can in his hand. He took a big swig.

'No, I'm not. You got what you came for, now git. Get a taxi or something.'

Pamela stamped her foot. Agnes was glad to see some aggression from the girl. She was obviously going to shout at the man again but she didn't get the chance. He grabbed her arm.

'I said, git.'

He turned her round and propelled her to the top step. Agnes wondered would he go so far as to fling her down them. Pamela didn't give him the chance. She ran down the steps and the front door banged behind her. The house door knocker rattled. At the bottom of the steps she looked back at the closed door, then up and down the street, as if uncertain which way to go.

Agnes made up her mind quite suddenly. She called, 'Pamela, would you like a lift?'

Pamela crossed the road and came round to the passenger side of Agnes's car. She opened the door.

'Get in, Pamela, if you want a lift home, or wherever you are going.'

Agnes's voice was bored. She had a lot of questions to ask this girl, a lot of questions. Pamela got in and slammed the car door. She looked both guilty and embarrassed. She pulled down the seat belt and clicked it into place.

'What are you doing here, Mrs Turner? Your car is different, I didn't recognise you.'

Agnes did not answer. She sat for a moment, gripping the steering wheel, her knuckles white.

'You knew who the man was, who was nearly choking Polly to death. You knew it was this man Andy. What hold has he got over you?'

Pamela suddenly clammed up, her face closed, sullen. Her lower lip stuck out, pouting.

'What's it to you, Mrs Turner?'

'He's supplying you with drugs, isn't he, this Andy? And, by what I heard him shout at you as you came out, he's expecting you to push them for him too. Do you realise he sells to eight-year-olds?'

'It's only for their mothers, not for them.'

Pamela almost shouted the words at Agnes.

Agnes thought she had better tell the girl that she had dined with her parents and that she knew about the tablets found in her pocket, the stolen money, her staying out till two in the morning. Then she remembered a very important question, something that seemed to her more important than any details of this sordid affair.

'Where is Polly, who did your parents get to take her?'

For the first time Pamela really looked unhappy, she looked at Agnes and tears did brim her eyes.

'The Brewsters, they were called. A little farm place. I had to go with them to see Polly left behind, part of my punishment. She was like, barking, crying when we left.'

'Can you take me there, to this farm place? Are your parents expecting you home?'

Pamela shook her head miserably.

'No, they think I'm at Bella's. You have to lie all the time. Bella's mother doesn't care where she is. She's allowed out all hours. Of course, I know she's sixteen, but...'

Agnes felt little sympathy for the girl beside her. She was not sure why she had not fought more for Polly. With parents like this girl's, Agnes was rather glad, probably for the first time in her life, that she was an orphan, brought up in an orphanage, with no madly tidy and strict parents. Only the nuns to cope with. They could be bad enough at times, but they were not so close, so involved.

'Well, Pamela, let's go to the Brewsters' place and check Polly is happy. Can you show me the way there? You know them well, I'm sure.'

Pamela nodded and looked at Agnes with a certain amount of fear in her eyes. She fiddled with her coat buttons. She tried to say something, stopped, then looked out of the side window, watching the late afternoon traffic and busy pedestrians.

'Well, Mrs Turner, we don't know them all that well but Dad said they had two dogs like Polly and he said it would be all right, Polly would be all right, happy, and I'd taken Mum's money. Oh, hell...'

'And what did you think, Pamela, did you have no say at all? As your mother said to me, she was your dog. Did you try to keep her?'

Agnes had already explained to the girl that her parents had quizzed her about Andy. She had not, however, said anything about his further exploits of vandalism. She could see little use in Pamela's knowing. Did she like the man, or was she so hooked on drugs that he had a hold over her? She was on a dangerous and slippery slope. If he could get her pushing drugs in her own school it would save him the trouble and danger of waiting outside for the girls to appear. Also, Agnes suspected, accosting the younger ones outside other schools – a fifteen-year-old would look much less suspicious than he did, hanging around the school gates with his marked face and his bicycle.

At last, on the road to Peacehaven, after what seemed to Agnes a fairly long drive, Pamela put her hand on her arm.

'Turn right, up this lane, it's a long way and very rough. Your poor car won't like it. The house is off the road to the left.'

Agnes started cautiously up the rutted lane which seemed to go on for ever. At last she arrived at a large yard, drove over the dried mud and up to the door of the big stone house. Everything looked pretty run down.

Agnes, accompanied by Pamela, went up to the front door, and rang the bell. Nothing happened. Agnes gave a loud rap. The door opened. A man opened the door. A pleasant-looking man with red cheeks and a little tuft of hair on each cheek.

'Hello, what can I do for you?' Then he appeared to recognise Pamela. 'Oh, you're Polly's mistress, or you were. Come and see how she's doing. Well, not so good really, won't eat. Frightened by my two, but she'll settle.'

He led them through the house. It was not an attractive place. A woman, rather fat and rosy like her husband, came into the hall carrying a bowl, heavy, containing what looked like chicken or some kind of animal food.

'Oh, hello. Just feeding the...'

She looked at her husband enquiringly.

'They've come to see Polly, how she's getting on.'

They walked further on through the house and out of the back door. Fields everywhere, but a rough square of grass, coarse and scarred, surrounded by a barbed wire fence.

'Keeps the cows out. There's Polly, look, across there by the old hen house.'

Agnes looked. Pamela looked. The little dog sat. Even from where they stood by the door, they could see how miserable Polly looked.

'Go to her, Pamela.'

Agnes's feelings were indescribable. As they approached, Pamela burst into tears. Polly's tail began to wag very slowly. She recognised Pamela. Agnes joined her and put her hand on the puppy. Polly was trembling, her whole body was shaking.

Mr Brewster came up, his face still jovial.

'She's really not up to our two bitches.

They're only playing, but she's not up to it. She's not used to their rough and tumble.'

Agnes looked more closely at Polly. She had no collar on and there was blood on her neck, not a lot, just a slight stain on her white fur.

'Has she been bitten, Mr Brewster?'

She knew she spoke sharply, but the answer she got from the jolly-looking man was quite relaxed.

''Spect they nipped her, you know – just playing.'

Agnes took the trembling puppy from Pamela's arms. Suddenly from the back door of the house, two black and white Jack Russells tore out, one leaping at the other. They made straight for their master, barking. Then spied Polly in Agnes's arms and starting barking harder and leaping up. They were obviously two well-fed, happy, boisterous youngsters, but not the companions for the puppy in her arms. Polly trembled more as they leapt up. Agnes clutched her tighter.

'Well, Mr Brewster, Pamela misses Polly and wants her back. Do you mind if we take her now? If you paid anything for her I'm quite willing to reimburse you, of course.'

Pamela looked at Agnes in complete disbelief.

'Mum and Dad won't–' she started to say.

Agnes cut her short, waiting for Mr

Brewster's answer, which he gave readily enough.

'No, of course not. Take her by all means. No, I didn't pay anything for her and to tell you the truth, the wife and I have been a little worried about the dog, not eating and all.'

'Thank you, that is kind, Mr Brewster.'

She walked back to the house carrying Polly. Mrs Brewster came out of the kitchen, wiping her hands on a tea towel.

'Can I get you folks a cup of tea?'

'They're taking Polly back. Missie here wants her back, so say goodbye to her.'

Agnes could see there was no active cruelty there, just a complete insensitivity to the needs of a dog brought up in a tidy, quiet home, no rivals, no other dogs, and thrust into an environment it was completely unable to cope with.

While she was thinking this, a large black and white cat tore past her and out of the back door, tail blown up like a brush. Mrs Brewster laughed and bent her legs so that the cat could get by.

'That's Minnie, she always flies at the dogs when they get fighting, she rules the roost.'

She patted Polly on the head. The puppy responded with an uncertain lowering of the head and a lethargic wag of the tail. Both husband and wife waved them off. As the car started, Pamela started to wail.

'Mum and Dad won't have Polly back, Mrs Turner. They didn't exactly want her in the first place, it was me that wanted a dog.'

In the rough lane leading away from the house Agnes stopped the car, turned and looked at Pamela, her face stern.

'Pamela, I will take Polly. She will be my dog. You need not tell your parents about the visit. Did they know the Brewsters?'

'Not really. Dad met him at work. He came in to fill some form out and Dad said–'

'And let him have the dog without going to see Polly's future home?'

Pamela nodded, then gazed ahead down the rough lane, her face white and serious.

'If I hadn't taken Mum's money, none of this would have happened, would it, Mrs Turner?'

Agnes, not normally given to lectures, felt it was time for one.

'Pamela, when you throw a stone into the middle of a lake, the ripples never cease until they have covered the whole lake. In this case Polly was involved and had to suffer the ripples. Now, where shall I take you? Home?'

Pamela was cuddling the little dog. Polly was still trembling, but looked more composed now, her eyes not so staring and fearful.

Agnes asked again, 'Do you want to go

home? Shall I run you there?'

Pamela shook her head vehemently. She looked pale and as apprehensive as the puppy in her arms.

'No. Take me to Bella's, please, Mrs Turner. They think that's where I am anyway.'

She directed Agnes to the street and house. It was not far along from the Robertses' house and of similar design and type. Pamela got out of the car. Polly tried to get out with her, but she gently put her back on the passenger seat. Before she shut the door she kissed the little dog on the head.

'It's my fault you've been through that awful time, nearly strangled, then living in that place with those terrifying dogs. It's all my fault!'

She shut the door and Agnes let the window down about two inches.

Pamela spoke to her through the window, her voice breaking with sheer emotion.

'I'll put it right, Mrs Turner. I will. I'll tell. I won't take his beastly stuff to the schools, no matter how much I owe him. And I'll come off the drugs too! I will, I will. Ecstasy and everything else. I've been so stupid, so stupid!'

Agnes did not like the sound of the words 'everything else'. Ecstasy was bad enough – and fatal in some cases.

'What else does he supply you with? Does Bella take drugs, and Tina?'

Pamela nodded, still looking through the car window at the puppy, who had curled up on the seat with eyes wide open.

'Yes. Just for kicks. We snort cocaine sometimes, or smack. But not much, only now and again. I could give it up tomorrow!'

Agnes sighed. How many people – particularly young people – had said that, and failed. Some had succeeded in beating the habit of course but...

'I'm going to tell Mum and Dad about Andy, and let them tell the police if they want to. We're not frightened of Andy.'

'Perhaps you should be, Pamela. He's a nasty man. Be careful, for goodness sake!'

8

Agnes was thinking of the treatment of the puppy, the desecration of her car. The broken window. Andy.

This dangerous man would not stop at anything if he thought his livelihood was in danger of being taken away.

As Agnes drove away she fleetingly thought of going to the police herself. But no, strictly speaking it was none of her business. These three silly girls had got themselves entangled in the drug scene. Let them get themselves out it!

On the way home she locked Polly in the car and went into the pet shop she had noticed several times on her way to Pretty Heads. She bought all the things she would need for Polly: a dog lead, tinned food, biscuits, a grooming comb, a shampoo. The latter contained, as the shopkeeper told her, 'something for the fleas'. Topping everything with a small squeaky toy, she loaded up and drove home, talking to Polly softly and stroking her head.

No one met her going in or in the lift and soon Polly was eating some of the tinned food, not with much enthusiasm – but at least she was eating it.

Agnes gave her two days to settle down, then gave her a bath. The little wound on Polly's neck had healed. Once the blood had been bathed away, there was little to be seen. That day too, a visit to the vet's.

'Oh, isn't this the little dog you brought in as an emergency?' Mr Singer was leafing through the pack of Polly's notes. 'The Roberts dog, isn't it?'

Agnes explained what had happened since then, the giving away of the puppy and also the fact that she was taking Polly and giving her a permanent home.

'Good. The little pup seems to have had

rather a rocky beginning, wouldn't you say, Mrs Turner?'

He instructed Agnes how to get the ownership changed on the microchip so that should Polly ever get lost she could be contacted immediately if anyone found her.

'Would you please change the name and address on Polly's notes, Mr Singer? She will need her yearly injection, won't she, and if she has any problems I would like to bring her to you.'

Agnes gave her address and felt much happier when she left the vet's. Polly was now her dog, and already she was losing her feelings of loneliness.

As the days went by, the change in Polly was lovely to watch. She put on a little weight and her coat improved and became smooth and shiny. Agnes took her for two walks a day. She did not meet any of the flat owners until Mrs Warburton saw her in the hall and remarked, 'Are pets allowed, Mrs Turner?'

Agnes had replied quite pleasantly, 'If they are not, Mrs Warburton, I'll move.'

Nothing had been said after that.

Luckily Polly did not bark or make any noise when Agnes went out, just retired to her bed and gave Agnes a wonderful welcome when she got back. It made all the difference to the flat and Agnes's doubts about whether she had done the right thing in buying it completely disappeared.

Agnes worried a little about Pamela Roberts. Andy, after all, was a drug pusher and, by the sound of him, wanted to extend his terrible trade by getting any 'client' who owed him money to do some work to enlarge his rounds. How could Pamela get away from him? Would she be able to stop taking drugs? How strongly were the three girls hooked?

However, the care of Polly did much to put the Robertses out of her mind. The way they had treated the dog, sending her off to an unknown environment, not bothering to check on her, all that was enough to persuade Agnes to leave it to them to sort out the problems with the police, or to confront Andy themselves, or whatever. Polly was safe and that was the most important outcome of the whole affair. She did realise that Andy might be just a very small cog in a larger organisation. Still, she thought, that was nothing whatever to do with her.

How very very wrong she was, as she was to find out at the beginning of the next week, on a sunny Monday morning.

She took Polly down in the lift, and then through the glass and mahogany door leading to the concrete steps that in turn led out of the back door to a strip of grass, rather tatty and unkempt, where Polly made herself comfortable. Later she would take her out to the country for a real walk on an extending lead.

When she came back she did notice that Louise Le Mesurier's milk was still outside her door. She looked at her watch, the milkman came early. Twenty to nine. Well, perhaps Louise was having a late morning, perhaps she had been to a party the night before and was catching up on some sleep.

She picked Polly up and got into the lift. As the lift doors swooshed to, the milk disappeared from her sight and for the moment from her memory, but alas, not for very long.

She fed Polly a very small breakfast of biscuits, replenished her water bowl and made herself her customary cup of coffee, put off since she had adopted Polly until after she came in from the puppy's first small outing.

At last Agnes was ready for Polly's real walk of the day, its timing influenced a little by the weather forecast after the morning news. Sunny but rain by midday. Well organised as she always was, she went to the rather pretty locker in the hall which was now designated as 'Polly's cupboard'. In it was the little dog's extending lead, her ordinary collar and lead, a stack of small plastic carriers with draw tops, poop scoops, plastic gloves. Agnes was very conscientious about picking up any mess Polly made, using the plastic glove or the scoop, popping it into the bag and drawing the string tightly and tying it.

Agnes went down the back stairs of the flats, not using the lift. She felt the exercise was probably good for her. Then she walked round to her car and set off for the country places where Polly could run around on her long lead. Agnes felt she would probably never let the lively puppy entirely off the lead. She was an excitable little animal and Agnes guessed she might easily take off after a rabbit, or even a bird scared out of the hedge. Agnes loved these walks with Polly and usually stayed out for an hour or sometimes more after she had found a safe place to park her car.

This morning she had had another apologetic telephone call from her garage, saying they were still waiting for the new door; one had arrived but the colour had not been perfect. Actually Agnes did not mind too much. She was getting used to the red car. She had carefully draped the passenger seat with an old bed sheet so that Polly would not spoil the upholstery with dirty paws, just as she had always done in her own car when Mac had been alive.

The morning was still fine and sunny as had been predicted. Agnes walked through the fields for an hour, sometimes walking quite briskly, sometimes slowly, occasionally stopping to give Polly time to savour the delicious country smells. Sometimes Polly would almost disappear into a ditch or hedge bottom, leaving just her fat little bottom and furiously wagging tail visible. She never caught anything in the hedge or ditch and Agnes thought there was probably nothing there to catch, only the fascinating scent of something.

When they got back again, Agnes looked at her watch. Ten to twelve, just right for her to clean Polly up a bit and prepare her own lunch. Using the back way again so that she could dump her little plastic bag into her dustbin, she climbed the few concrete stairs to the ground floor of the flats, picked the little dog up and made for the ground floor lift, feeling after her long walk that to climb up all the stairs to number 6 would be a bit much.

As she came through the glass and wooden doors into the hall of Flats 1 and 2, she noticed at once that the milk was still outside Louise's door. Perhaps she had just forgotten to take it in. Somehow Agnes felt uneasy about the bottle still being there. She determined she would ring the door bell and at least see if Louise was all right, the neighbourly thing to do she felt, but first she must cope with Polly.

Upstairs she put away the extending lead, put on Polly's ordinary collar, and checked the water bowl. The puppy took a few laps of water then retired to her bed, lying as she mostly did, on her back with her legs spread out showing her pink belly.

'No modesty, Polly. Now I won't be long.'

Agnes changed her shoes, kept on her coat and locked her front door. The lift took her smoothly down. She stepped out. The bottle of milk was still there, its silver top catching the light from the hall window. Agnes picked up the bottle and rang the door bell and waited. Nothing happened. No sound from inside the flat, only the constant rumble of the passing traffic. She tried again. Nothing. Perhaps Louise was out? Agnes bent down and pushed open the letter box, tried to peer in. A draught brush obscured the view, but to her surprise as she pushed, or tried to push, the brush aside with her fingers, the door opened. It was not locked. Suddenly Agnes had a feeling of foreboding, fear. Should she call someone else? She tried to banish the fear as irrational and cautiously entered the flat, calling, 'Louise, are you there? Louise, it's Agnes!'

No answer. The flat seemed unnaturally silent.

Agnes slowly crossed the little hall, guessing where the kitchen was. She placed the bottle of milk on the table and looked around. The kitchen was tidy, the curtains at the window drawn. Agnes went into the sitting-room, dark because of the drawn curtains. No one. The only sign of life, a single wine glass on the coffee table, beside it a bottle of white wine, two-thirds full. Agnes called again and again before entering the main bedroom. This time the curtains were not drawn closely and allowed the sun to light the room clearly.

There was Louise, lying diagonally across the double bed. Agnes immediately thought, remembering her fairly large intake of wine on the occasions she had been with her, she might be tipsy.

'Louise, wake up, wake up!'

She moved nearer, further to the end of the large bed, then she saw Louise's head. The fair hair matted with blood. The face turned towards the bed end, her eyes wide open but sightless, dead.

Agnes leant down to look more closely. Louise's head, the back of her head, was crushed in; slivers of bone were visible and small greyish jelly-like particles of brain. It was a gruesome sight. Agnes had seen plenty of terrible injuries in her nursing days – car crashes, road accidents, falls – but nothing had prepared her for this. The back of the skull was completely flattened. There were no signs of life.

Louise had on a white blouse, the collar and upper part stained with blood, skirt uncreased and in place, black sheer nylons, her shoes still on her feet, her legs partially supported by the bed. Agnes felt she must have been hit, brutally hit from behind, maybe never seeing her assailant, then fallen on to the bed.

Agnes realised she was shaking. She left the bedroom and went into the kitchen where she had noticed a white wall telephone. Automatically she dialled 999, gave the address and, trying to steady her voice and to sound normal, she said, 'There has been a murder here,' replacing the receiver before they could ask her name. The bottle of milk still stood on the kitchen table where she had put it when she first entered the flat.

She crossed the hall and put the front door on the latch so the police could get in without ringing. Then she left, got in the lift, let herself back into her own flat to be greeted by a joyful welcoming Polly. She knew she should have waited, explained, but she did not want to get involved any more than she had to be. They could and would come to question all the flat occupiers, including herself of course.

She would tell them it was she who had telephoned them, then let them ask what they liked. She would answer just the questions they asked, nothing more. She didn't want to tell them everything she knew because she had a suspicion, just a suspicion, that perhaps – perhaps – she herself had been the intended victim. The Robertses might have gone to the police, Andy might have found out and sought his revenge. He perhaps, and still only perhaps, had mistaken Louise for her – the change of car, the resemblance, the hair, the figure, the clothes. It could be, it could be!

Agnes poured herself a drink. She was no longer trembling. She sat and waited for the inevitable knock on her door or the peal of her door bell. A slight feeling of enjoyment came over her. Poor Louise, she thought, it was a shame she should lose her life but it was Andy who must be found and made to pay the proper price for what he had done or for what she suspected he might have done.

That was as far as she would let her thoughts travel. The police might find a man or a woman who wished Louise dead for some reason and had killed her. A totally different murderer with a totally different motive. After all, Agnes realised she knew little of Louise's past life. They had mostly talked of trivial things, clothes, make-up, television. But Louise Le Mesurier had been an attractive woman. Perhaps she had a lover, a jealous lover. She certainly had never mentioned a current man in her life.

Well, Agnes thought, let the police search first. They might even trace it to Andy, this killing, but somehow she doubted it. After all it was she and only she that knew who had thrown the stone though the window, scraped the car, all intended, aimed for and at her, Agnes Turner, not the French widow. Andy had nothing against Louise and had, if it were he, merely killed the wrong woman.

The questions, the interviews, the statements continued for a week or more. Each flat owner took it differently. Arthur Leeming was jovial and co-operative but knew nothing about the lady and couldn't understand why the DI or his colleague would not join him in a drink when they came to his flat.

'I know you are on duty but for goodness sake, a small one wouldn't hurt!'

The Major was furious about it all, complained that it was an invasion of privacy. His wife and he didn't know the woman at all, hadn't spoken to her, only a vague 'Good morning' now and again.

Miss Horrocks was, as she put it, 'being driven into a nervous breakdown by all these questions'. She couldn't bear it. Then usually tears and a rush up to Agnes's flat to literally cry on her shoulder. Agnes was kind to her and ministered to her with tea and biscuits or occasionally a glass of sherry or, in extremes, a brandy.

9

Three weeks went by and gradually the reporters stopped buzzing around the front door when anyone emerged.

Flat 2 was closed and everyone, including Agnes, felt a vague feeling of – was it fear? Perhaps just apprehension – when they crossed the lower hall to the front door.

Everyone had answered all the questions put to them. Agnes probably knew, had known, Louise Le Mesurier a little better than any of the others. No one except herself had ever been out with her. The only time they had met her was at the small drinks parties each had given. Although Agnes was the latest person to come to the flats, the police had asked more questions of her than any of the others, but she was not prepared for the question they asked just after the third week of the murder.

It was Sunday morning. Major and Mrs Warburton went to church, as did Miss Horrocks. They did not go to the same church. This fact Miss Horrocks made very clear to Agnes almost on the first Sunday she was there. Apparently Major and Mrs Warburton were what Miss Horrocks called

'High Church' whereas she was determinedly 'Low Church', stating firmly to a
completely disinterested Agnes that she
considered incense and all those vestments
and 'dressing up', as she put it, to be highly
wicked and 'a long way from the cross'.

Agnes's assurance that she was neither
High nor Low, and indeed did not go to
church at all, did not help. This had been
met only with a sniff from Miss Horrocks
and the would-be argument on her part fell
to the ground with scarcely a whimper.

On this Sunday, just over three weeks after
the death of Louise Le Mesurier, Agnes
returned from Polly's walk. Both Polly and
she were fairly damp.

The rain had started half-way through the
walk. Polly quite enjoyed getting wet and
loved being dried. This always ended up
with a game, Polly hanging on to one end of
the towel and Agnes the other. This Sunday
morning the game was just going on. Agnes
had already changed when there was a ring
at the front door. Agnes felt a wave of apprehension similar to that she experienced
when crossing the lower hall.

Should she let anyone in?

The Warburtons were out, Miss Horrocks
was out. Quickly she picked up the telephone and rang Arthur Leeming's number.

'Someone is ringing my flat from the front
door, Arthur. I've looked out of the window.

It's a man standing there. What shall I do?'

Arthur rose to the occasion rather as Agnes thought he would. Before he spoke, Agnes could hear the clink of a glass being set down on a table.

'Right. Let him come in and I'll come up, be having a drink with you. Then we can see what he wants. He can't murder both of us, can he?'

He laughed his rather resounding, fat laugh.

'Oh, thanks, Arthur, so much, I was a bit nervous!'

Agnes put the telephone down and pressed the intercom, but not the entry button.

A cultured voice answered the small click the intercom made.

'I'm Louise Le Mesurier's brother. She spoke of you on the telephone, Mrs Turner. I just have a small problem you may be able to help me with.'

There was no trace of a French accent there. In fact, the voice was English public school, rather than French in any way.

Perhaps he was educated in England, Agnes thought, and pressed the entry button, after saying, 'The lift in front of you will bring you up to my floor, Mr...?'

Agnes's door bell rang and she hurriedly opened it to Arthur Leeming who came in carrying a bottle of whisky and a glass, rather to Agnes's amusement.

'You needn't have brought your own whisky, Arthur!' she said, smiling. She shepherded him through to her sitting-room, placing a hastily produced dish of olives beside him, and went back to the front door.

The man who stood outside was strikingly good-looking, and had a family likeness to Louise.

'Please come in. I didn't catch your name?'

'Pierre, Pierre Demain.'

He looked towards Arthur Leeming, who rose and shook his hand.

Louise's brother sat down in the chair near Arthur. Agnes suggested perhaps he would like a drink.

Pierre Demain shook his head and waved away the suggestion with a very French gesture.

'We understand you have a problem. Maybe I, or ... we can help you with it?' Agnes included Arthur in this and he nodded in agreement. Agnes was so glad he was there.

She had no idea how she could help this elegant, handsome man, nor what sort of problem he might present her with.

Whatever it was, he was finding it difficult to start enlarging on it. He straightened his tie several times and ran a finger round the inside of his collar before he began.

'It's to do with a rather expensive diamond ring, Mrs Turner.'

'Well, the police will have that. They did a search of the flat.'

Pierre Demain shook his head and waved his hand again.

'No, no. You don't understand. The police have not reported finding such a ring and I am reluctant to ask them about it.'

'Why? Some skulduggery?' Arthur asked, laughing.

Pierre looked slightly surprised.

'In a way, yes. My sister lost it and claimed a hundred and fifty thousand pounds in insurance compensation, then found it again. I just wondered where she had hidden it. You see, she never confessed to the insurance company that she had found the ring.'

After a time a very sorry tale came out. Pierre Demain took some time to tell the story. Agnes felt there was shame there and a real need to put things right now his sister was dead. Perhaps though, she realised, he might not want to return the ring, perhaps he was not as honest as he sounded.

Arthur Leeming, getting slightly mellow on his own whisky, found the story Pierre told was rather amusing; he grimaced once or twice and was the recipient of several reproachful glances from Agnes. The thought of an insurance company losing money seemed to delight him.

Apparently when Louise had lost her third husband, she had been devastated but the question of money had not immediately arisen in her mind, for she believed that he would have provided for her. The expensive engagement ring, she had known its price. Like a child, she had accepted it as proof that she was marrying a wealthy man. In actual fact she was, but alas a man who could not stop gambling. They had been married only a few years when his untimely death from a particularly virulent type of cancer revealed a bank balance depleted almost to nothing.

Pierre would not, or perhaps could not, say whether Louise had genuinely lost or misplaced the ring which was now her only asset. But she had claimed the insurance and then later had found the ring.

Agnes pointed out that it was surely quite possible, if Louise had found the ring, that she had indeed told the insurance company, repaid the money and then sold the ring. At this her brother had sadly shaken his head.

'Repaid the money, Mrs Turner? You alas don't or didn't know my sister. Money ran through her fingers like water, it was gone.'

He was obviously upset about what Louise had done, but Agnes still could not see how she could help him. She said so.

'It was a forlorn hope, Mrs Turner, but I thought, hoped, she might have worn it when you were together. You might have admired it and she might have given some clue as to where she kept it, or hid it for safety.'

Agnes shook her head. Louise had never even mentioned the ring to her, but a thought flashed across her mind. Supposing, as she suspected, Andy was Louise's murderer – had she had it on that morning, and had Andy stolen it? Agnes was certain Andy would do such a thing, and would probably have the means to get rid of it. He probably would not get the huge sum of money the ring was worth, not selling it on, but he would get a very acceptable amount of money.

'You live in England, Mr Demain?' Agnes asked.

She was not particularly interested but she was suddenly preoccupied by a memory; a vague memory.

'No, I live in Paris. This flat is no use to me. I shall put it on the market as soon as I am able, but first I must do a thorough search for the ring. It may be somewhere, in an ornament or at the back of a drawer, I don't know.'

Arthur Leeming broke in suddenly.

'In a teapot, my wife hid things in teapots. First place the burglars look, I expect.'

104

'Yes, yes. I will look, even in the teapot.' Pierre Demain got up. 'I must go, I have taken enough of your time.'

Agnes put up a hand to detain him.

'Mr Demain, was the ring a large diamond with two emeralds, one each side, then a smaller diamond each side?'

'Yes, exactly, that was it, a beautiful ring.'

Agnes tapped her nail on her front teeth, a habit she had when she was trying to remember something.

'Then I did see it. She wore it to a dress show we went to. I can remember it on her hand. It was so large and ornate I took it for a piece of costume jewellery. I didn't think it was real.'

'Then this is good news. She still had it, still wore it. Maybe, I will find it. I will put it right for her – the deception haunted her, I know.'

He left with much murmuring after he had gone from Arthur, about insurance companies who could well afford to lose a bit and the man being a fool to think of paying them back, or trying to put his dead sister's affairs in order when the whole thing was probably forgotten or written off as one of the insurance company's few losses.

Agnes hoped Arthur Leeming would not tell the 'ring' story to anyone else, especially the police. She did go so far as to suggest it would be better not to mention the unfortunate occurrence at all, as obviously Mr Demain was trying to keep his sister's deception a secret. His only reply was a non-committal 'Humph' as he picked up his whisky bottle and glass. Thanking her for the drink, which she did not remind him he brought himself, he then walked rather unsteadily to the front door.

Agnes wanted to think, wanted to forget Pierre Demain and his search for the missing ring. It wasn't so easy.

Two mornings later she and the Frenchman almost collided as she came in with Polly and he came out of Flat 2. He greeted her with his usual charm.

'Good morning, Mrs Turner. No luck, I am afraid.'

Agnes looked puzzled for a moment. 'Oh, I'm sorry, perhaps...' She stopped, unable to think of anything adequate to say.

'I shall leave tomorrow, return to Paris. I can't do any more. Perhaps you and Mr Leeming would have lunch with me tomorrow? I would be most grateful if you would, most grateful.'

Agnes was about to say no, though felt she could not speak for Arthur as well, when as if by magic the lift doors opened and the man in question appeared. The invitation was repeated and promptly accepted.

'Oh, that would be very nice, wouldn't it, Agnes? It's very nice of you. Is that the last we shall see of you, and have you found the ring?'

Pierre Demain shook his head. He hadn't found it and he had searched in every possible place, drawers, cupboards, ornaments, teapots. He gave Arthur a small and rather rueful smile.

'Well, I must go. Shall we meet here tomorrow, say about twelve thirty?'

Agnes felt impatient about the whole thing, the lunch invitation, the visits of the police, the questioning. She was anxious to get on with her own investigation. At least she had a suspect. Had she realised how much further this lunch date was to take her along the road in her own investigations, she would have welcomed it with much greater enthusiasm. But of course she didn't know and she went into the lift with Polly, feeling that she had been trapped into accepting by Arthur Leeming's untimely appearance.

10

The restaurant that Pierre Demain took them to was unknown to Agnes, but then, of course, she had not been living in Brighton long enough to have tried many eating places. This was a small place, rather dark, but warm and cosy. Pierre Demain was a good host. He was driving and was very abstemious with regard to drinking wine.

Unlike his sister, Agnes thought and felt a bit guilty at the thought.

Their host told them he would have to come back in a week or two to meet the auction house who were clearing the flat.

The food finished, they were sitting having coffee and Agnes's favourite liqueur, kümmel, not usually a luxury that she would indulge in, especially at lunch-time. They had moved from the dining-room into a small area given over to coffee drinkers. It was near the street window and one could see the cars and people moving by in the afternoon's rather misty air. Suddenly Agnes saw a car, dark blue, fairly new-looking, a coupé, the top open. But it wasn't the car that caught her eye, it was the driver. Andy. Just as he drew level with the restaurant the traffic forced him to slow down.

Agnes prayed he would not look around him – if he did, it would be quite possible he might see her. He didn't. The car edged forward and Andy moved past. Agnes felt her pulse quicken. Andy looked different, better dressed, and the car – that was a very new addition. No bicycle would be leaning against the school walls now by the look of it. The ring, was this the result of Andy finding the ring in the flat of the woman he had killed?

Lunch over, Pierre Demain drove them back to the flats. It really had, thanks to his charm and good manners, been a most pleasant interlude. They said their goodbyes in the lower hall of the flats. Pierre was leaving for France at five o'clock. He was not sure of the date the auctioneers were coming to clear the flat, but he would have to be there, he said. Then they would send him a catalogue of the furniture, china, silver etc.

'So we may meet again sometime,' he said with his charming smile.

Back in her flat, putting a collar on the wildly welcoming Polly ready for her delayed walk, Agnes could see the blue car in her mind's eye and thought again, from bike to car. The money had come from somewhere and where else she wondered, but from Louise Le Mesurier's ring? What to do now? Pamela, she needed to see Pamela again, but how could she get hold of the girl without her parents knowing? Perhaps Pamela had packed in the drugs scene, dumped Andy, said she would have nothing more to do with him. Agnes hoped not. She had no other way of keeping tabs on Andy except through Pamela.

Then she suddenly thought of Bella, Pamela's friend. She knew where she lived because she had taken Pamela there. Would she be a better person to get in touch with? How much was Bella involved? Could Bella pay more readily for her supply, if she was using drugs? If so, she would not be as useful as Pamela. Well, Agnes argued with herself, most teenagers could not raise the kind of money they needed if their habit was big and growing daily. She would try Bella first. Meet her – where? Leaving school, try to get her alone, away from her school-mates.

A nice feeling engulfed Agnes. No longer did she feel bored, useless. She was alive again, full of thoughts as to how she could solve so many pressing problems and punish the evil doers.

The first visit to the hairdresser's after Louise's death, Agnes had felt, would be rather overwhelming. She was right. Exclamations abounded:

'Oh, Mrs Turner, we couldn't believe it.' 'Such a nice lady!'

The endless questions, who did it, why did they do it, was anybody suspected, bothered Agnes.

'Poor Melanie was so upset. She kept thinking of her poor head, how they described it in the papers, so awful!'

Melanie was the girl who cut, styled and tinted Louise's hair.

Agnes did her best to stave off the questions. One or two of the customers joined in as well, and when the time came, Agnes was glad to leave.

The next visit was a little better and they talked about other things as well. But Valerie did make a remark that gave Agnes food for thought and reinforced her feeling that if Andy was the killer, he had mistaken Louise for herself.

Showing Agnes the back of her head with the mirror, Valerie said suddenly, 'Mrs Turner, it was strange that although I did your hair and Melanie did Mrs Le Mesurier's, the style was so alike, wasn't it?'

Agnes murmured some discreet reply and waited till she was under the drier to sort out her thoughts on the subject a little more objectively.

Agnes always found her time under the drier at the hairdresser's a good moment for reflection, for getting her thoughts in order. The hum of the machine cut one off from the trivial conversation that usually went on in the hairdresser's.

She felt beautifully isolated from any outside noise or distraction. Even the passing traffic, people coming in to make appointments, was almost shut off. It was rather like watching television with the sound turned down.

Agnes began to think about Andy, how he could possibly have made the mistake of thinking one woman was the other.

Names!

They were her first thought. The name of the murdered woman, featured in the papers, would mean nothing to him. He presumably did not know either woman's name, hers or Louise's, unless Pamela had told him. Le Mesurier would be no different from Turner if he was not acquainted with either.

Appearance too? There in the comfort of the drier Agnes remembered dashing across that busy road to rescue the puppy. She let her thoughts drift back to that morning. The forgotten hair lacquer, then the words to Valerie–

'I think I'll put a headscarf on. It's breezy out there.' Something like that.

So, he had only seen a little of her fair hair. Louise normally wore a hat, so the same amount, or almost the same amount, of fair hair would be visible again. The tweed suit that Louise wore strongly resembled a suit Agnes had rather resurrected to use for walking Polly.

It was all possible. The change of car could have muddled him. The fact that she had almost stopped using the front door because of Polly would mean he would not see, or know, she was the owner of the dog; he would only see Louise's entrances and exits and her own without Polly.

The ring came next into her thoughts. She found it surprising that Louise should have been so dishonest as to claim the money, yet not tell the company that she had found the ring. Still, money might have been short at the time. According to her charming brother, it had preyed on her mind. He wanted to return the ring to the insurance company. Was he telling the truth?

Anyway... As she remembered now, Louise had worn it at the dress show. Did that show a guilty conscience? But that was not really the question. There was Andy's car. Had he bought it with money obtained from drug dealing or from murder? Of course, it might not be his car.

The 'Ping' went on the drier. Her period of protected thought was over.

The conclusion, Agnes felt was – must be – that Andy had killed Louise thinking it was her and found the ring, probably on Louise's finger.

Well, the last thought that came to her as she ducked out of the drier was a rather uncomfortable one. When he found out Louise was not the woman who knew he was a drug dealer, not the woman he wished to silence, would it mean that she, herself, was in danger?

Probably.

As Valerie put the finishing touches to her hair, she chatted away.

Agnes missed most of the chatter, pre-occupied as she was with her own thoughts, but she just caught Valerie's final remark.

'Of course, they'll never catch him, will they?'

And as Agnes paid and left the salon, she felt Valerie was probably right, as far as the police were concerned – but then, Valerie didn't know someone else was stalking the murderer too. Someone who knew, or was almost certain she knew, exactly who the murderer was.

Driving home, still in the red Porsche, she kept an eye out for the blue car but did not see it. Her next objective was to try to talk to Bella – preferably alone, not with Pamela.

Bella seemed to act as Pamela's alibi when Pamela wanted to be somewhere her parents forbade her to go, or with someone they disapproved of.

It was, Agnes thought, worth a try. A talk to the girl might prove useful. After driving Pamela there, she knew where Bella lived. Should she call? What excuse could she make to the girl's parents for wanting to see their daughter?

As it happened, fate seemed to be on Agnes's side. The first time she approached the house about a week later, at about half-past three. Bella was just getting out of her parents' Volvo. The parents stayed in the car. Bella made for the front door, waving to her mother and father, putting her key in the lock. She disappeared inside.

The car started jerkily, throwing up a small cloud of gravel. The parents drove off.

Bad driver, Agnes thought, and waited till the Volvo was some way away. She parked her car about three houses up the pleasant tree-lined road. She waited a few minutes then walked up the short drive to the house.

Agnes rang the door bell. No answer.

She pressed the bell again, a little harder and longer.

The door opened.

Bella appeared at the door.

There was a white rim on her upper lip, where she had been drinking milk. She licked it off before she spoke.

'Yes?' she asked.

11

The girl standing in the doorway, licking the milk from her upper lip, was not at all like Agnes had expected. She thought she would be another Pamela, or Tina, the girl who had run away, or like the girls she had seen coming out of the private school. This girl, Bella, was certainly different: taller, her young breasts fuller, her legs long, well shaped. For a moment she thought the girl could be Bella's older sister, she looked at least eighteen, but no, it was Bella. She smiled suddenly, showing white, even teeth. She opened the door wider and asked Agnes in.

It soon became obvious that she knew who Agnes was but not, by the sound of her first remark, why she had come to her house. She was poised and quite at ease entertaining an adult in her house with her parents out. She ushered Agnes to an arm-chair in a pleasant, well-furnished sitting-room, then said with easy confidence, 'I'll get Mrs Fellows to make some tea.'

She left the room, was gone only a few minutes, then she came back, sat down on the settee and curled her long shapely legs under her. Her movements were rather feline and, rather to Agnes's amusement as she thought this, a large long-haired ginger cat jumped up on to the settee beside Bella. The girl looked across at Agnes, grinned and rubbed the cat's stomach. It was lying upside down, four feet in the air, purring loudly.

'I'm a cat person myself, Mrs Turner, but I believe, according to Pamela Roberts, you are a dog person. It was great how you rescued Polly from that place her parents had sent her to. Pamela thinks the sun shines out of you.'

116

It was obvious, as Agnes let Bella chatter on, that Pamela had told her all about how Agnes had helped get Polly back and had then given her a home, but there was no mention of Andy's cruelty to the dog. Strange. Could it be that Bella was more friendly with Andy, or maybe used him more as a dealer than the others, worked for him, perhaps? So maybe Pamela had not told her about that incident.

A rather fat motherly-looking woman pushed the sitting-room door open with her foot, came in and plonked the tray down on the coffee table. Half a dozen ginger biscuits scudded on to the tray from the plate and she said, 'Bother,' and collected the biscuits up and put them back on the plate. The teapot, milk jug and cups and saucers were all of pretty matching china.

'And there's that.'

She pointed a stubby finger at something on the tray.

'You left it on the kitchen draining board. You know what your mother will say if she sees it. I'm off now.'

She already had a hat and coat on. She gave a vague smile in Agnes's direction and went out, banging the door behind her. A further bang, Agnes presumed, meant she had left the house. Whether this was her normal behaviour or whether she was in a bad temper because of getting tea for them,

Agnes couldn't guess but, as if she read her thoughts, Bella laughed and rubbed the cat. 'Noisy old fat oldie she is, eh, Ginger?'

Then the girl did something that caused Agnes's heart to give a little jerk and beat a little faster. Bella picked up something from the tray, almost hidden by the plate of ginger biscuits. A ring. She slipped it on to her middle finger and as she lifted the teapot Agnes got a good look at it. A large diamond, flanked by two large green emeralds, then two small diamonds, one each side. The ring! The ring that Louise had worn to the dress show or, if it was not that ring, one exactly like it. What was it doing on the finger of the girl pouring tea opposite her? It suited her white pretty hand.

Agnes had called on her to try and find out something more about Andy. Was the ring the first clue? She took the cup of tea handed to her and refused the offered biscuit.

'What a pretty ring, Bella,' she said.

Bella looked at the ring and twisted it round her finger. 'Yes, it is pretty, isn't it? It's only costume jewellery though, not real, at least I don't think it is.'

The diamonds sparkled in the spring sunshine filtering through the window, as if to give the lie to Bella's remark. It was a beautiful ring.

Agnes recognised the distribution of the stones, the setting, everything about it. She longed to ask more about it, but did not in case Bella should clam up. She need not have worried. Bella was very forthcoming.

'Tell me why you came to see me, Mrs Turner. About Pamela, is it? Is she in trouble again? You know she's got a really bad smack problem? She'll take money from anywhere to get it. I feel sorry for her. Her parents are potless.'

'Do you mean she's on heroin, Bella?'

Bella nodded, still twisting the ring round and round on her finger. This news about Pamela surprised Agnes. Surely the parents would know, would notice something un-usual? But the ring was her greatest puzzle and in a way the greatest impediment. Had Andy given Bella the ring? If so, she could hardly ask the girl to say anything against him. Agnes leant forward to get a closer look at the ring. Bella stopped twisting it.

'Do let me see, it's so charming. May I look at it?'

Bella took the ring off and handed it to Agnes, a questioning look in her brown eyes.

'They do make costume jewellery well these days, don't they?'

Agnes slipped the ring on her finger. The diamond flashed.

'I had a ring. I bought it for myself. A ring

exactly like Princess Diana's engagement ring. A big blue stone surrounded by small diamonds. It really looked like the real thing, unless you examined it closely.'

Agnes took the ring off and put it on the tea tray. Bella did not attempt to pick it up and put it on again. She refilled Agnes's teacup and her own, took a ginger biscuit and dunked it and thrust the whole biscuit into her mouth, cupping her mouth with her hand.

'Was that a present or did you buy it yourself?'

Agnes tried hard to make the question sound casual. Bella let one curled-up leg fall off the settee and began to swing her foot in its ugly thick-soled black shoe to and fro rhythmically.

'I stole it actually, fancied it and stole it.'

Agnes decided to take the remark in the same cool way it had been made. She sipped her tea and put the cup back in the saucer before replying with a disbelieving smile on her lips, designed to provoke Bella into proving she was telling the truth.

'How could you manage to steal such a pretty piece of costume jewellery? I expect the woman's furious at leaving it wherever she did. You couldn't have taken it from her finger, I imagine?'

Bella grinned and, like Agnes, almost as if in imitation, she took a sip of her tea before she replied. Her long-lashed dark eyes narrowing as if with hidden laughter, she put down her cup.

She linked her hands behind her head, her eyes became more serious, she shook her head, looked round the room as if deciding just how much she would say. Agnes felt the tension welling up in the girl.

'Andy Weedon is a low-class evil shit.'

The words came out with calm venom.

'Then why do you have anything to do with him, Bella?'

'Oh, Mrs Turner, come to the party, get real. So many of us have bought drugs off him, especially Pamela, and he's got us hooked. He's got us right where he wants us.'

Agnes was silent. Her mind was in a whirl, the ring uppermost. He must have killed Louise or he wouldn't have the ring. That was where Bella had stolen it from, but how? She had to ask.

'Bella, did you steal the ring from Andy – what did you say his name was, Weedon? How did you get it, where was it?'

Bella yawned, her tension retreating. She was obviously bored with the conversation and the business of Andy Weedon. She got up, went to the mantelpiece, picked up a packet of cigarettes, took one out and lit it with a gold lighter lying beside the pack. She took a long luxurious draw and began to talk, assuming, Agnes thought, that her guest wanted to know more about Pamela than about Andy Weedon, but Agnes sat back and listened, refusing the cigarette Bella offered her.

'Not supposed to smoke, I'm not. So why do the olds do it and leave the things around?'

Agnes was equally interested in Pamela Roberts and the drug supplier, both had to be dealt with, especially now, if the ring was anything to go by. She might be dealing not only with a dealer, but also a murderer. Excitement flooded over her as she listened to Bella's story. Now she was getting somewhere, she hardly needed to interrupt the girl's flow of words at all, just a discreet question now and again, to get the facts more clearly sorted out, but mostly she just listened.

Bella began at the beginning, rather as if she wanted to tell someone all about it. In some ways Agnes felt the girl was showing off, enjoying telling the story which featured her as the leader, Pamela as only a silly schoolgirl.

The three of them, Tina aged fifteen and a half, Pamela just fifteen and Bella sixteen, had gone to a rave in a garage near their homes. Pamela could get out quite easily by lowering herself out of her bedroom window on to the flat-roofed garage beneath. She was the one with the strictest parents. Tina's hardly bothered where she was and Bella's were great party-goers. As their daughter was sixteen they gave her an immense amount of freedom, at least so Agnes thought as she listened to the exploits the girl got up to with boyfriends, especially those a bit older, who had motor bikes or cars. Freedom it certainly was.

None of the girls, according to Bella, was into drugs at all, not until they met Andy Weedon. He offered them a couple of Ecstasy tablets free, only two. Tina took one, and Pamela the other.

'I was tired out by about one thirty, but they were still dancing like mad. I didn't think much of it really, Mrs Turner. There was a man there selling bottles of water, I could see he was just filling the bottles at the tap and selling it as mineral water.'

She laughed, then her face became more serious.

Andy had come up to them again and asked them did they want more tablets.

'Not freebies this time though, girlies,' he had said.

As none of them had any money left, they could not buy any.

'See you next time. Bring the cash and I'll fix you up.'

That was how it all started.

It began to be a habit. They would rustle

up some money somehow. Bella could usually sweet-talk her father into a sub. Tina too had decent pocket money and could get more, but Pamela had to steal it from her mother – she'd even taken the money put out for the milkman one morning. The paper boy got blamed for it and Pamela's parents starting putting a cheque out for the milkman.

Bella had laughed again when she was telling that part of the story and Agnes had broken into her laughter: 'I don't think that's awfully funny, Bella.'

The girl had shrugged her shoulders and made a little grimace at Agnes.

'No, you're quite right, it wasn't funny, especially as the paper boy got the sack.'

Andy Weedon began to hot up the salesmanship and appeared at the school. Ecstasy was his main bag, but some of the girls were snorting cocaine, not many were shooting up, not at first, but it grew. Some of the older girls got found out and were expelled. Pamela tried heroin. She seemed, as Agnes listened, to be the weakest of the crowd, buying more Ecstasy than the others, and wanting to try the harder stuff as well.

As Bella chatted on, spelling it all out as if she had been longing for ages to do so, Agnes pictured Pamela's house – the neatness, the banishing of her dog – and she wondered just how much her stupid drug-taking was due to her parents. To her surprise Bella answered her question as if Agnes had spoken it aloud.

'Mind you, Mrs Turner, if either of my parents had given Ginger or George Rats away to a horrid home, I'd have pinched their money, set fire to their car.' Both cats were on her lap as she spoke. Agnes felt the girl meant what she said.

Agnes now had a much clearer idea about Andy's drug-dealing activities, but the ring was still a real puzzle. Why was Bella wearing it? Had Andy given it to her? Agnes hardly thought so, unless he too thought it almost worthless. But then, if he had thought that, why bother to steal it, especially from Louise's finger? A gruesome task if she was already face downward on the bed, covered in blood and, from the state of her skull, very dead. No, there was something strange here. She had to find out what was going on.

Agnes was beginning to distrust all the stories she'd heard, even the one told by Louise's smooth-tongued French brother about the insurance company. If he was telling the truth and the ring really was worth a hundred and fifty thousand pounds, would he declare it or was he really after the money? Who was telling the truth, who had deceived Louise? Pierre Demain, Andy

Weedon, Bella?

Suddenly Agnes put the blunt question to the girl opposite her who looked so innocent, so young, stroking the two cats with her long fingers and black-painted nails, and who seemed to be able to solve the problem.

'Tell me the real truth about the ring, Bella. You're just making up a story about it at the moment.'

The rather brusque tone, the words 'real truth' made the complacent smile disappear from Bella's face. She looked down at the cats and her lower lip quivered a little. Was that acting too, Agnes wondered?

'Well yes, Mrs Turner, it was a lie. I use drugs too and have to pay Andy. It's easier for me with my more generous parents, more pocket money. He started me on cocaine and now I've got to do what he says.'

'Well what does he say, about the ring I mean? Why have you got the ring? Did he give it to you?'

Bella shook her head, got out a crumpled tissue from her pocket and wiped her eyes with it.

'We are all three in a mess, Mrs Turner, a mess, particularly Pamela who owes him most. He says he will make her go with men, you know, if she doesn't pay him, or help him. I don't know if he means it, I don't think he does.'

'What about the ring, Bella, where did he get the ring and why did he give it to you? Even if it's only a fake one, why did he give it you – or did you really steal it?'

Bella tore the tissue into little bits, screwed them up into a ball, then looked at Agnes. In spite of the tears in her eyes, as she put one finger up and pushed the hair behind her ear in that nowadays typical teenage gesture, she was still so pretty, so mature, that Agnes hoped Andy was not using her for anything other than peddling.

'It's my uncle, my Dad's brother. They haven't spoken for twenty years. They had a quarrel before I was born and, well, he's a jeweller. He has a shop on the other side of Brighton. He, Andy, wants me to take the ring, see how much it's worth, just in case it's ... you know, real.'

'Does Andy want your uncle to buy it?'

Bella shook her head. 'That wasn't the idea at all, just to put a valuation on it and then Andy could sell it to a man he knew, who would say nothing.'

Suddenly Agnes was tired of listening to Bella, tired of the stupidity of these three teenagers, all of whom came from reasonable and certainly not deprived backgrounds. She made up her mind and much to Bella's astonishment said, 'Very well, Bella. It's only quarter-past four. Let's go

127

over and see your uncle and get him to tell us about the ring, tell us if it's just an attractive piece of costume jewellery or the real thing.'

The girl sprang to her feet, scattering the cats from her lap. Her face lit up, she really wanted this.

'Oh, Mrs Turner, if you would come with me, that would be wonderful.'

The journey across Brighton was something of a nightmare. Their start had been a little delayed by Bella's insistence that the two cats must be fed and safely shut in before they could be left.

'It's their meal time and they won't understand. Mum and Dad are going to a drinks party. They won't be back till about eight. I can't leave the cats hungry.'

Of course the delay met with Agnes's complete approval. Anything to do with animals' comfort and well-being always came first with her.

Polly, too, had to be collected on the way and given a short walk on the back yard grass then fed and watered.

Finally they were free to set off and battle with the stream of cars, motor bikes, vans and lorries.

Agnes began to worry a little that the jeweller's shop might be closed before they got there. She was also very anxious to know if the ring was a 'cheap imitation' or not.

She was almost sure it was the ring she had seen on Louise Le Mesurier's finger at the fashion show and if it was worth a fortune she'd know it was Louise's for certain.

'Left now, please, Mrs Turner, and then right,' instructed Bella. 'You'll see the shop on your left. It's only small, but very exclusive. Uncle Steven is a posh jeweller. I wish Dad and he would work things out.'

Agnes turned into a slightly smaller street, to her left, then to her right.

She saw the small jeweller's lighted window, and drew up outside. As Bella had said, it was exclusive. A very small window was lit from the back, a green velvet curtain carefully draped. In the front was displayed a gold necklace with small diamonds set in alternate links. The stand around which it was featured was in the form of a velvet neck. A few items, no more than six, were dotted about, mostly gold. Over the window, in gold letters on black, were the words 'Goldstein Jewellers'.

Bella pushed open the door as Agnes locked her car, having given her usual words of reassurance to Polly: 'We won't be long, Polly.'

Before they had set out Agnes had insisted that she should show the ring to Bella's uncle and claim that she was getting it assessed for a friend of hers who had found it in a box of trinkets. Bella had agreed to

129

this as long as she was allowed to hear what her Uncle Steven thought the ring was worth and, of course, Agnes returned the ring to her when they left the jeweller's shop.

Agnes had thought as she had taken the ring from Bella and placed it in her handbag, how many lies and how much deceit and guilt it had already caused. Even she herself was prepared to lie about her part in its history.

A bell tinkled as Bella pushed open the door. A white-haired man looked up. He was standing behind a glass counter, examining a fine gold chain. He dropped the chain and came round the counter, arms open wide, and embraced his niece.

'Bella, Bella. My little Bella! So long since you have been to see your old uncle!

Bella introduced Agnes to her uncle, and after a good many more pleasantries Agnes managed to explain the reason for her visit.

Bella burst in with, 'Nunc, I told Mrs Turner you were the best jeweller in Brighton and knew more about precious stones than anyone else. Isn't that true?'

Her uncle smiled broadly at Agnes, lifting his shoulders, shrugging the palms of his hands upwards in the Jewish fashion, obviously pleased.

'If she says so, who am I to contradict such a lovely and pretty person, eh?'

He proffered chairs. They both sat down opposite him. Agnes passed him the ring. As he took it in his hand, he became all jeweller. He took what looked to Agnes like a chamois leather and rubbed the white metal of the ring, gold or platinum, she wasn't sure.

There was a long silence while he turned the ring this way and that, put a small glass to his eye and the ring close to his nose, again turning the jewel this way and that. Then he suddenly spoke, but only to say, 'Excuse me, please, ladies.'

He crossed the shop and disappeared into a back room.

'That's his office, very important place to Nunc!' Bella whispered. She was obviously very fond of her uncle and proud of him.

After a time Mr Goldstein emerged. He looked preoccupied and yet pleased with himself. He spoke directly to Agnes, holding the ring between his thumb and forefinger and moving it, making the big diamond flash in the lights of the little shop. He seemed reluctant to put it down. As last he laid it gently down on the glass counter.

'Mrs Turner, your friend is very lucky to have found this – in a box of trinkets, you said?'

Agnes nodded, feeling distinctly guilty. She did not lie easily to anyone she liked. She turned to Bella, but the girl's attention

131

was focused on her uncle.

'Yes, Nunc. Well, is it valuable? That's the thing!'

He nodded, his eyes still fixed on Agnes. He folded his rather white hands together as if to get the last ounce of drama from his words.

'Mrs Turner, these stones are nothing short of ... let us say, magnificent. The large diamond is perfect, as are the emeralds. It is not, strictly speaking, an antique ring. I would judge by the filigree effect at the side of the small diamonds and the setting in general that it was made in the seventies. Needs cleaning, which would bring out the green of the emeralds even more brilliantly.'

Bella could not contain herself any longer. She burst in.

'Nunc, stop all that. How much is it worth in money?'

Her uncle looked at her reproachfully but continued, quietly.

'I think, Mrs Turner, should your friend wish to sell this object, the selling price would be in the region of one hundred and thirty-five thousand pounds and for insurance purposes, one hundred and fifty thousand pounds.'

Agnes was not surprised. After all, that was the figure that had been quoted by Louise's brother. But Bella was ecstatic.

Agnes was afraid that in her excitement

she would give the game away, but she didn't. She just smiled, almost giggled.

'Thank you so much, Mr Goldstein. I thought it was a very charming ring.'

'It is also a very expensive one.'

The jeweller placed the ring in a black leather ring box, the name of the shop in gold on the white satin lining of the lid. The ring nestled in the black velvet of the box, looking even more expensive and impressive in its proper surroundings.

Although he said he would certainly not charge for the estimate of the jewel's worth, Agnes insisted on paying him for his expertise, and did so.

More kisses and embraces and 'Come and see me again, Bella!' and then they were outside the shop. Agnes handed the little box back to Bella once they were in the car. She felt rather reluctant to part with it.

Bella's pleasure puzzled Agnes. Why should she want to give the ring and the resulting cash to a boy who was a drug pusher? Then Bella told her something which made her partially, but only partially, understand.

Andy Weedon wanted the money to take him to an expensive private clinic in London where he'd heard of a doctor who was having great success at removing birthmarks using revolutionary laser treatment.

'Andy hates that mark so much. It is pretty

133

horrible, I don't blame him for wanting to get rid of it. Maybe it's that that makes him like he is. If I had to live with a mark like that, who knows what I'd be like.'

Agnes turned to agree with her but then Bella did not know the man she pitied was also a murderer. A cold-blooded murderer.

Agnes again felt the old feeling. She was in possession of more facts than anyone and that was just the way she liked it.

12

The drive back across Brighton to Bella's house was much quieter traffic-wise. Even so, Agnes drove rather slowly. Polly had jumped off Bella's lap and had retired to the back seat, where she was stretched out, fast asleep.

Bella gazed at and caressed the little black ring box. She snapped open the lid once or twice to admire the ring, nestling in its little slot of velvet. She smoothed the white satin lining. The gold letters were precise and easy to read, the satin puffed up and shiny.

'It looks much better in its box, doesn't it, Mrs Turner? Andy will know that I really did take it to my uncle because his name is on it, my Uncle Steven's name, I mean!'

She showed the name, Goldstein, to Agnes.

Agnes stole a glance at Bella, wondering about her.

'Do you mean he might think you had lied about it?'

'Well, he might. One hundred and thirty-five thousand pounds is a lot of money, isn't it? He'll be able to get a car, as well as get his birthmark done.'

Agnes felt there was a hint of fear in the girl's voice when she spoke about Andy. Perhaps it was because the awful man was capable of withdrawing the drug source from her, and probably many of her friends.

'He may, this Andy, have passed me in a car the other day – a blue one, I think it was. Dark blue, rather a new car by the look of it.'

Agnes made this remark casually as if she was not particularly interested. But she was wondering if the car had replaced the bike, because he had found enough money in Louise's flat to buy it. Before or after he had bludgeoned her to death. Agnes shuddered slightly as the picture of Louise dead and battered lying on the bed flashed before her memory again.

'Oh, that blue car! No. He borrows that from his brother sometimes. His brother is a bit of an airhead. Makes Andy pay when he uses his car though. Not just for the petrol and oil, but a rent, kind of like hiring it out.'

Bella seemed to Agnes to know a good deal more about Andy than she had at first revealed. She wondered if, underneath all the fear, perhaps Bella regarded Andy Weedon as her boyfriend. It seemed hardly likely.

As they arrived at Bella's front door, there were no lights on, except the porch light, which probably came on automatically.

'They're not home yet. Didn't expect they would be, drinks parties usually end about eight, unless they start chatting.'

Agnes wondered whether there would be a meal for the girl. Funny how families lived nowadays, she thought. The tea things would still be on the table as they had left them, the place in semi-darkness. Her mind switched quickly to her own teenage years before she had left the nuns in the orphanage. Maybe she hadn't missed much, at least compared with today's standards.

'You are not going to mention my name, Bella, in connection with this ring, I mean?'

Bella shook her head very positively.

'Oh no, Mrs Turner. I'm certainly not, if you don't mind. Thank you for going with me though. Uncle would have had a fit if he'd thought it belonged to me, wouldn't he?'

She smiled widely.

Agnes nodded, pleased that the girl was so adamant about it. Bella added, explaining the reason, 'I want Andy to think I did it all, so he owes me one, you know what I mean? In case I need anything from him.'

Drugs, I suppose, Agnes thought as she drove away, but at that moment there was nothing she could do about it, not until she had caught and dealt with the purveyor of those drugs.

When Agnes arrived home she felt completely disorganised. She was a person who liked her day to be orderly. Polly's early walk, coffee on her return with whatever breakfast she wanted, usually toast and marmalade and fruit juice. Then dress ready for shopping if there was any to be done, then change again into clothes and shoes suitable for Polly's long walk. Home to a glass of white wine and lunch. This was her main meal unless of course she had asked someone to dinner in the evening, which was not often now because she was becoming rather a television buff and did not like missing any of her favourite programmes. For some strange reason she didn't enjoy them as much if they were videoed or repeated.

So she had built this routine for herself, slightly altered with Polly's arrival, but while Polly had brought some change she'd also made her life less lonely and much more enjoyable.

Today her visit to Bella and Bella's uncle had thrown everything out of gear. On her arrival home, she tried to get back to normal. Polly's walk was a shorter one than usual. When they got back Agnes fed her dog and prepared herself supper. She found two slices of chicken breast in the fridge, made a salad, heated some soup and turned on the television. With the tray on her lap and Polly asleep and replete at her feet she began to feel she had caught up with herself and her comforting routines.

By bedtime she had tried to put Bella, Tina and silly Pamela Roberts out of her mind. What she wanted now was a plan to punish and, if necessary, get rid of the man responsible for their problems and for killing and robbing someone who had nothing whatever to do with the scene he lived in. His treatment of Polly, too, was not forgotten in all this.

It was not easy for Agnes to get to sleep. She lay staring at the window, wondering how much luck and coincidence would help her. They usually did, she might almost say, always did, but would this time be the same? Suppose he did not come skulking round the gates of the schools, then she would have lost him, perhaps for ever. No, because all she'd have to do would be to go back to Bella. Agnes felt that where Andy went,

Bella might follow. She would keep an eye on him.

She also had to take into consideration that Andy Weedon might, if he could, quickly sell the ring and go off in search of this specialist laser treatment Bella had talked of. Agnes had no idea how long it would take, where it would be done. Again, she might have to cultivate Bella a little more. She would be sure to know. The supply of drugs to anyone buying from him would be affected by his absence. It was a pity the ring was wrapped around with so much secrecy. Pierre Demain, Bella, Andy, Bella's parents... How very lucky it was for the man who had stolen and murdered, perhaps because of it.

Days went by and nothing happened, no word from Bella. Agnes had driven by the two schools where she had seen Andy before. Nothing, no sign of him. Agnes waited and fretted. The police appeared to be getting nowhere. Louise's brother came and the flat was cleared.

Everybody in the flats wondered if Louise Le Mesurier's flat would ever sell when the would-be buyers found out what had happened in the bedroom. Agnes, however, had more pressing things on her mind. She wanted Louise's killer brought to justice, her kind of justice.

Then an unexpected letter arrived from an old friend. Agnes had lost touch with her years before and very much regretted it. Not only was it lovely to hear from Madge, but the letter, though in no way connected with Agnes's present preoccupation, was also to prove very useful in rather an unexpected way.

Agnes opened the letter with some curiosity. She did not recognise the handwriting. The postmark was London. The letter read:

Cornwall Hospital
Pits Lane
Chelsea SW

Dear Agnes,

I have recently heard that you have moved to a flat in Brighton. Do you come up to London ever? If so I would so love to see you. So much has happened since we met when you were looking after Lady Bellamy.

Dear Bernard died of a heart attack nearly a year ago. You can imagine how I miss him. Then I was discovered to have a nasty breast lump and have had three operations, so I am not quite the woman I was!

However, if we meet I can tell you all about our 'goings on'. Some happy, not all sad.

Your old friend of happier days,
Madge Hillier.

Agnes was saddened by the letter. Always afraid of pushing herself, she had a habit of waiting for people to contact her rather than contacting them. She wrote a note saying she was coming to London in two days' time to do some shopping, which was true, and she would call in the afternoon if that was convenient. She would quite understand, she put in the letter, that Madge might have other visitors that day and if so she was to let Agnes know – she could always come another day.

No telephone call came. So two days later Agnes found herself walking up the steps of the Cornwall Hospital and Clinic, wondering what she was going to find. She hoped Madge was responding to her latest operation successfully.

She approached the reception desk. The nurse, or receptionist, was dressed American-fashion, white hat with two stripes perched on smooth dark hair, a smart, well-fitting, belted white coat and white stockings and shoes. Her perfectly lipsticked lips parted in a receptionist's smile.

'Mrs Hillier, certainly. Room 6.'

She pointed up the long white corridor, carpeted with a tasteful thick green carpet. A white-coated man – a doctor? – emerged from a room and hurried into another room. 4, 5... Agnes hesitated then took hold of the door handle, her heart beating a little faster than usual. She knocked gently, a voice said, 'Come in', and there was Madge Hillier.

Agnes stood, holding the bunch of flowers in her hand. The doctor, the man in the white coat, came out of the room next to number 6.

'Right Mr Weedon, we'll start the treatment tomorrow, the colour of the mark will fade slowly, so don't expect too much too quickly.'

A voice answered him.

'OK, I won't.'

It was Andy's voice.

Then the door was shut and the white-coated surgeon – doctor? – hurried up the corridor away from Agnes.

The coincidence had happened. Andy Weedon was in the next room to the one she was visiting. How this would help her to succeed in punishing the man she knew was both a murderer and a drug pusher, she didn't yet understand, but she knew the answer would come.

She closed the door gently behind her, having crossed the room.

'Madge, how are you?'

Madge Hillier sat forward in the bed to greet her.

'Agnes, so lovely to see you again, so lovely!'

13

Madge Hillier had changed a great deal since Agnes had last seen her, at least three years ago.

Then, she had been a robust, red-cheeked, rather plump country woman.

She and Bernard, her husband, had seemed inseparable. They both loved country pursuits – shooting, long walks, gardening.

It was lovely to see two people so in accord, and it was rare to spot them on these country walks without their two dogs gambolling along beside them.

Their house, a large stone-built, comfortable-looking place, mirrored their activities and way of life. Inside, like outside, it was rather untidy but welcoming. The dogs were allowed everywhere. Muddy pairs of wellington boots were lined up just inside the front door. These memories flashed in front of Agnes as she crossed the room to greet Madge. Now a much thinner, paler Madge but with the same sweet smile and open-armed greeting, the same warm low voice.

'How lovely to see you, Agnes, I hope you did not mind my writing to you, so much has happened since we last met, sad things and glad things. There's always a mixture, isn't there?'

Agnes was not a demonstrative person, but she returned Madge's hug, then sat on the side of the bed for a moment, still holding Madge's hand in hers. Madge made light of her illness and her operations.

'They say they've got it all away.' She indicated her breast with the flat of her hand. 'But they always say that to comfort you, I suppose, don't they?'

She was to have treatment and that was it. She would say little more and Agnes did not press her. She changed the subject, but could not think of a cheerful one to talk about.

'You must miss Bernard so much, Madge, and are you still in your lovely house?'

Madge shook her head. She had moved to London, on her daughter's advice. Agnes remembered her elegant daughter Marcia, married to a Frenchman. She tried to remember his name. It slipped into her memory – de Curzan, that was it!

'I live in Lowndes Square, a flat. I don't like it, it seems gloomy, but perhaps it's just me. It's convenient, central.'

'And the dear dogs – were they retrievers, Madge? I can't quite remember – and the little one.'

Madge nodded.

144

'Two golden spaniels, noisy devils, and Willie was a Jack Russell. He died of old age. Marcia took the boys, the spaniels. She has a nice house outside Paris. The spaniels speak fluent French now and are very happy!'

She twinkled a little at Agnes and it pleased her to see that Madge's old sense of humour was still with her, and her laughter still infectious.

As she got up from the bed and crossed to sit in the comfortable bedside chair, Agnes faced the wall which divided her from the next room. Only that wall divided her from Andy Weedon, murderer, thief and drug pusher. She could tell the police, but too many people were involved, too many lies had been told. Louise had lied about the ring being found, so had her brother. In a way, she herself had lied to the jeweller. The girls and anyone who bought drugs from him would probably deny it. She was almost sure that Bella would protect him. All those lies would keep him safe. Everyone seemed to be protecting him in a way.

As to the murder itself, who could prove it was he? No, not the police. She had never relied on the police and she was determined she never would. Something would happen that would put him in her power, it always did.

For the moment Agnes dismissed the man

from her thoughts and gave her entire attention to Madge Hillier.

'When your treatment is over, Madge, and you are able to get away, will you come and stay with me, for as long as you want to? The sea is just across the road from my flat and there is a lift. You will need a change, unless you are going to stay with Marcia and her husband?'

'No, they are a family unit. They both work and love their jobs. I wouldn't go there, though of course they have asked me to. I would love to stay with you, Agnes, you always mean what you say.'

'I do, Madge, I really do. I should love to have you!'

Agnes left the hospital almost reluctantly, hating to leave Madge behind. Perhaps it was the nurse in her, she thought, but she longed to be able to make Madge feel better, look better.

She glanced at the door next to Madge's. It was firmly shut, but there was a spy hole in all the doors for the nurses to check their patients every so often. She longed to raise the wooden flap and look inside, to see what Andy Weedon was doing in this expensive room, frighten him in some way, but she knew it was a foolish idea. She turned away from the door and continued down the corridor, thanking the nurse or receptionist at the nursing station as she passed her. The

146

girl gave her a quick automatic smile as she passed.

Agnes stepped out of the front door of the hospital, feeling suddenly depressed. The change in her friend Madge may have had something to do with it, but mostly she felt it was caused by the thought of Andy Weedon safely indulging himself in expensive hospital care with stolen money.

She quite realised that the removal of the birthmark, if it was successful, would not serve to disguise his identity; indeed, it was quite possible, as Bella had suggested, that the stain on his face was something he was deeply affected by and that he only wanted it removed because he hated it. Indeed, Agnes felt she could understand this. Had she been so marked, she was sure she would have felt the same, but that did nothing to excuse the manner in which he was raising the money to have the treatment. He had no thought for the misery he was causing the girls, the children, and there was no knowing how many lives he had ruined with drugs.

The drive home to Brighton was as traffic-ridden as usual and Agnes arrived home later than she had intended but Mrs Jenvy was quite happy. She had given Polly her 'long walk', she said rather proudly. Polly greeted Agnes with her usual enthusiasm. There were no telephone calls to monitor.

Agnes was glad to be home.

A week went by. Agnes rang Madge Hillier every evening, just talking about trivial matters, encouraging Madge to talk about her treatment, how she felt, and more cheerful things, old familiar memories of Bernard, Marcia, the dogs, walks they had taken together. Agnes hoped it helped.

Madge seemed to welcome the chats so much, and truthfully a lot of Agnes's own loneliness was banished by the regular talks, though she was not usually very keen on the telephone. After a week, though, Agnes was getting impatient for a sighting of Andy. She wondered whether he would be out of hospital about now and back in Brighton.

She had no idea how long his treatment would take, whether he would attend as an out-patient or stay in the Cornwall Hospital. Then a letter arrived that looked as if it might shed a little more light on the drug-pushing operation. It was from Pamela Roberts and was just a request, a very urgent request, for Agnes to see her as soon as possible. She didn't give a reason.

Agnes replied at once, suggesting the next day at about four o'clock. She wrote, did not telephone, as Pamela had perhaps been afraid to telephone in case her parents heard or traced the call. They were strict and they were watching her. Quite rightly, Agnes supposed, but Pamela seemed to be deceiving them constantly, with the help of Bella. She would be interested to know why Pamela was so anxious to see her, and to hear what she had to say.

On the dot of four the front door bell rang. Agnes lifted the door phone and pressed the lever.

'It's Pamela, and I've brought Bella with me. Is that all right, Mrs Turner?'

Pamela's voice sounded nervous and breathless.

'Yes, of course. Come up, both of you.'

Agnes waited until she heard the lift door click open and 'whoosh' shut, then she opened her door. Polly rushed out of the bedroom, tail wagging, delighted to see them. Pamela bent down and picked the little dog up. Polly adored this.

'Oh, Mrs Turner, she looks wonderful, so different to when we brought her out of that horrid place. She was so thin and miserable.'

Greetings over, Agnes took the girls' jackets and sat them down in the sitting-room, excusing herself while she went into the kitchen to make the tea. Both girls were quite silent when she came back into the room. They drank a cup of tea, had a slice of the creamy Sally Lunn cake Agnes had got for them, talked a little nervously about school, Polly, Bella's cats – anything, it seemed, to avoid broaching what Pamela really wanted to tell Agnes.

At last Bella, obviously the braver of the two, said, 'Come on, Pamela, tell Mrs Turner about your aunt and her son and everything. Go on, tell her!'

With one or two interruptions from Bella at the start of the story, Pamela seemed relieved to talk and tell what had happened.

Her mother had a sister whose husband had deserted her – 'ran off with another woman', Bella had interrupted – and who had a son, now eleven years old. He went to a Church of England school near Peacehaven, where the pair lived – in, according to Bella, abject poverty – helped out by Mrs Roberts now and again when she could do so without her husband knowing.

'He's so stingy,' explained Bella.

A week ago Mrs Roberts and Pamela had driven over to see her sister. The boy was home from school with a bad ear. Usually Pamela did not see her cousin who, if not at school, was always out with his mates. This time, however, on the visit she was describing with agonising slowness to Agnes, was different.

'He'd got a new CD and he asked if I'd like to hear it. Mum and Auntie Susan were being dead boring and talking about cleaners and clothes and so I went upstairs and he played the CD. Simply Red it was. Not new, but I'd only heard it on radio. It was good, I'd have loved one for myself, but it was dead expensive so–'

Agnes broke in. She could not listen to Pamela droning on and on and saying absolutely nothing of any interest.

'What exactly did you want to talk to me about, Pamela? Get to the point.'

At last, and without any more prodding from Bella or Agnes, it all came out, still slowly and with a wealth of unnecessary detail. Pamela was not a concise story teller, but what she told was very interesting, especially to Agnes.

After playing the CD Mark, the cousin had dragged another out of his school bag and thrown the bag over to the bed on which Pamela was sitting. Mark had zipped up the top of the bag again, but hadn't noticed the small compartment on the front was open. As it landed next to Pamela a few, about six she thought, small plastic packets had slid out, each containing two tablets. She had picked one up, guessing they were Ecstasy.

'Oh, yeah, yeah. You won't tell Mum, will you, she'd go ballistic! You can have two if you like. They're seven pounds a tablet. I'll give you two freebies, if you keep quiet about seeing them.'

He grabbed the bag and more spilled out, some tiny packs of white powder and about six first-class postage stamps.

Pamela had heard about microdots of LSD being put on stamps, so anyone who wanted to try the drug just licked the stamp and had either a good trip or a bummer. She was impressed. Mark was only eleven and carrying a bag like that, she felt he must know a 'Mr Big'. She had asked him straight out where he had got his stuff from. He just shook his head and carefully put the packets back in the school bag. Pamela had decided to risk a question, a name.

'I bet you got them from Andy Weedon.'

The boy had looked completely unmoved.

'Andy who? Never heard of him, who is he?'

'And did he tell you anything else, Pamela?'

Agnes felt the two girls were trying to get the heat off Andy and were pleased to find out there was someone else involved besides their supplier.

Pamela nodded. Apparently she had questioned the boy, who did not want to say anything about his source, but in the end she had made him tell.

'He lives in Peacehaven, has a big house there, big house and a big black car, a BMW, I think it is.'

'So do you think that is where Andy Weedon gets the drugs he takes round the schools, or do you think it's not only his source but that he works for this man, like he makes the children and you work for him? Is that what you think?'

They nodded. Suddenly Pamela burst into tears.

'I want to come off it, Mrs Turner, all of it. I can't though. Mum and Dad don't even know I'm on anything. They'd kill me if I told them.'

'Did the boy tell you the name of the man at Peacehaven?'

Pamela shook her head, her eyes red with crying.

'No, all I got out of him was that the house was named Homely or something like that. What can you do to help me, without letting anyone know?'

Agnes shook her head. 'Nothing, Pamela, unless you really want to give it up yourself.'

Agnes got up, a hint that she wanted the girls to leave. She shut the door behind them with relief. Silly young people, she thought, wasting their precious youth. What could she do indeed! The answer came to her as she carried the tea tray out.

If they were so weak they couldn't give it up, she must cut off the supply, kill the source! Obviously there was more than one drug pusher in the area.

14

Agnes had at last got back her own car. After much trouble and toing and froing, the new door was the exact colour of the rest of the car and the scratches that had been on the bodywork had been completely erased.

She was glad to have it. The red one had not been at all to her taste and she intended to celebrate its return to her by going to Peacehaven to see if she could locate the house the teenagers had mentioned. 'Homely' was the only clue they had been able to give her. No number, no road and no precise location. Not an easy puzzle to solve.

'He lives in Peacehaven,' The idea that Andy Weedon's supplier lived there was far fetched and probably quite wrong, but it was the only lead Agnes had and she felt it would be rather exciting and interesting to try and find a house with the unlikely name of 'Homely'.

The drive to Peacehaven was pleasant and as Agnes set out at about ten in the morning, the traffic was not too hectic. The tourist season would soon be increasing the flow of coaches and cars, motor bikes and caravans. The morning was perfect too, sunny but not very warm. The houses she passed on her way were bright with daffodils. It seemed to be a wonderful year for that harbinger of spring and even some of the grass verges were sprinkled with them, perhaps planted by an imaginative county council. They certainly looked big expensive blooms, too big to have got there by accident.

Agnes looked at the names of the houses she passed. Some had none, just numbers. Some did not even have a number. Some had only a partially obliterated name on the outside of the door, but none even came near the name Homely. Agnes wondered if the girls could have made a mistake. It might perhaps be Homestead, Home House, Home Cottage... Just as she was coming to that conclusion, she noticed a red letter box on her side of the country road. A postman was shovelling out the letters into a bag, a red Royal Mail van just ahead of him, its back door open.

Agnes drove up near him, switched off her engine and got out of the car. If anyone knows the district and house names it should surely be a postman! She went up to him just as he was closing and locking the postbox door.

'Homely? No, I think you mean, Home

Leigh, Sir George Brennan's place. He lives up there – look, you can see it from here.'

He pointed to the rise in the ground beside him. Above it was a path which wound upward and upward. Way above there, a copse of trees almost hid the large, rather splendid-looking house, white-painted with tall brick chimneys, poking above the trees.

'Can one drive up to the house on this path?' Agnes asked.

She had only to back her car a little to be able to turn into the narrow roadway.

'Sure, the road gets a little wider a bit higher up. Then away from the house, it's a proper road, past the cliff and down to the motorway.'

Agnes thanked him and was about to turn away when she thought maybe he might know a bit about Sir George Brennan, might deliver his letters.

'Long way for a postman to deliver letters up there?' she said.

The postman, about to walk to his van, laughed, continued the few steps and slung the bag into the back of the van and locked the door.

'Specially on a bike! No, I deliver there, Sir George is a councillor, magistrate. Pillar of society like, has a lot a mail. Goes abroad and all sorts. Pleasant sort of bloke really. I go up in the van.'

He eased himself into the driver's seat, waved a hand and the van started up and moved off, smoke puffing out of the exhaust.

Agnes got back into her car and sat for a moment thinking. Then she decided to reverse the car and go up the narrow steep road past Home Leigh, just to have a look at the house. After all, Pamela and Bella had got the name of the house partially right, perhaps it really was worth looking into. Up in that house might be a man controlling, supplying, obtaining drugs with more than one Andy Weedon, pushing them in the schools and clubs and at raves.

Agnes drove up the narrow road. The postman had been right. It soon opened into a road of more importance, with a better surface. As she progressed upward the view of the sea opened out in front of her, then, as the wood emerged, the view was on her right side. Higher still and as she rounded a corner, the house came into sight. Manicured lawns, beds of flowers already blooming in the spring sunshine. More daffodils, tulips, jonquils, a hedge of pink daisies, planted so thickly their pink blooms almost obscured their green leaves. A garden kept perfectly and where money was no object. Even as she drove past, a gardener pushing a wheelbarrow came from the back of the house. Otherwise, no sign of life. She carried on, and started the descent to the main road. A plan was already forming in her mind, perhaps inspired by the sight of the house or maybe by the words of the postman, spoken rather in admiration: 'Sir George Brennan. Councillor, magistrate, pillar of society.'

Wasn't it just that kind of man who...? Agnes stifled her imagination. He might be everything the postman said and nothing more, but on the other hand...

Agnes was determined to go back up that steep path, call at the house, but she knew that with a man of Sir George Brennan's standing she would have to telephone and make an appointment. She was already planning what she would say. Sir George Brennan's reaction to her words would tell her a great deal about him, of that she was very sure. She looked forward to it. Life was no longer boring.

A long telephone call to London that early evening to Madge was more cheerful than she had expected. Madge had been told that she could now stop her radiotherapy and could go to a convalescent home in a week's time. Marcia, her daughter, was still insisting she go to Paris, but Madge was adamant.

'They both have their own lives, it's not fair. Marcia has painting classes in her house, five days a week. Her husband works hard all week. Anyway, I don't want to go there, Agnes. I want to live in my own flat, like you do.'

'Madge, in a week when you're pushed out of the clinic, come here. My spare room looks over the sea, I'd love to have you.'

Even though Agnes had offered more than once, Madge still made little dissenting noises. Agnes was sure she was keen, but didn't like to impose.

'Anyway, think about it, Madge. I'll come up and fetch you, no bother. I'm coming up to London day after tomorrow, more shopping. I'll call in and see you. Do think it over.'

The shopping bit was a lie, but she felt Madge would say something like, 'Oh no, not all this way just to see me.' Agnes genuinely wanted to have her to stay until she was better and stronger and the effect of the treatment had worn off a little. Perhaps it was the nurse in her still lingering. She had felt surprisingly close to Madge, and it was as if the three-year gap in their friendship had never happened.

The visit to London was a break from Agnes's plans to entrap Louise's murderer and the seemingly endless drug problems. Madge was persuaded to come and stay with her.

'Just for a few days. It's so sweet of you, Agnes!'

159

Agnes was determined to make it longer than 'a few days' but played along with Madge. She wanted to help as much as she could to steer her through the week or so after the treatment had stopped, while the various effects of that treatment were lessening a little. As a nurse in the cancer clinic she had been all too clearly aware of those effects.

Three days later, after her visit to London, she telephoned Sir George Brennan. A woman answered the telephone.

'Could you perhaps state your business, what you wish to speak about?'

Lady Brennan had a soft, well-modulated voice.

Agnes prevaricated a little and said that she would rather not discuss the matter on the telephone but that her worry was to do with the behaviour of several young people she knew. This seemed to generate a little more interest at the other end of the telephone. There was a slight rustling of paper.

'Perhaps the day after tomorrow at three o'clock. Would that suit you?'

Agnes agreed to this time, thanked Lady Brennan effusively and put the telephone down. The quickened interest at the mention of young people was perhaps significant.

Agnes had not only rehearsed carefully exactly how she was going to lead the

160

conversation, but had even written it down and then read it aloud, wondering whether to introduce names, particularly that of Andy Weedon. She decided against naming any of the schools in particular or the girls whose names she knew. She was slightly nervous of naming names, but Andy Weedon's sudden riches might upset Sir George, so his name must be mentioned. Perhaps just a reference to 'Andy' might be enough.

She had assumed the person who had given her the appointment was Lady Brennan. She did not quite know why, perhaps the air of quiet authority and confidence had had something to do with it. Agnes wondered if she knew that her husband was connected with the drug trade, or was she only involved in his life as a pillar of society?

Anyway, whether she were in or out, whether she had any knowledge of her husband's side trade, if he was in fact a drug peddler, was of little matter one way or the other. Agnes was after bigger prey, a murderer and a thief. The drug trafficking was bad enough, but at least the participants could refuse it; poor Louise had had no such choice. Her life had been taken away from her without choice, she had not even known the man who had ended it all for her, not even known his name and in all probability not even known what he looked like. And, after all this time since her death, the police had arrested no one. Perhaps, Agnes thought, with some of the help she was capable of giving them about Louise's assailant, they could have gone further, found out more, but she trusted her own powers of detection more than theirs. She had Andy Weedon in her sights and now Sir George Brennan.

The day arrived and she drove towards Peacehaven and Home Leigh with high hopes and a sense of delicious excitement. As she drove into the wide sweeping drive of Home Leigh, she was impressed again by the beauty of the garden. When passing it before she had only seen glimpses, but now she could see walls tumbling with purple aubretia, yellow privet had been used sparingly and cleverly to brighten the rather shaded end of the house. No expense had been spared in this part of the garden and probably the garden at the back of the house was just as pretty.

As she got out of her car, the same gardener came round the side of the house. He was with, Agnes guessed, the man she had come to see. She glanced at her watch, three o'clock on the dot. The man walking beside the gardener was white-haired, the front pressed into a deep wave which did not move in the breeze, as if he used lacquer to keep it in place. His figure was good, not thin but tall and muscular. Agnes noticed he looked first at the Porsche, then at her.

He came forward, holding out his hand.

'Mrs Turner, right on time, very punctual!'

He seemed slightly embarrassed, as if he would have preferred to meet her in the house. He turned quickly, making a motion with his hand towards the gardener as if to dismiss him, indeed the gardener seemed to understand for he turned and ambled off.

'Lovely car you have, Mrs Turner, one of my favourites, the Porsche. Reliable, fast and luxurious.'

Agnes agreed with him by merely smiling as he ushered her into the hall, quickly crossing it into the library.

The room looked like a library in a film. The polished floor was scattered with expensive-looking rugs. The large desk where Sir George went and seated himself was, Agnes guessed, real Chippendale. The walls were lined with leather books tooled with gold titles. They looked as if they might have been bought by the yard and never opened, let alone read. The fireplace was huge with electric logs glowing and above it hung a portrait of Sir George Brennan himself, in mayoral robes, one hand resting on the arm of the chair, the other holding a book. Sir George again looked embarrassed as Agnes gazed at it – in fact it was difficult to look away from it. It dominated the room.

'I was Mayor of Brighton a few years ago, Mrs Turner.'

He glanced up at the large portrait, then swung his mahogany revolving chair back to face her.

'My wife persuaded me to have it done.'

Agnes was seated in a similar, but not revolving chair on the other side of the desk.

'How can I help you, Mrs Turner?'

Sir George steepled the fingers of his two hands. He had a gold ring on his right little finger in which was set deep in the gold a large flashing diamond.

Agnes composed herself and started her well-rehearsed speech, her prepared questions.

'Sir George, I believe you are greatly respected in the town. I have heard a lot about your campaigns for youth clubs, the local free tennis club, your being responsible for running the sailing club and a great many other such good works.'

Sir George preened, straightened some pens and pencils on his desk and waved his hand in a small dismissive gesture. He was obviously pleased.

'Oh, Mrs Turner, one does what one can, you know.'

Agnes felt she had done enough flattering and could now start on the reason for this afternoon's visit.

She mentioned her friends, not naming them, who were worried about their daughters and their unruly behaviour, then went on to tell him that both the girls were able to get Ecstasy when they were partying – and, without much trouble, other drugs as well. Sir George looked quite horrified as he listened to all this, his eyebrows raised, his lips pursed.

'And you say the parents haven't suspected their daughters are taking drugs, Mrs Turner? How like parents of today, no sense of responsibility!'

'The two I know of are fifteen and sixteen and well able to hide what they want to hide, Sir George.'

She then went on to tell him about her visits to the schools where she had seen the man they called Andy, selling drugs to girls at the private school and children at the primary school.

At the name of Andy, did she detect a slight start? She was almost sure she did; now was the time to make the final thrust. She waited, letting him make the expected remark.

'Did you not think of going to the police?'

Agnes shook her head positively.

'No, the police must have drug pushers and drug takers reported to them every day, Sir George. They would take little notice of me, I am afraid. Someone of your standing would carry more weight. Besides, there has been a change taking place that interested me.'

'A change? In what way, Mrs Turner?'

Agnes then started on the part of her tale that she felt would disturb him if he were the drug source, the man the pushers had to buy from if they wanted to carry on their trading.

'Well, this man Andy's circumstances have suddenly changed. When I first saw him he was riding a bicycle and looked shabby. I also noticed that he had a disfiguring birthmark on his face. These two girls told me he has been to the Cornwall Clinic in London to have the mark removed. Now, that's an extremely expensive private hospital. How did he get the money? His trading must have altered, become much more lucrative.'

The effect on Sir George was electric.

'Andy Weedon at the Cornwall Clinic! I know it well – was in there myself. He's got money from somewhere!'

Agnes felt a surge of triumph. How did he know the name Weedon? It had slipped out. Sir George did not even notice he had said it. If Andy had risen, as it were, from rags to riches, it must mean to this man that Andy was diverting some of Sir George's profits to his own advantage or had maybe even found another source and was operating independently. He got up and paced the floor.

His face had reddened.

'Thank you for telling me about this, Mrs Turner. This man must be stopped, you were right to come to me, quite right.'

There was a knock on the door.

'Would you and your visitor care for tea, dear?'

It was the same quiet voice that Agnes had heard on the telephone. She answered quickly, feeling Sir George was in no mood to play with teacups.

'No, Lady Brennan, thank you so much, but I am afraid I must go.'

Sir George walked her to her car. He seemed preoccupied and angry at the same time.

As she drove away, Agnes felt well satisfied with her visit and its result. Now all she had to do was wait to see what the furious Sir George would do to Andy, or come to that what Andy would do to Sir George. She hoped he would not remember letting slip the name Weedon but even if he did, what matter. She was sure he would assume she hadn't noticed it. Well pleased, she drove back to her flat looking forward to taking her sweet and uncomplicated friend Polly for her walk. Why, she thought for the hundredth time, were animals so easy to get on with? Was it because they had no language to argue with? Did they argue amongst themselves in a way she didn't understand?

They seemed not to be devious, perhaps this was their greatest charm.

She thought too of the house Home Leigh. Was it Sir George or was it his wife who was responsible for that beautiful garden? Out of the stagey library window she had glimpsed the herbaceous border. The lupins just beginning to come out, the azaleas pink and glowing. The rows of winter pansies, all colours, flanked by multicoloured cape daisies. How could a man whom she suspected strongly of dispensing drugs to young children and teenagers, ruining their lives, how could he live amongst such beauty and not be affected for good? Agnes realised she was being naïve; she was no philosopher, not much of a thinker. But one thing, one thought, one love had been hers. Animals.

Once, when she was about eleven, one of the nuns at the orphanage had said, asked her, almost sternly, 'If there was a puppy in a river drowning and a baby alongside it, I believe you would rescue the puppy!'

'Of course I would, certainly I would, babies are horrid!' had been her determined reply. The nun's had been:

'Glory be to God, what will you say next!'

Now at sixty-one she still felt the same way.

When she got back from her walk and was just getting her supper, the telephone rang.

Agnes did not get many telephone calls and she thought it might be Madge. It was Bella. She sounded excited.

'I've seen Andy. The mark's nearly gone, sort of mottled but much paler. He's got a lovely car, a maroon BMW.'

Agnes felt she wanted to warn her, but what was the use, self-willed Bella would go her own way.

'Be careful, Bella, and don't take any of that awful Ecstasy, remember that girl who died.'

'Oh, Mrs Turner, she was allergic probably, or she didn't take enough water. Anyway, I've only got two.'

Agnes had one more try, knowing it was useless, but feeling she must.

'Think what else he's selling, Bella, not just Ecstasy.'

'I know, Mrs Turner, but now he's got all that money from the ring, maybe he'll give up the drugs. It was a lot of money, wasn't it?'

'No, not by today's standards, Bella, and he wouldn't get as much as its full worth, then the car and his time in that clinic, he might not have much of it left.'

Bella sounded as if she didn't believe her.

'Well, thanks anyway, Mrs Turner. We're going to a rave tonight. I promise I won't take any more E – only the two, promise.'

Agnes had to be satisfied with Bella's

169

light-hearted reply. Andy had probably spent nearly all the money already. She was sure Bella was keen on this awful man, though she would not quite admit it. She could only hope the girl would not get hooked on the harder stuff. Horse shit, coke, smack, dream coke, crack. How many names for so much horror. She wondered, should she go and tell Bella's parents, or was it better to try to keep the girl's friendship and influence her that way?

The best way of all was to destroy the root of it all, Andy Weedon and Sir George Brennan, if he were guilty – but how to do that? That was the all-important question. If Sir George resented Andy's prosperity enough to do something about it, her plan would work. In the unlikely event that he should continue to allow Andy to prosper, she realised it would be up to her to come up with another plan.

15

Mr Leeming, Arthur, caused a ripple of surprise in the flats by calling a meeting in his flat. The number 1 residents, back from visiting their daughter in Australia, were included. They were very shocked at the news of the murder that had happened while they were away.

Arthur Leeming made a little speech, after handing round drinks and welcoming back Mr and Mrs Wilcocks, who were older than Agnes had expected. Mrs Wilcocks carried a stick and walked very slowly. Mr Wilcocks was rather bent with a rugged aged face and sparse white hair.

Having made his speech he sat down and looked around the assembled seven. His suggestion was received in surprised silence. Apparently the estate agent had been finding it difficult to interest prospective buyers in Louise's old flat. Arthur Leeming thought they should all try and persuade Pierre Demain to reduce the price by several thousand pounds. After the silence there was almost universal dissent. Only Miss Horrocks agreed with Arthur Leeming's suggestion, but Agnes felt for all the wrong reasons.

'Oh, she will haunt the place, the French lady, she will. Someone will see her all bleeding in the bedroom. She's bound to come back!'

Agnes turned away from Miss Horrocks who had caught hold of her hand and was looking pleading, expecting her agreement.

'Oh, of course not, Miss Horrocks, given time people forget these things, they just forget.'

Arthur Leeming leaned forward in his chair and stroked his thighs with his flat open hands in a familiar gesture. His lower lip stuck out.

'Well, I dunno, Agnes, whoever wants the flat, even if they come from miles away, they've got to be told, by the estate agent I mean. Perhaps making it cheaper would be a good idea.'

'We can't tear the block down just because someone was killed in one of the flats, Arthur. If you make one cheaper the others must be the same.'

Agnes's voice was cold. In her mind she was thinking of Andy Weedon. If the killing reduced the value of all their flats, that would be something else Andy would have to pay for – and she would see that he did.

'No, don't let's ask them to reduce the price. It happened and that's that. The flat is just the same as it was before.'

The meeting broke up, with Arthur Leeming still muttering as they left.

As Agnes stepped out of the lift the next morning three men were just leaving the vacant flat.

Agnes knew the man leading out the two others.

'Good morning, Mrs Turner, may I introduce you to your new neighbours. Mr Adams and Mr Bailey. This is Mrs Turner who lives in number 6, the top flat. She bought the flat through our firm!'

The two men shook hands. One of the men, Mr Adams, was slightly made up.

Not too obviously, just a touch of eye-shadow, a trace of lipstick and a pony tail.

Mr Bailey was more macho. Both seemed to Agnes pleasant men, about thirty-five or perhaps more.

'Mr Bailey and his partner Mr Adams have decided to buy the flat. When the contracts are exchanged it will be all sealed and settled.'

'Oh, good. I hope you will be happy. It is a very nice flat. I am sure you will enjoy it.'

The estate agent shepherded them out. Agnes was pleased the flat had sold, but she wondered how the rest of the residents would react. Well, they must sort it out as they thought. Perhaps Miss Horrocks would prefer two homosexuals to a ghost! One couldn't be sure. Arthur Leeming and the dear Major and his wife would probably say they didn't want to be in the same block as a pair of poofs. The people back from Australia, well, she couldn't think how they would take the new occupants. She didn't know them well enough but Agnes felt that after they found out, they would have their say and that would be the end of the matter. No one would leave. They might threaten, but nothing would come of it.

How strange people were, Agnes thought.

How dear Madge would love to be well and free of her cancer. How she would love to be able to live in health with anyone, homosexual or not. She went out into the street to her own car. The estate agent was just driving away from the kerb across the road. He looked pleased with himself. The two buyers of the flat were walking away together, maybe towards their own car. One had his arm round the other's waist, and they were talking animatedly.

Had they paid less for the flat? The estate agent she presumed would have had to tell them about the murder. Agnes realised she could not have cared less. She knew all the other residents would worry the question like terriers with a bone until they found out. What could they do about it, what good would it do them?

When she came back from shopping, as she got into the lift, she met the Warburtons going up to her floor. She said nothing about her meeting in the hall; let them find out for themselves. She felt she wanted nothing to do with it. She had enough problems of her own to cope with. Who had bought the French widow's flat and how much they had paid for it certainly did not figure amongst those problems.

They were complaining. They usually were complaining about something! This time it was that the new postman was not coming up the back stairs and putting their mail through their letter boxes, but leaving it all on the hall shelf and not delivering it at all.

'Well, that means I'd better go down and look in case there is anything there for me,' Agnes said, thinking there might be a letter from Madge.

She let the Warburtons out of the lift, then took it down again to the hall. There were two clothes catalogues for her and underneath them a square, opulent-looking envelope with a first-class stamp. She gathered up the three and went back up to her flat.

The letter, or rather the invitation, surprised her. It was from Sir George Brennan asking her to a drinks party in exactly one week's time at Home Leigh. The invitation card was as opulent as the thick expensive envelope.

Formal Sir George and Lady Brennan ... 6.30 p.m. ... RSVP ...

Agnes decided she would go. She might, at such a gathering, find out more about Sir George. Who his friends were, how he managed to live in such style. Yes, it would be well worth going!

In the meantime she decided to get in touch with Bella and find out if she had any more news of Andy.

Agnes telephoned Bella at home during

175

the evening. As usual she answered and, also as usual, said that her parents were out. She was chewing something as she was speaking.

'I'm just having my supper and watching television.'

'Oh, I'm sorry if I interrupted you, Bella.'

Agnes was genuinely apologetic. She hated being interrupted herself at meal times. She heard Bella give a giggle at the other end.

'Oh, don't worry, Mrs Turner. It's only a cold chop and crisps. I can usually find something in the fridge. I could go and get fish and chips but it's too much bother.'

Agnes was, as usual, rather scandalised by this. Bella accepted Agnes's invitation to tea the next day and Agnes determined to give the girl a decent meal.

When she came she had little to tell about Andy. Yes, she had seen him. His 'mark', as she put it, was now much fainter, he was delighted and was still attending the Cornwall. Yes, he was also delighted with his car. It was very posh. On the subject of drugs she was silent and would not say anything about Pamela or Tina or any of the others having got any more from Andy. She ate with gusto and then announced that she had to go. She was going to a rave with friends. Ecstasy would feature there, Agnes knew, but she did not approach the subject at all.

After the girl had left Agnes thought a lot about Sir George Brennan. If he was a 'Drugs Baron' he would certainly be furious that Andy Weedon was apparently operating independently and would do anything to get back his territory, anything.

16

On the day of Sir George's party Agnes arrived promptly. Several cars were already parked in the extensive drive. As Agnes drove up to the front door a large man approached the car. He looked to Agnes exactly like one of the 'heavies' on television who act as doormen at clubs where fights are expected or as bodyguards. Wide shoulders, hair so close cropped as to look almost as if it were shaved. However, he was very pleasant.

'May I park your car, madam?'

Agnes got out, leaving the keys in the ignition.

'Lovely car, a Porsche, madam. Really luxurious.'

He stroked the bonnet as he came round to the passenger side. Agnes smiled politely. She was rather pleased not to have the responsibility of the parking as two more cars were already waiting to come through the gate.

Agnes mounted the steps to the house. The front door was open.

As she entered the large sitting-room, Lady Brennan came forward immediately to greet her. Agnes was surprised that she even knew her name as she had only talked to Sir George. His wife had seen Agnes only for a moment.

Had her husband said something to her intimating that Mrs Turner knew more than she should about their business, or was Lady Brennan simply an accomplished hostess? She looked, as she came forward to greet Agnes, both aristocratic and detached.

'Oh, Mrs Turner, how nice to see you! Would you like a drink, and is Hilton dealing with your car for you?'

Agnes answered yes to both questions and Lady Brennan led her across the room to where the two barmen in short white coats were dispensing wine, whisky, gin, vodka. Sparkling glasses stood in rows on the white tablecloth.

Agnes chose a white wine and her hostess then led her back across the room, winding her way skilfully through her guests.

'This is Mr and Mrs Shelbourne. They live in Hove, probably near you. Mabs, Henry, this is Mrs Turner, and may I say diplomatically,' she laughed, 'Mabs and Henry

178

are not madly in love with Hove, so you can perhaps convert each other.' She glided away.

'Oh, now she's started something, Mrs Turner. You have a flat on the front at Hove?' Agnes assented and they were soon involved in a lively argument on the good and the bad sides of Hove and flats in Hove. Agnes moved from one bunch of guests to another; there must have been about thirty people there. At a sign from Sir George they were shepherded through to another smaller room where a big table was spread with food. Sliced turkey and chicken, smoked salmon, quails' eggs, stuffed eggs, small hearts of lettuce and peeled tomatoes, avocados sliced thinly and arranged in half moons. At the other end of the table, sweets of all sorts and flavours. Beautifully done and served by the two barmen who had left the drinks table for the moment to serve the food. All very nice, but Agnes could think of a better way of spending a sunny evening. She at last asked someone where the powder room was and escaped from the food table, making her way across the hall to the door indicated by a fellow guest who was obviously a friend of the Brennans and knew the house well. The door of the downstairs cloakroom was locked, so Agnes went upstairs to look for another.

The door of one bedroom was open and it

had an en suite bathroom. Agnes went in, opened her handbag and freshened her make-up. She stood for a moment looking in the mirror and wondering just how soon she could leave without seeming to be churlish. She looked at her watch. Twenty past seven, a little early to leave.

How slowly time goes when you are not enjoying yourself, she thought rather glumly. She must stay a little longer. She replaced the make-up in her handbag and stepped out onto the landing. The noise of mingled conversation and laughter came up from the downstairs room as she shut the panelled door of the bedroom behind her and made her way to the top of the stairs, passing the closed door of what she guessed was another bathroom or bedroom, then another, then another. This last door, she observed, had a key sticking out from the lock; the handle was the same as the bedroom, but the key looked different, cheaper. As she paused for a second by the door she heard a slight noise, like something falling from a shelf, not anything heavy. She hesitated, then curiosity overcame her and she tried the handle – perhaps a cat was shut in there. The noise happened again, just a soft 'plop'. No distressed miaow or scratching. The key was in the locked position. Agnes turned it, and opened the door. It was a broom cupboard. Two shelves above, full of cleaning materials. A pile of dusters wrapped in cellophane slid to the floor to join the ones that she had heard fall. A Dyson carpet sweeper, flex neatly wound stood in front of her, beside that a larger carpet shampoo machine, by that a Hoover, rather more old-fashioned. These were drawn forward to the front of the cupboard. It was what was behind this row of cleaners that transfixed Agnes. The body of Andy Weedon was seated under the bottom shelf, in an almost foetal position, knees drawn up, head pressed down on the knees, his fair hair covering his face.

Agnes peered close in the dimness of the recess into which the body had been manoeuvred. She could see the fair hair but not the face. The purple birthmark, now much paler and, as Bella had said, mottled, was quite visible. His blue shirt stuck out from the collar of his jacket as it had done that day when she had seen him swinging Polly round at the end of the lead. His arms were thrust in between his knees, the hands she could not see, but by the very stillness of the body, she could tell he was dead. But not quite satisfied she put out a hand and touched his neck. It was ice cold.

Agnes found herself trembling not because she had seen a dead body, but because whoever had put it there might have seen her seeing it. She closed and

181

locked the door, leaving the key in place as it had been before. She came down the stairs. The chattering was still as high and shrill, broken by occasional bursts of laughter. She crossed the hall, went into the downstairs cloakroom that the other guest had pointed out to her. It was now empty. In this room she again looked at herself in the mirror. She was pale. As she was putting a little blusher on her cheeks the door opened and Lady Brennan walked in. She smiled brightly.

'Why can people like Elizabeth Taylor or Joan Collins keep their lipstick perfect while they eat, Mrs Turner – or may I call you Agnes?'

'Of course you may, Lady Brennan.'

Agnes had forgotten her hostess's Christian name, but to complement her remark she got out her own lipstick and pretended to apply it even though she had already done so upstairs. Her heart was still hammering away from the shock of what she had seen, but she was beginning to calm down a little.

The two women walked back into the big room together. Most of the guests were strolling away from the buffet and the barmen had returned to the drinks table. Agnes walked up to it. She felt she needed a drink.

'What would you like, Mrs Turner –

Agnes?' Lady Brennan asked.

'I would love a brandy and ginger ale if I may.'

Agnes would not usually have asked for such a drink when she was driving, but she could see the one glass of white wine she had chosen still half full, on the bookcase across the room where she had left it, and she felt she could risk the brandy. Her companion surprised her by saying, 'Do you know, that's exactly what I would like! Agnes, you must come to dinner with us if you would care to, then we can really talk.'

Agnes left the party at eight fifteen, though about half the guests were still there. Her mind was a maze of questions without answers.

Who had killed Andy Weedon and how had he died? She had not been able even to guess at the cause of death. Who had hidden him in such an unlikely place? Everything pointed toward Sir George Brennan. Protecting his territory? Looking after his own interests? Furious to learn that Andy had acquired so much money? She could not feel sorry for Andy, all he had achieved with his life was to make girls like Pamela and Tina permanent drug addicts, not to forget the younger schoolchildren. No, she felt the world was a better place without him.

As she left the party another man brought her car to the door for her. He was a huge man, tougher looking than the first one. Agnes wondered whether they were in fact bodyguards for Sir George and his household. If so, why did he need them? Could they, or would they, do the killing? Would they dispose of the body? The fact that the body had been hidden in the cupboard seemed to point to the fact that he had been killed that day, otherwise surely there would have been an attempt to get Andy out of the house and taken to wherever they planned to bury him. The risk they had taken was so huge.

The more she thought about the body, crushed in the corner, folded up, the more she became convinced that the killing had not been planned, but committed by someone out of control. Somehow to Agnes that imaginary someone did not fit the character of Sir George Brennan. One of his henchmen perhaps?

Or had someone killed Andy and dumped the body in Sir George's grounds? With their connections he would hardly summon the police. He would have to hide it, dispose of it.

Agnes did not sleep well that night, even after a long and pleasant walk with Polly. Another thing puzzled her. Why had Sir George asked her to the party? Maybe to thank her for the information she had given him about Andy? Lady Brennan had been most effusive when Agnes had bid her goodbye and thanked her for attending the party. She had kissed her a quick air kiss on the cheek, a quite unexpected gesture to Agnes. Well, she would see if that invitation materialised. If it did, she would accept out of sheer curiosity.

In the night, unable to sleep, she got up to make herself some tea. As she stood waiting for the kettle to boil, she had to admit to herself that this was not the lonely life she had feared. She seemed to be gaining friends and acquaintances from all quarters and she was enjoying herself. She made her tea and took the tray through to the bedroom, with a biscuit for Polly, who was sitting up in her bed wondering what was going on in the middle of the night.

17

Agnes heard nothing for two days. Sir George Brennan must have disposed of the body by now, probably the night of the party. He could hardly leave it where it was. The cleaner would have a shock if she opened the door to get the vacuum cleaner out and found that! But how? Perhaps somewhere else in the house. It was a big house with plenty of rooms in which to hide a corpse. Or in the boot of a car, or in a garage. She remembered the two tough-looking men who had been so obliging with her car. They looked capable of handling anything or anybody. She was sure she would hear from Bella or Pamela because they would not have been able to contact Andy. Every time the telephone rang she expected it to be one of the two girls.

On the third day, she answered the telephone just after her long and lovely walk with Polly. It was Madge, a little sad and despondent. She had to have another scan. She was evasive and Agnes did not press for details. She felt Madge was both upset and disappointed at the thought the scan might involve more treatment or surgery.

Agnes did her best to help and reassure her.

'Madge, try not to worry, they are only making sure you are all right and the moment they discharge you, the spare room is ready for you.'

This did not have the effect she had hoped. Madge burst into tears. Agnes wished she was there to put her arms round her, comfort her. Agnes had left nursing so long ago she was not familiar with the treatments that were given nowadays. However, one thing she knew had not changed, that was the need for tender loving care, and that she felt she could give to Madge and would the moment she could. Another scan was a little scary even to Agnes, but hopefully it was just a precaution and nothing would be found to need more treatment. She replaced the phone and almost immediately it rang again.

'Oh, Mrs Turner, something terrible has happened. I can't tell you over the telephone. Can I come and see you now? I can come straight away, I've skipped school. I have to see you.'

It seemed no time for trying to put the girl off, telling her to turn up for school. Agnes just said, 'All right, I'll wait for you,' and put the receiver back on its rest.

She was amazed that Bella, by the sound of the horror in her voice, must have somehow found out about the death of Andy Weedon, but where could the body have been moved to and found so quickly? Somewhere public? Yet there had been nothing on the television or in the papers saying a body had been found. She could only wait for Bella to turn up and tell her what she knew.

So many of his 'clients' would miss their supply but after all it had only been three days. But she supposed some might need a fix pretty regularly if they were on heroin or cocaine. She wondered too if there were any other pushers who would take Andy

Weedon's place. If Sir George was the power behind it all, surely he would be anxious to put a replacement on the school run. If it covered most of the schools in Brighton, then quite a lot of money would be involved, quite a lot of children waiting for him.

Agnes felt there was no doubt Sir George was guilty, his slip in calling Andy 'Weedon' when he professed to know nothing about him had confirmed her suspicions. Then the small matter of the body in the cupboard pointed the finger of guilt even more firmly at the magistrate and councillor, Sir George Brennan.

The door bell rang. It was Bella, a very tearful Bella by the sound of the voice over the door intercom. Agnes let her in then greeted her with an open door as the girl stepped out of the lift. She looked shattered, her eyes red and swollen from crying. Usually a tidy, neat dresser, she looked anything but. Her coat was draped over her shoulders, one arm of the coat inside out, her school tie undone, the collar of her white school blouse poking up on one side while the other was buried in her blazer.

'Come in, Bella, try to stop crying, please.'

Agnes sat the girl down on the settee and put an arm round her shoulders. She was wondering how Bella had found out about

Andy, or was it just his disappearance from the scene that was upsetting her? She soon learned that Bella obviously knew nothing about Andy, where he was or, most importantly, what had happened to him. This was apparent from her next outburst.

'Oh Mrs Turner, it's awful, awful, awful. They say she could die, she's unconscious. I've been to see her, they said I could. I talked to her, they said to talk to her, but it didn't do anything, she's got tubes in her mouth and in her arm. She looks like she's dead!'

Agnes gradually managed to get the details. Pamela had got some E's, quite a few tablets, and decided not to sell them but keep them for herself. She'd gone to the rave with Bella and her parents had no idea that she was out.

'Do your parents know about this, Bella?' Agnes interrupted at this point.

'I had to tell them, Mrs Turner, I was with her. When she collapsed I went to the hospital with her, they rushed her away from me into a sort of casualty room.'

Bella spilled it all out. They had, of course, asked for Pamela's name and address and rung her parents. Bella heard the nurse's conversation on the telephone, heard her say, 'Your daughter's here in the Brighton General.' They came at once of course. They were, as Bella put it, 'freaked out' completely. Then when the doctors turned them out of Pamela's room to do some more treatment, they became aware of Bella. Mr Roberts really set on her, said it was all her fault, their daughter would never have stolen out at night without a lot of encouragement from her.

'In a way I suppose they were right, Mrs Turner.'

Bella began to sob again, it had hit her hard. She went on, trying to control her tears.

'My parents came, I rang them. At first they didn't seem to understand what I was talking about, then they caught on and came right over to the hospital, they were devastated. They were pretty decent about it all. Mum made a booboo though. She put her arm around me and said, "It might have been you, darling." That set Pamela's mother off of course.'

'How is Pamela now? Has she come round or is she still in a coma?'

'She's still unconscious, in intensive care – oh, God knows what's going to happen...'

Agnes let Bella talk herself out about the whole horrific scene. The rave and the awful moment when Pamela collapsed. How awful she looked. Perhaps, Agnes thought, this will cure Bella of taking drugs any more, perhaps not.

At last she decided she must tell Bella to

go home, try to comfort her parents. The girl looked at her in surprise as if that aspect of the drama had not occurred to her.

'Now Bella, you've taken the day off school. Go home and tell your mother and father you intend to take no more Ecstasy now you have seen for yourself how dangerous it can be.'

After the girl had left Agnes sat thinking over what Bella had told her. How could these men do these terrible things just for money, create a chain of events that could only cause pain, illness and often death? If not death then a ruined and useless life. What she had hoped would happen to Andy Weedon had happened. One cog in the vile wheel had been taken out, but the machinery would grind on without him, someone equally unscrupulous would take his place. His death had only happened because some larger cog in the wheel had suspected him of taking away some of the money that should have been paid to them, the Lords of the Racket.

Louise's ring had a lot to answer for. Agnes could see it in her mind's eye, the big diamond flashing, the beautiful green stones. It made her shiver a little to think of it.

Bella hadn't mentioned Andy Weedon. Agnes supposed her concern for Pamela had momentarily pushed him into the background. She had been certain when Bella telephoned that she'd wanted to talk about Andy and his disappearance. Agnes was glad she had not blurted anything out about his death before the real reason for Bella's panic and dismay had come out. His death would affect Bella more than Pamela's, she thought, but to them he was not yet dead. That fact must come out sooner or later, but when?

Days went by and Agnes watched the television news and searched the newspapers for any mention of a body being found. She felt the distinctive marking on his face and neck, still there, though less obvious now, would make identifying him fairly easy. Although that would depend on whether the body was found locally.

He could of course be buried somewhere, but eventually the fact that he had disappeared must be noticed. Agnes remembered Bella saying he borrowed the blue car from his brother. That was one relative who must be wondering where he was. They might think he was in London having more treatment for the birthmark, but surely his parents, if he was in touch with them, or his brother would have been told if that were the case. It was a mystery and a nasty one, indicating that Sir George Brennan had ways and means of getting rid of anyone not playing the drug game to his rules. Not a man to cross. Where did his supply come from? Perhaps Andy had underestimated the power of the gang he was in.

He obviously was not very bright to have flashed around his new-found wealth. He must have realised Sir George would get to know about the large amounts of money he was able to spend and think at once that he was on the fiddle with Sir George's precious merchandise. He would of course have told no one about the ring. Yes, a stupid as well as a wicked young man who deserved in Agnes's view exactly what he had got, gruesome though his death had been.

Agnes began to feel she was becoming too involved with the whole drugs scene. These rather stupid young teenagers, their seemingly unseeing parents. The Robertses, over-zealous. The Goldsteins' odd way of leaving their wayward daughter too much on her own and to her own devices. She needed a break and she determined to devote that break to Madge who was facing the result of her scan. Marcia her daughter and her son-in-law would come to be near her, Agnes was sure, but this would worry Madge more than give her comfort. She was always reluctant to take either of them away from their home and work. Agnes decided to spend two days and nights in London to be near Madge, to help her through the new scan and its results.

When she arrived in London, having arranged for Polly to be cared for by Mrs Jenvy, her usual 'dog sitter', Madge was delighted to see her.

'I'll book into a hotel for a couple of nights, Madge. I'd like to be here with you. I feel the scan will be all right.'

Madge made a little grimace.

'I wish I could believe that too, Agnes, but there is still a little lump there,' and she pointed to a place under her arm. Her eyes filled with tears, not of self-pity – that was not Madge – but rather of fear.

There was no need for Agnes to book into a hotel.

The Cornwall Clinic had a small annexe for relatives of patients. Agnes did not claim to be related to Madge. However, the receptionist booked her into a room in the annexe without argument, remarking kindly that friends were often just as important and that as Mrs Hillier's nearest relative lived in Paris she felt Agnes could rate as a relative.

The two days and nights were not particularly pleasant ones.

The surgeon talked to Madge, as they do, with great optimism: 'Yes, there is a new lump which will have to be removed.' But he explained that there was a good chance it was not malignant and that she would possibly be able to go home – or to a 'half-way' house as it were – soon after the operation.

Agnes went back to Brighton, feeling that it would be rather longer than she had hoped before she could have Madge in her flat to look after her.

Being in the clinic and going so frequently past the door leading to the room where she had seen Andy Weedon – or at least heard him speak – brought back the picture of the curled-up body in the broom cupboard and made her wonder anew where it was now.

18

As Agnes parked her car outside her flat, she braced herself, ready to tackle the problems she had left behind her only two days ago. It seemed longer. Polly seemed to think that way too, for she greeted Agnes as if she had been away for weeks. Mrs Jenvy had to be paid and listened to. How good Polly had been, eaten her dinner and done her bizzies each day on her walks. Mrs Jenvy was too reliable and altogether too precious to hurry or ignore so it took a little time for her to say goodbye for the moment to Polly and promise Agnes, 'See you on Tuesday, Mrs Turner.'

At last she had time to pick up her mail and press the telephone recorder for messages.

The first and only message was from Bella.

'Oh, Mrs Turner, I've rung and rung, have you been away? Pamela died, she came round and talked, told her Mum and Dad everything, then suddenly she was … it was so sudden, so unexpected…'

Bella was crying now and the message faded away.

Agnes was shocked, badly shocked. She had somehow assumed that Pamela would recover, that she would be one of the lucky ones to survive the effects of the drug. But no. No wonder Bella was devastated, to lose a fifteen-year-old friend, dreadful. And the Robertses. Agnes felt she could do nothing today. She was tired after her time with Madge, the uncertainty about the result of the tests on her friend, and now this dreadful news of Pamela, poor silly little Pamela. All this and the rather hectic drive from London had really tired her out.

She sat down and took off her shoes, thankful that Mrs Jenvy had given Polly her long walk. Agnes closed her eyes. It would be her birthday next week, she would be sixty-two – as the nuns would say, 'Pushing seventy, Agnes, not young any more!'

She got up and made for the dining-room.

What she needed was a brandy and ginger ale, a pick-me-up.

'You are thinking rubbish, sixty-two is nothing.'

She firmly remonstrated with herself. She would feel better tomorrow, then she knew what she would do. Find out who had taken Andy Weedon's place at the school gates. Someone would have, she was sure it was too lucrative a round to let go, and if let go, the children who were only beginning on their experimental drug taking might slip through the net and be lost forever. The others, more firmly hooked, might try elsewhere. The likelihood of there being a replacement she felt was great. She would do that, but now, as she sipped her drink, all she wanted was to go to bed.

There was just Polly's short walk before bed. Coming out on to the top landing from the back stairs, she bumped into the Warburtons who were just coming out of the lift. The Major stopped her, ignoring Polly.

'Agnes, these new chaps in number 2, those two, I am rather afraid they are ... you know!'

'Very nice couple, aren't they, Major?' Agnes said and escaped into her own flat with Polly.

The next morning Agnes felt better, more optimistic about Madge, more philosophical about poor Pamela. As she went through her morning routine she could not make up her mind what to do. Get in touch with Mr and Mrs Roberts to say how sorry she was – or was it too soon for that? Should she just write a letter of condolence? She could not make up her mind. The short walk with Polly helped her a little and on her return, she telephoned Bella, but it was Mrs Goldstein who answered.

'Mrs Turner, yes, Bella has told me a little about you, you were most kind to poor Pamela, I dare not think how her parents must be feeling. Thank goodness Bella is not into this awful drug scene, she's a sensible child really.'

Agnes decided to be frank with Bella's mother, who seemed to have no idea that her daughter was well into the drug scene, as far as Ecstasy went anyway. Agnes was pretty sure that Bella was not yet using heroin, crack, coke or any of the harder stuff, but how sure could she really be? Bella might be deceiving her just as much as she managed to deceive her parents. She hoped not.

'Bella's here if you want to speak to her, Mrs Turner.'

Bella came to the telephone. She was more composed, but sounded very down and after 'Thanks, Mum,' as she took the telephone receiver from her mother, she

198

said, 'Oh, Mrs Turner, it's all in the papers. Could I come and see you this morning?'

Agnes had plans of her own, so suggested another time. She wanted to keep the resolution she had made last night. Go to the two schools she knew about this afternoon – and perhaps another school she had noticed nearby – and look out for Andy's replacement. This morning she was not going to have Polly done out of her walk, and anyway on that walk she wanted to think out her plan regarding Sir George. She wondered if asking them round to drinks might be a good idea or even, as Lady Brennan had done to her, suggesting dinner.

She did not want to waste the morning listening to Bella's lamentations and self-blamings about her poor dear friend Pamela Roberts. Of course Agnes realised it was quite awful for the girl, who was little more than a child herself. Death at that age is more terrible, more unexpected, more dramatic.

Agnes felt genuinely sorry for Bella, but just now she did not want to deal with that side of drug taking, she wanted to deal with the pushers.

As Polly ran about, chasing after imaginary rabbits or even blowing leaves, Agnes looked on the undulating fields and downs, trying to understand why, at fifteen, you needed more stimulus than that offered by the world around you. What drug could make you feel better than the gifts you already had? Health and, more important than perhaps anything else, youth and the years before you to explore, travel and fall in love?

Agnes had her lunch in a small country pub, a place she had been to before where the host gave Polly water and a bowl of food. She sat in the sun, quite warm now it was May. At about three o'clock, she drove back to the flat, parked Polly in her basket, gave her some reassurance about her return and got a meal ready for the evening, then set out to monitor the schools' gates, just to check.

She managed to cover all three schools. The younger children came out slightly earlier than the private school. She sat watching the gates of Ernest Williams School as the children ran out, some into the arms of their mother, some pushing and shoving each other across the path, some walking solitarily. No man approached either of the school's entrances. None of the children appeared to be looking around for anybody to come up to them.

In the second school, the one she hadn't been to before, she did notice something. One of the children, a solitary one, stood leaning against the stone support of the school railings, his bag at his feet, the strap of the bag held in his hands. He was fair-haired, about ten years old and he looked bored, lethargic and rather pale. Agnes watched him and sat in the car on the other side of the road. She had a good view up and down the pathway; most of the children had gone now.

Suddenly, a car drew up just short of the entrance, a dark blue coupé. A man got out and walked up to the boy, who gathered up his bag when he saw the man approaching. He also thrust one hand into his pocket. Something was exchanged, but the man's back was towards Agnes. She couldn't see what it was, but she could guess. The man turned round and was facing her. He didn't look towards her car, but she recognised him. He was one of the men who had been with Andy when he was nearly killing Polly. Suddenly she remembered Bella's remark. Was it Bella or Pamela? She wasn't sure, but she did remember what had been said about the car.

'Oh, that's his brother's car, he lends it to Andy sometimes.'

There was the car, the dark blue car which now Agnes recognised as well. So Andy's replacement was none other than his own brother. Well, they were all of a type, she could see again this man making howling noises as he watched his brother swing Polly round and round. Did he know Andy was dead? Perhaps not, Agnes thought as she drove away.

It was time to go to Westwood School to see if any of the girls were hanging about waiting for Andy, or perhaps for someone else to turn up in his place.

As she drew near, the school seemed totally deserted. No blue car, no girls waiting around. The doors at the top of the flight of stone steps leading into the school were closed.

Agnes paused for a moment, almost stopping her car, but doing so on the opposite side of the road.

Suddenly, the doors opened and a girl – just one girl – came out. It was Bella and she was waiting for someone.

Agnes could hardly believe her eyes!

A man, Agnes recognised him as the man from the blue car, Andy's brother, came up to Bella. He had something in his clenched hand. He opened his hand as he reached the girl, showing her what it was he held. Bella put out her hand to take whatever it was from him, but he re-clenched his hand and drew it back, shaking his head vigorously. Agnes could almost hear him saying, 'No, no.'

He waved the other hand to and fro as if to emphasise his refusal. Agnes guessed, watching the scene, that he had the drug but

Bella had no money to pay for it. Poor Bella. So much for her remark to her that she only took dope now and again and that she could 'take it or leave it,' as she put it. As Agnes watched she became more disgusted with Bella. She was literally pleading with the man, in Agnes's opinion lowering herself to his level, to let her have whatever he was selling and, Agnes supposed, pay when she could. Perhaps Andy would have let her have whatever he had been selling, and owe him, pay when she was able, or perhaps do a bit of pushing at the school or at other schools. Agnes simply could not stand it any more. She got out of her car and crossed the road to Bella's side.

Bella did not see her until she was almost beside her. The man with the drug still clenched in his hand said, 'Who's this, Bella? What do you want, you old cow?'

'Mrs Turner, I can't talk to you!'

The remark seemed to galvanise the man into action.

'No, you can't talk to her. You've done enough talking to her already by the look of it. I'm off. Goodbye!'

He turned, jumped down the two steps on to the path, sprinted along to his car and jumped in. As he started the engine, a plume of smoke came from the exhaust and there was a bang, but the car started, if rather jerkily, and was soon away and out of sight. Bella let out a little wail as if she was in pain. It was a cry of real anguish. She sat down on the little wall at the side of the steps; the dusty shrub above her pulled at her hair but she hardly seemed to notice it.

'Mrs Turner, Mrs Turner, you don't know what you have done. I'm not just on Ecstasy. I'm on smack, heroin, have been for weeks now and I can't do without it. I must have it. Andy will give it to me when he comes from that clinic, but I can't wait.' She wailed again. 'I can't wait, what am I going to do?'

'Come along, get in the car. You are coming home with me to talk to your parents, Bella, right now!'

Agnes led the protesting girl across the road to the Porsche. Once in the passenger seat, all the girl's resistance seemed to crumble except for one or two remarks: 'You don't understand, Mrs Turner. It's terrible when you try to stop, it's awful, awful,' and 'I only needed it perhaps once a week, now it's every day. You get cramps and shivers and sweat and want it so much.'

Agnes felt deeply sorry for her but drove steadily on to Bella's house, praying the parents would be there for their daughter to tell her story. They seemed to be socialites, out a lot for drinks and dinner parties. Of course they were fond of their daughter, Agnes was sure they were, but in thinking that she was well able to look after herself, able to cope with growing up, with all its attendant problems, anxieties and frustrations, that was where they fell short, at least in Agnes's opinion.

Both Mr and Mrs Goldstein were in, drinking tea in the kitchen together. Bella led Agnes through, then stopped short of the kitchen door. She looked younger than her sixteen years at that moment, young and very vulnerable. She looked from Agnes to her parents.

'Mum, Dad, I want to talk to you, tell you something.'

Bella turned to Agnes and held out her hand towards her.

'You remember Mrs Turner, don't you? You met, no, you nearly met. You were just off to the Haynes', or somewhere.'

Was there bitterness in that remark? Agnes thought there was.

Agnes looked in surprise at the girl beside her. Did she perhaps resent being left to her own devices so much, blame them a little for the mess she had got into?

'I want to talk to you, Dad, Mum. Mrs Turner's here with me, she knows all about it, or some of it.'

Her parents looked both surprised and a bit mystified. They looked at each other, eyebrows raised.

'What is it, Princess? Shall we go through to the sitting-room? We can't talk in the kitchen, can we?

Agnes had to take over, trying to do so without appearing overbearing, and they agreed to stay where they were.

'Shall we sit down, Bella, have a round table conference?'

Agnes tried to lighten the tension a little. Bella's chair made a harsh scraping sound as she pulled it forward. She put both arms on the table and sank her head down on them. Mrs Goldstein got up suddenly, taking the flowered teapot with her.

'Whatever the conference is going to be about, I'm going to make another pot of tea. Mrs Turner would probably like one and I need another cup.'

She got to the sink and filled the kettle, looking over her shoulder and half smiling. The water splashed her hand.

'Bother. Bella, this is nothing to do with boyfriend trouble?'

Her daughter rolled her head to and fro on her arms. Her mother switched on the kettle and stood, waiting. Agnes felt they were getting absolutely nowhere. Mrs Goldstein waited until the tea was made and then came back to the table and sat down, but not until she had taken saucers and cups from the cupboard and put them on the table. She poured milk into the two extra cups and her own. She looked at her husband who shook his head. Agnes felt they were playing for time, felt she was in a play or a television soap, anything but reality.

'Bella, tell your mother and father what you should tell them. They will know what to do and how to help you.'

Bella raised her head, sat up straight, looked at Agnes for support and encouragement, then said, 'I'm on heroin, Mum, Dad. I only take a little, now and again. I think, I thought, I could kick it, but I can't.'

Agnes kept quiet. She was interested in the way Bella's parents would react to their daughter's confession. For a second or two there was complete silence. Then it was Mrs Goldstein who spoke first.

'Darling, I can't believe this! Heroin! It's dangerous, isn't it? I mean, did Pamela take that as well as those pill things? And she's dead, Bella, she's dead!'

She turned and took her husband's hand and held it.

'Did you know about this, Mrs Turner? Bella said you took Pamela's dog, or rescued it or something?'

This remark seemed to fire Bella into a rage. She leapt to her feet, tears streaming down her face. The chair fell over. She didn't seem to notice its fall.

'You see, you see, you see! You never listen to what I say, either of you. You're always out. Drinks parties, dinners. You don't care what I do or where I go any time of day or night. You just don't care. I hate you both.'

She stormed out of the kitchen; upstairs her bedroom door crashed to with a bang. Mrs Goldstein got up as if to follow her, but her husband kept hold of her hand. They seemed upset, but still puzzled.

'No, dear. Leave her for a moment. Let's talk to Mrs Turner. She will perhaps be able to help us. Would you, please?'

He turned to Agnes. His face was quite white and drawn.

'Where has she been getting the drug from? The same place as Pamela Roberts, I suppose. Did you know about it?'

Agnes could say quite truthfully that she did not know Bella was taking heroin until this afternoon. She did not repeat any of the information she had gathered about Andy. She just told them what she knew about the habit the young ones had of taking stimulants at parties and raves. This, they of course knew, but they did not seem to realise that Bella might be able to get the tablets too, or to think she might want them.

'I could kill whoever sold them to her, kill him.'

Bella's father began to pace up and down the kitchen, banging his clenched fist into the palm of his other hand. He seemed the more affected of the two.

Agnes thought as she got up to leave, Well, one pusher has been killed already and replaced. It's the bigger fish, the large many-tentacled octopus, that needs to be killed.

She felt sick of the whole miserable business.

'You must spend more time with your daughter,' she said almost brusquely.

They both agreed.

'Oh, I'd better cancel the Parkers' dinner party,' Bella's father said.

'Yes, I really think you should,' Agnes said, and was sure they both missed the sarcasm in her tone and manner. Mr Goldstein went to the telephone then turned to his wife with a rather bemused look.

'What shall I say, dear? Shall I say you are not well?'

'Why not say Bella's not well, Mr Goldstein?' Agnes suggested. Again they missed the sarcasm, or she imagined they did. Parents, she thought! Mrs Goldstein accompanied her to the front door. Then she did show a little emotion, tears even.

'Thank you, Mrs Turner for being so kind and caring and forgive us for ... I don't know, we've always tried to give her everything she wanted.'

Agnes felt a momentary sympathy for the woman and took her hand in hers.

'Perhaps that's why she wanted even more, Mrs Goldstein and a little more of both of you.'

She got into her car, worried about leaving

Polly for so long, but Polly was all right, ready for her walk and as welcoming as always. Strange, Agnes thought, as she put on her lead, if it hadn't been for Pamela, I would never have had Polly and now Polly is well and happy and Pamela is dead.

As Agnes came back from her walk with Polly, she noticed that the errant postman had again left the little pile of mail on the hall shelf instead of delivering it to each flat as he was supposed to. Agnes sighed and hoped his actions wouldn't spark off another meeting. The postman not delivering properly always irritated the Warburtons and Arthur Leeming. They seemed to love having a meeting to air their various grievances and usually it only needed a small thing like this to start a landslide of other complaints.

She sorted through what was left on the shelf. A small dress catalogue for Louise Le Mesurier. Sadly she put it on one side. Louise would have certainly picked it up had she been alive. Her interest in clothes was paramount.

There was one letter only for Agnes. She recognised the expensive envelope immediately. The Brennans, she was almost sure. There in the hall, crossing to the lift, she ripped the envelope open. It contained only a short note from Lady Brennan, asking her to dinner. She crammed the letter in her pocket and picked Polly up. Polly was not enamoured of the lift, it frightened her a little, so Agnes carried her.

Once in the flat and with Polly catered for, she sat down and read the note more carefully. Four days' time. Should she go, should she accept? Curiosity overcame her distrust and even fear of Sir George. He had killed one man he suspected of grabbing his ill-gotten gain and spending it on himself. Agnes decided she would go, make some reference to Andy, perhaps, and see what Sir George's reaction would be. She put the note on her telephone table, feeling that the invitation was at short notice, so she would telephone her acceptance instead of posting a note.

Agnes remembered Lady Brennan's rather casual mention of an invitation to dinner, but had taken it as mere politeness. But no, she had obviously meant it, indeed there had been an air of sincerity and almost detachment from her husband's flamboyant manner that had made Agnes like the wife much more than Sir George himself. Even so, Agnes could not make up her mind. Was Lady Brennan a part of the drug scene? After all, she was living in luxury in a beautiful house. Did she know where the money was coming from? This dinner party might be the answer.

What to wear, she wondered. Should she

ask when she telephoned her acceptance, was it a formal dinner party, or a small intimate one? No, she thought, she would not ask; as the invitation had been at fairly short notice and the note handwritten, she would take it to be small, and no need to dress up too much.

A much more difficult task had to be performed before that though. She had to write a letter of condolence to Mr and Mrs Roberts. Her visits to their house had been anything but enjoyable. What a mixture, she thought. Mr and Mrs Goldstein Mr and Mrs Roberts, Bella, Pamela and Andy. She had certainly picked up a crowd of acquaintances and one near friend in Louise Le Mesurier. Now three of them were dead. She certainly had been wrong in thinking her new lifestyle would be tedious and lonely. Sir George and Lady Brennan, the newest of all, how long would they last, as acquaintances, or would they perhaps succumb to some accident connected with drugs?

19

Agnes took great trouble on the night of the Brennans' dinner party to look her best. She chose her dress with care. A pale lavender frock, sleeveless with a short long-sleeved jacket, the V-neck edged narrowly with a silver trimming which matched the trimming on the cuffs. A thin silver chain set off the neck neatly and a similar chain acted as a bracelet. Agnes rather liked understatements and this jewellery was, she felt, a good example of understatement. Lady Brennan, at least, would be certain to have large diamond rings, to Agnes's mind something of an overstatement in jewellery.

'If you cannot compete then don't try to!' Agnes didn't know who had originally said this, but she heartily agreed with it.

Having put on her make-up and generally finished making the best of her appearance, she sat down and looked at herself in her dressing-table mirror.

Agnes was interested in how she looked, but not fanatical. She used night cream regularly. Whether it had done anything to keep the wrinkles at bay she was not at all sure. She peered closely at her face. Round her eyes there were decidedly signs of ageing catching up, and also round the lips – lips did not improve either by sixty-two! The lines on them would not let the lipstick give the mouth a shining look that youth gave them. Agnes shook herself.

Good points? Her hair always comforted her. In youth, it had been mousy and so fine and difficult. Since she had had money, she had paid well for styling and constant care and attention. Then, as she put on a tiny trace more blusher, she gave herself points for where she was going tonight. Who but herself would venture to dinner in a house where on the last visit she had found a corpse in the broom cupboard? A rare smile curved her lips. What would she find out tonight, why had she been asked? She realised she was mixing with dangerous people. Three people dead already!

She switched off the dressing-table light and got up.

'Once more unto the breach...' she said to herself. As she said it, the telephone rang. It was Lady Brennan.

'Mrs Turner, Agnes. George has just had a good idea. He says Hilton will come and fetch you, then...'

She gave a little laugh, as if to lighten her words slightly.

'Then you can have two glasses of wine instead of one and a liqueur even. He could be there in ten minutes, slight exaggeration on George's part, quarter of an hour, then he can drive you home. I'm so looking forward to seeing you again. Does that idea appeal to you?'

Agnes simply had to say 'Yes'. Why not? It was a bore always having to think about what one could allow oneself to drink when driving. She was very strict about one glass of wine only when she was driving herself home from any party or function. Lady Brennan had sounded pleased when she had agreed. Agnes made a little grimace into the mirror before she turned away. She hoped she wouldn't land up in the broom cupboard! She dismissed the thought with a laugh but the thought was there. If she had known what was going to happen at this party, would she still have gone?

Hilton arrived in just over the quarter of an hour Lady Brennan had predicted. Agnes locked her front door, having said her usual, 'Won't be long, Polly' to reassure the brown-eyed animal lying on her bed, looking as usual slightly reproachful, head on one side, ears back.

It undoubtedly was pleasant to be called for. She got into the luxurious car and sat back full of rather mixed feelings, but determined to find out as much as possible about Sir George and his involvement in the drug trade. Also, she did not omit his wife from her thoughts. After all, she lived in affluence. No expense was spared in that beautiful house. She had at her disposal the cars, the beautiful furniture, so was she, perhaps, just as guilty as her husband? Or perhaps she hated the way his money was earned. She must have known about Andy Weedon's body being in her house, she must have been in some way party to its disposal. These things Agnes wanted to sort out and punish. She was glad Andy Weedon was dead, but whoever killed him would not go scot-free, she would somehow see to that.

The car drew up smoothly at the door of Home Leigh. Her driver leapt out of the car and came round to open her door for her. Agnes smiled and thanked him. This evening he was wearing a chauffeur's cap which hid his bullet head and made him look less like a bouncer.

Lady Brennan, Elizabeth, was effusive in her greeting and led Agnes through to the sitting-room. Sir George and two other men rose as she entered the room.

'Ah, Agnes isn't it? Lionel, this is our friend Mrs Turner. Agnes, Lionel Compston and this...' Sir George motioned towards the other man beside him, 'is Gerald Leach.'

Both men were curiously alike, about five foot nine or ten in height, slightly rotund and both bald with a fringe of greying hair round their heads. Both also looked newly shaven with skins smooth and pink. They all sat down, including Elizabeth Brennan who had rather stood back while the introductions were going on. Now she looked pointedly at the drinks tray.

'Ah, yes, yes. What will you have to drink, Agnes?'

Agnes chose gin and tonic with lemon and ice. As she sipped the drink she found it too strong for her and turned to Sir George, who was now deep in conversation with his two companions. Lady Brennan took the glass from Agnes and glanced heavenwards.

'George's gin and tonic would strip paint off walls, Agnes. Let me mix you a reasonable one.'

They both went over to the drinks tray and her hostess mixed her a drink. This time it had a reasonable amount of gin in it. The two women went and sat on the settee together, and eventually the men gave up their threesome chat to join them. The conversation became general, though not particularly interesting. Lionel Compston talked, Agnes thought, rather proudly about his private plane.

'It's called an Islander and I've kept the name, made on the Isle of Wight. Nice little job, Mrs Turner — useful sometimes too, isn't it, George?'

He slapped his rather fat thigh as he said this. He was feeling his drink, Agnes thought, and she wished he would go on, say more about the usefulness of the Islander. George Brennan looked irritated and shook his head at him, as if he would like him to shut up. Agnes broke his train of thought by telling him she had had a house on the Isle of Wight at one time and knew the man who had designed the Islander's livery. This turned the conversation a little but it did not lessen Agnes's suspicion that the plane might have been used to dump Andy Weedon's body somewhere out at sea. After all, if the body turned up somewhere, carried there by the tides, it would hardly be recognisable. More drinks were served, but Agnes stuck to the one gin and tonic and made it last till they all trooped through to the dining-room.

Dinner could only be described as superb, consisting mostly of fish. A starter of melon and prawns was followed by a main dish of lobster and tiny new potatoes. Asparagus with a sauce which blended perfectly with the lobster. Hot bread rolls and butter, which the three men demolished. A side salad of avocado, tiny spring onions, peeled cherry tomatoes and the white hearts of tiny lettuces. To Agnes, the perfect meal!

'I've not included any meat, it's not good for you. I have enough trouble with George's high blood pressure, so I've given you a healthy meal, diet-wise. I know you men would rather have roast beef and Yorkshire pudding!'

There was a glint of mischief in Elizabeth Brennan's eyes as she said this and the two male guests made suitable noises about how they had enjoyed it.

Sir George was not as untruthful. Being the host he could speak his mind.

'Well, it was all right, darling. All right for you girls, I suppose, but you know I like a bit of beef or lamb! Still we can make up for your healthy meal – these look delicious!'

The maid had cleared away the plates and was bringing in individual bread and butter puddings, swimming with cream and smelling hot and sweet. The men tucked in.

'Any more where this came from, Elizabeth dear?'

Elizabeth rang; three more were brought in and were just as quickly demolished.

Coffee was served in the small sitting-room, with liqueurs. Elizabeth obviously thought her husband could be trusted to serve these in the small glasses on the tray.

There was an enormous range of liqueurs and Agnes chose her favourite – kümmel.

After drinking their coffee, the men got up, as if to a prearranged signal.

'Now girls, you don't mind if we leave you for a short while, do you? We have a bit of business to discuss, so I do hope you will excuse us. We won't be very long.'

They filed out of the room. There was a short silence, then a door closed which Agnes took to be the library. Then all was quiet. Elizabeth Brennan leaned back and sipped her crème de menthe. She looked more relaxed now the men had gone. They had 'left them in peace', as she put it.

At first they talked about general things. Agnes complimented her on her beautifully kept garden and the house itself. She really meant what she said but her praise did not seem to have much effect on Elizabeth Brennan. Agnes felt she was waiting to say something totally different and at last she put an end to talk about houses and gardens. She leant forward, opened a silver cigarette box on the table in front of her and took out and lit a cigarette. Agnes was surprised. She had not seen Lady Brennan ever smoke a cigarette during her visits to her house. Elizabeth smiled.

'I'm sorry, Agnes, but what I have to say makes me feel I really need a cigarette to steady my nerves a little.'

Agnes made no comment in answer to the remark, just waited for her hostess to speak and let out whatever it was she needed to have a nerve steadier to say. She watched her draw on the cigarette two or three times, then roll the lighted end to and fro on the ashtray's edge. At last she made up her mind to speak and Agnes was so shocked for a moment she could not even reply.

'Agnes, I want to kill my husband and I need your help.'

It took a few seconds for the sentence to make sense in Agnes's mind. She half wanted Elizabeth Brennan to repeat it so that she had more time, but her senses told her that she had understood exactly what had been said. She was going to ask 'Why?' but she was not given time.

'That girl Pamela has died and many more will die like her, others will become so addicted to the substances he deals in that they will become useless shells, burnt out, often for the rest of their lives.'

She stubbed out her cigarette violently in the ashtray.

'But how can I help you, Elizabeth, in what way ?'

Elizabeth Brennan took the handbag from behind her. Agnes remembered thinking it rather odd that she had been carrying it with her in her own house. She took out a clean white envelope and shook out a selection of different pills on to the polished surface of the coffee table. They rattled a little as they fell. Her face was stony. She looked up at Agnes, as if to say, 'I know what I'm saying and I mean every word of it.'

'Now, will you listen carefully, Agnes. It is here that I think you can give me your professional nursing help.'

She put one finger on an orange pill.

'That's for George's blood pressure, it's very high – has been for years.'

She moved the others, one by one with her finger.

'That one is his daily aspirin and these two are what he calls his pee pills, you know. Now you see the aspirin and those two are circular, white and easy to replace with another kind.'

Agnes was silent. She really had nothing to say.

Next from the handbag Lady Brennan took a very small plastic bag, about two inches by two inches. In this Agnes could see three white tablets very like the aspirin and the diuretic tablets.

'These are amphetamines. If I replace those three with those three, will it be enough to kill George or not?'

'Has your husband got heart trouble as well as the high blood pressure?' Agnes felt slightly dazed.

The answer was a very polite nod.

'Well, yes, then, that might be enough to kill him if his heart is weak – but surely, Lady Brennan, you don't intend ... surely you could talk, try to make him know how you feel.'

'No, no. I have tried and tried. He is very important and well known in many parts of the world. Agnes, he must go.'

Agnes's curiosity overcame her shock. At last she asked, 'But why me, how do you know I wouldn't give you away?'

'Oh, that was easy. I saw you open the broom cupboard upstairs and look in. You must have seen the body, you must have seen it, didn't you?'

Agnes nodded. She could not deny it. She had no idea that Lady Brennan had seen her.

'Yes, something made a noise in the cupboard. It was some dusters falling off the shelf. I thought it must be a cat in there, that's why I looked.'

'And never reported it to the police. I waited days, even after Lionel had got rid of the body from his plane. I knew then it was safe to tell you what I was and still am determined to do.'

There was a sudden rumbling of voices and the sound of footsteps. Elizabeth Brennan swept the pills back into the envelope and put that and the little plastic bag with its three tablets in her handbag. She placed a hand over Agnes's and smiled reassuringly.

'I always give him the pills, normally about lunch-time. He never even looks at them. He wouldn't take them if I didn't give them to him.

'Hello, darling. Finished?'

Sir George came in rubbing his hands,

223

looking very pleased with himself, as did the others.

The maid came in with another tray of coffee. The men poured themselves large measures of whisky. Elizabeth and Agnes had another liqueur. It all became very cosy and light-hearted, making Agnes feel as if she had only dreamed the conversation that had gone on before the men had returned. At about eleven o'clock Agnes took her leave. Feeling the way she did after the drinks she had had, she was very grateful to be driven home by the massive Hilton.

Some drunks, young and noisy, passed as she was putting her key in the lock. They took one look at Hilton standing behind her and went on without even a rude gesture or cat call. He saw her up to her flat and only left with a polite 'Good night, madam,' after she had put the further key in her flat door. She walked Polly, still feeling rather in a daze. Only when she was at last in bed did she dare to let herself think of the conversation she had had with her hostess.

It was almost unbelievable that that gentle, rather pretty, aristocratic woman could have planned such a neat and clever killing. Agnes realised too that she had made herself an accessory. Well, she didn't mind. Andy Weedon, the pusher, was dead and now, maybe, the most powerful member of that despicable team might be liquidated too. Pamela, in a way, would be avenged.

Agnes wondered though how Bella would fare. Andy was gone and soon the drugs which had filtered down to Andy would be gone too. It would be easy to find another Andy, but certainly not easy to find another Sir George. Would Lady Brennan ever have the courage to carry out what she threatened? Seeing her face and hearing her voice again in her memory, Agnes felt she would have both the determination and the courage.

In the morning Agnes felt a nagging worry which would not easily be banished. She had given her opinion to Elizabeth, that three amphetamine tablets might kill her husband, but suppose they didn't? Suppose they just made George feel very ill? Would he suspect that she was trying to kill him? Agnes tried to calm herself. She had only given an opinion. She could be wrong. Elizabeth must realise she could only say 'maybe' to her. Had her words been too encouraging? She could not dismiss the feeling from her mind that she should have refused to give any opinion at all. Perhaps the gin and tonic, the table wine and the liqueurs had made her give a more careless reply than she would have normally. Well, it was no use worrying about it now, but she wished heartily that she had not involved herself in the affair at all, had just brushed the question aside with a smile even and said something like, 'Oh, I am sure you don't really mean what you are saying, Lady Brennan.' That would not have resulted in what she felt now would be a constant worry to her.

20

Bella telephoned the next day and asked if she could come and see Agnes after school tomorrow. She sounded very down, so Agnes said, 'Yes, if you tell your mother and father where you are going. I'll make high tea for you. What would you like?'

This was not greeted with Bella's usual zest. She rather liked her food and loved fish and chips.

'No, don't bother, Mrs Turner. I don't want anything to eat.'

Agnes left it at that. She was just off to the hairdresser's and decided she would get some cream cakes on her way back which might tempt Bella.

Bella arrived at about four thirty, the next afternoon. She never looked her best in her school uniform and apart from that she looked pale, thinner and wan. She threw herself down in a chair, dropped her school bag beside her, covered her face with her hands and began to cry, the tears running between her fingers, making no sound at all.

Agnes sat down beside her and tried to take her hands in hers, but she would not take Agnes's hand, nor remove her own from her face.

'I don't want to live any more, Mrs Turner. Truly I don't. Andy's gone off somewhere. He's not in the hospital in London. I think he's gone away to another country, you know, like America or Australia. Or else he's dead. He could be dead because his brother has been coming to the school with drugs and now he's got Andy's BMW He could be dead.'

Agnes felt in a way she would like to tell Bella the truth, that indeed he was dead and buried deep in the ocean where nobody would ever find his body, but of course she couldn't. Anyway the girl was young. If she was in some odd way in love with Andy, she would get over it and find someone else.

'And have you bought anything from his brother, Bella?'

Bella shook her head but could not meet Agnes's gaze. She lowered her head and looked at the floor.

'Have you, Bella?'

'Yes, I just got some grass. I had to have

something, Mrs Turner, I really had to have something.'

'What, even after Pamela, knowing what it did to her?'

Bella got to her feet and started to walk around the room, pushing her hair over the top of her head.

'You don't know what it's like, Mrs Turner, you just don't!'

Bella's hair was inclined to frizz and when she pushed it up, as she was doing now, it made her look very wild and desperate.

'Bella, I know I don't know what it's like because I have never had experience of drug withdrawal, but if what you tell me is true and you are not on a daily dose, then surely it cannot be so bad?'

Bella turned away from Agnes, facing the window so her face was hidden. She was shaking and still combing her fingers through her hair. Suddenly she turned to Agnes.

'It's not true, Mrs Turner. It's not true! Andy started me on a new pill. I can't remember. It was purple and he gave it to me instead of Ecstasy. It was wonderful, wonderful! One girl told me it was like Ecstasy, but had acid in it as well. That's what made it different and stronger and really great, you felt–'

Bella broke off. Agnes felt even more strongly that the death of Andy – whoever had done it – was well justified. She was glad, glad, glad he was dead. There would of course always be someone to take his place. There always was. But at least one rat was out of the rat race!

Bella could not, or would not, eat anything. All Agnes could do was telephone the Goldsteins and tell them their daughter was in a really bad way and needed help from their doctor and whoever the doctor could recommend to help her.

They both came on the phone, one after the other. They sounded almost as desperate as their daughter.

'We've got an appointment with our doctor tomorrow, Mrs Turner. Bella won't talk to us at all. She just says we don't understand.'

Bella went to the bathroom to try to repair the ravages of her weeping and after hugging Agnes, left – Agnes hoped for home.

Next day, quite unexpectedly, a tiny touch of excitement happened to stir the residents of the flats. Agnes arrived home with Polly to find Miss Horrocks waiting for her. She was obviously slightly agitated and burst out her news to Agnes in breathless haste.

'Oh, Mrs Turner, what do you think? The police are coming here to ask more questions about poor Mrs Le Mesurier's death. They rang up. I expect you will have the message on your answering machine.'

The police had been very quiet of late about solving the riddle of Louise's death and, with the flat being sold, Agnes had not really expected to hear from them again. She felt their investigations might and probably would be going on. The police did not give up easily on such a brutal attack, but she did think they had pretty well exhausted the questions they could ask the flat dwellers who, apart from Agnes, had seen and heard nothing of interest to them. What they could want now she had no idea. Miss Horrocks said she dreaded them coming. She had nothing more to tell them. Agnes asked her what they had said on the telephone and when were they coming.

'Oh, at five o'clock, Mrs Turner, and the man said it was new evidence which had come up, or something like that.'

Agnes turned on her answering tape when she got into her flat. Miss Horrocks had been more or less correct. The only thing she had left out was that the man on the telephone was Detective Inspector Manning. He sounded polite and rather apologetic about having to requestion the residents but suggested that they all meet in Mr Leeming's flat, at that gentleman's suggestion, at five o'clock this afternoon.

Agnes looked at her watch. Half-past four. Polly had to be fed and her own meal prepared. Well, cold chicken and salad with some soup would have to be her meal. She suspected that Mr Leeming, Arthur, would do his best to spin out the meeting as long as possible and that Major and Mrs Warburton would demand to know what the new evidence was that made it necessary for more questions about the murder, nearly resulting in Mrs Warburton having a nervous breakdown – a remark the Major often made when the horrible affair was mentioned. The people in number 1, who had been away at the time, would probably not be asked to attend, so there would only be the five of them. No point, she was sure, in asking the new couple in Louise's flat to join them.

Agnes saw a car arrive at the front door. A man got out followed by a younger man. The car drove away and the front door bell rang and was answered by, Agnes guessed, Arthur Leeming. The detective was prompt. It was ten past five as Agnes made her way down to the flat.

Detective Inspector Manning was a good-looking man. Clean-shaven, dark-haired with a touch of grey at the temples. The younger man stood while everyone was directed to chairs and then sat next to his superior. He too was clean-shaven, with a red-cheeked boyish face and light brown rather untidy hair.

'This is my colleague Detective Constable Felton. We just want to fill in a little background to the questions my colleague DI Sutherland asked at the time. Now, Mrs Turner, you knew Mrs Le Mesurier better than anyone else in the flats, I understand.' His biro was poised.

Agnes repeated all the things she had said, answered all the questions she had been asked at the time of Louise's murder. Then the questions changed a little and each person was asked the same, the notebooks being written in after each one of these rather surprising questions.

'Miss Horrocks did you see any visitors call on Mrs Le Mesurier at any time – men or women – or see cars arrive? Perhaps if you happened to be sitting in your window – such an interesting view you have.'

Miss Horrocks bridled a little and said she didn't really take much notice of guests or even cars that arrived at the flats. She was much too busy, she said.

'Doing what?' Agnes whispered to herself.

The rest didn't bridle at all, though the Warburtons looked quite shocked and murmured something to the effect that they minded their own business and kept themselves to themselves.

Arthur Leeming was his usual suggestive self.

'Men, you mean? No, I didn't see any men

232

coming to the flat, although she was quite a good-looking filly, but she must have been fifty-plus – too old for me!'

He went off into his rather breathless laughter and then offered everyone a drink, as he usually did. All refused.

The Detective Inspector and his younger colleague rose to leave. Agnes wondered what they could possibly have gleaned from the interviews, which seemed to her to have added nothing to what the police already knew. Louise Le Mesurier appeared to have had few friends. Maybe some had called when Agnes was out walking Polly, but so what?

Arthur showed the policemen out, then they couldn't escape without the offered drinks. Whisky and gin and tonic and Miss Horrocks' usual small sherry were dispensed. Then, bringing the drinks to the table, Leeming looked round at the assembled flat dwellers, eyebrows raised.

'Well, what was that all about, then?'

Nobody knew or understood why the Detective Inspector had come and what the new evidence consisted of. Soon the meeting broke up in spite of Arthur Leeming's pressing suggestion that they should all have another drink.

Back in her flat Agnes at least felt pleased that the police had not closed the case. Only she knew that they would never find the killer, because he had gone the same way as his victim – got what he deserved, in her opinion. She felt no regrets at keeping this knowledge to herself. Had they caught Andy before someone else had, the punishment would certainly not have fitted the crime.

A few years in prison, and would they ever have found out about the drug side of his habits? Would someone have protected him from that side of things, not for his sake but for their own? Still, she could not understand the questions asked this evening by Detective Inspector Manning. Did he think that Louise entertained lovers at her flat, and that one of them had murdered her? But that theory would surely have been investigated at the time of her death? Why now, after all this time, were visitors to her flat important enough to necessitate questioning the residents? Neither had there been any reference to this new evidence. What new evidence?

Poor Louise. It was almost as if she had never existed. Her flat was now occupied by people who didn't know her, and they didn't even mind that her body had been found in the very flat where they were now happily living.

Agnes, as she normally did, turned to Polly to help banish sad and depressing thoughts from her mind. She fed her and when she had finished, watched her pushing the almost empty bowl around the kitchen, tail wagging. Cheerful!

Everyone expected another call from Detective Inspector Manning, or at least some kind of explanation about the nebulous 'new evidence'. Days went by and they heard nothing. No more questions, visits or telephone calls. Probably, Agnes thought, investigations were still going on that they knew nothing about. Perhaps they thought Louise was running a sort of brothel, why else should they be interested in who called at the house?

It was sad, and she wondered whether her brother in France was being questioned in any way about his sister. Since the flat had been cleared and sold, they had never heard from him again. Perhaps he was glad to be rid of a place which had housed such a horrifying scene. Agnes could not work out how close the brother and sister had been. Louise, as far as she remembered, had not mentioned her brother. Perhaps she had done so, and Agnes had forgotten. She did recall though how many people had recognised and spoken to Louise at the dress show. None had appeared to be a particularly close friend by their greeting. More acquaintances. Louise had been a rather mysterious person, perhaps?

Arthur Leeming had been the only person

235

who tried to make Manning tell more than obviously he was prepared to do.

'Can you tell us any more about why you have reopened the case today?' he had prompted. 'What new evidence have you turned up that makes us–'

'We have certainly not, as you put it, sir, reopened the case, because we have never closed it. As to the new evidence, that is something which, at the moment, we cannot disclose.'

None of the others, including of course Agnes, had asked any further questions.

Arthur Leeming had looked slightly put out, but had regained his good temper by the time they left. Certainly they would all have liked to know what the new evidence was, and why the visit? But after the answer Arthur had received, no more was said as to the how and why. Except by the Warburtons, who left murmuring under their breath about 'the intrusion'.

21

During the next week Agnes had a telephone call from Lady Brennan inviting her to tea the next day. Agnes hesitated, wondering whether, if she accepted, her hostess would bring up again the topic of the lethal pills she intended to give her husband. Perhaps not. After all, Agnes had given her opinion rightly or wrongly and there was nothing else for her to say.

Elizabeth Brennan, sensing Agnes's hesitation, said, 'Oh, do come, Agnes. I'm lonely and bored and I do like your company. George has taken himself off to Holland and we can talk girls' talk if we want.'

Agnes accepted the invitation and was pleased when Elizabeth added, very kindly she thought, 'Oh, I'm so glad. By the way, I hear you have a little dog, do bring her. Dogs hate being left out and don't much like being alone either.'

She arrived at Home Leigh at about three thirty. There was no Hilton to park her car and indeed it was not necessary because there was only one other car parked in the wide sweeping driveway. Agnes drove her Porsche in beside it, got out and locked her car with her locking device; the resulting small 'clonk' which told her that the vehicle was safely locked was always a reassuring sound.

As she turned to cross the drive, she noticed the car beside her. A brand new maroon BMW. She paused a second, thinking, was it Pamela or Bella who had mentioned to her that Andy had bought himself a new car, a maroon BMW? She was sure they had said... Yes, she remembered thinking that he must have disposed of the ring already to have been able to make such an expensive purchase. Well, by the look of it, Sir George had confiscated the car as his, bought with side-tracked drug money. He, after all, presumably knew nothing about the ring. This car might of course not be Andy's, but she was pretty certain it was. The brother had probably only had a chance to drive it once or twice believing Andy was still alive. But the ruthless Sir George had soon settled that little debt, as Agnes felt he would settle all such debts.

She rang the front door bell and a girl let her in. Agnes recognised her as the coffee server at the dinner party. She smiled at the young woman who gave a rather stiff smile in return and said, 'Lady Elizabeth is in the garden, Mrs Turner.'

Agnes crossed the hall and went through the french windows into the garden. Lady Brennan was bending over the roses, dead heading with a small dainty pair of secateurs. She looked up as Agnes approached, put down the almost full trug on the grass near her feet and held out a welcoming hand to Agnes. Polly, secure on her nylon extending lead, greeted her first.

'Oh, what a dear little creature! Polly, isn't it?'

She bent down and let Polly lick her face.

Polly started smelling round the grass paths, tail wagging furiously, showing great appreciation for the fact that she had been invited.

'How nice that she is not docked. I like them with their tails. I think it was cruel to dock them. I'm glad it's stopped.'

'Me too. Sometimes they bit them off – I mean, the humans bit the Jack Russells' tails off – horrible and cruel.'

Elizabeth Brennan picked up the trug, put a hand on her back just above her hip joint and made a face.

'Ugh, getting old is getting old, isn't it, Agnes? The joints don't like it at all. I've done enough for one day, I think.'

As they walked back into the house, leaving the trug of rose heads on the little wall that bordered the steps up to the french windows, Elizabeth Brennan went on talking. She seemed relaxed and happy. Agnes thought this aristocratic-looking woman looked so right in her garden, a trug on her arm, nipping off the dead heads of her roses. She wondered whether, if anything happened to her husband, she would be able to carry on without the massive amounts of drug money she imagined had already been earned by illegal shipments and sales.

As if she had read her thoughts Elizabeth turned from pressing the bell to summon tea to be brought and smiled at Agnes, a reassuring and confident smile.

'Agnes, all this – the house and another one in London – all belongs to me. I was a rich woman when I met and fell in love with George Brennan. His firm failed and he turned to this vile way of making money -a vile way!'

Agnes shook her head, but had to admit she had been thinking along a similar vein.

The little maid came in wheeling a trolley with tea things. On the bottom of the trolley was a bowl of water, obviously for Polly. Both women sat down and watched Polly taking a good long drink.

Then Elizabeth poured two cups of tea and handed one to Agnes, who shook her head as the sugar was offered to her.

'I feel I can talk to you, Agnes. It's so nice to have someone to chatter to. I only hope I don't bore you?'

She passed a plate to Agnes. On it were six or seven very small and delicious-looking scones with cream, and what looked like strawberry jam, bulging a little out of their centres. Agnes took one. Polly looked up expectantly, but when she was not offered one put her head down on her paws and went to sleep, giving her usual little snore which amused Elizabeth.

'Delicious scones, Elizabeth, did you make them?'

Her companion nodded, but otherwise

did not answer.

There was silence for a moment or two and Agnes felt Elizabeth was pondering whether to tell her guest more about her past, perhaps to justify her determination to put an end to her husband's life. Agnes hoped she would not have to act as a confidante. She herself was so different, she always kept her own counsel, told no one anything, told them nothing about what she was going to do or had done.

Elizabeth poured more tea and after the silence the words poured out.

The tale she told was not particularly different from many others. She had been the only child of rich parents, well educated. George was her first boyfriend. Rather a flamboyant out-going man. 'Full of him-self', her father had called him, and neither parent had approved of her marriage; they tried to put her off, begged her to wait a little while. Travel round Europe, see the world. All to no avail.

So she married George and for many years her parents had had to admit they had been mistaken. His firm, an engineering firm, had flourished and by middle age, all seemed well. No children. That was a sadness to her parents, but Elizabeth was not a great child lover longing to hold a child in her arms. It was rather her parents longing to be grandparents. However, they were reconciled.

Then George's firm took a nosedive. How or why, Elizabeth did not know or understand. She had more than enough money for both of them, so what did it matter?

It mattered to George, who became morose and bitter, and the marriage nearly broke up, but not quite.

Elizabeth's parents died and she was left with more money. This George resented even more. He became more difficult, more bored. He was desperate to get back his old status as a businessman, running a thriving concern.

Then he met Lionel Compston and Gerald Leach. Everything changed. George became his old self again. A new business, a new concern. Trips abroad. Holland, France, Denmark, once to China and Japan. When she asked what the 'business' was, he told her something vague, world-wide engineering, and 'You wouldn't understand, dear.'

She didn't, until she found out what the big deal was. Drugs. How the consignments got here and were distributed, she never knew. Once they lost a huge shipment 'millions of pounds in street value'. But the blame drifted to someone else.

What she finally found out was that there were thousands of small-time deals, with schoolchildren, shop assistants, factory workers. All types of class and degrees of wealth were covered by people like Andy Weedon. Then he was killed. George, Lionel, Gerald or someone else did it. Anyway, he had to be hidden in the house until the plane took the body well out to sea and dumped it.

That finished Elizabeth. She knew it had been done because George got it into his head, probably rightly, that Andy was selling the drugs, George's drugs, at a higher profit than he was telling George and making enough money to spend lavishly.

'Then that Pamela girl, and another boy of fifteen, died in a Brighton club or party of some sort. There is no end to the harm George is doing. He's addicted himself but you'd never know. He must go, Agnes.'

As Elizabeth talked, Agnes said nothing. As usual the wealth of knowledge she possessed about the whole sorry affair was her own and Agnes wanted it to stay like that. That was her power, that was the way she liked it to be.

'Really, how dreadful, Elizabeth,' or 'I can quite imagine how you felt,' or, 'Yes, they deserve it,' was all she contributed.

She listened with interest to the long story, and was never bored.

Later they walked in the garden with Polly, who enjoyed the new smells and new places. The subject of Elizabeth's past and – of more interest to Agnes – her future, was

dropped. The business of the pill replacement was not brought up again until just as
Agnes was leaving.

'I forgot to tell you, Agnes. I am sorry to
bring the subject up again. George has had
a bypass, a heart operation – you will know
all about such things.'

Agnes nodded, reluctant to even speak of
the intended attempt to end Sir George's
life.

'Well, will that mean that the amphetamines are more likely or less likely to work,
kill him?'

Agnes had to answer and thought carefully
before she spoke, trying to make her reply
non-committal.

'I really cannot answer that, Elizabeth,
because I don't know. But please think
carefully before you do this, you may regret
it for ever, you know.'

'Agnes, what would you do to a dog that
tore the throat out of lambs or killed sheep?
You'd have it put down, wouldn't you, even
if you loved it or had once loved it?'

Agnes could not reply for a moment. Then
she said, 'Yes, I suppose I would, Elizabeth,
but I think I would let someone else do it.'

Elizabeth shook her head very positively.

'Oh no, Agnes, it's my responsibility and
mine alone. Don't worry any more about it.'

Polly jumped into the car and Agnes got in
after her. Elizabeth watched her drive out,

waving her hand and smiling, but the look of determination had not left her face. She would do what she had threatened to do, Agnes was as sure as she could be of anything. She looked at Polly. If she chased and killed lambs, sheep, cats, could she have her put down, she wondered? But when it came to humans she was not at all sure that drug dealers, pushers, drug takers, were worth fighting to preserve, cure, make better. She herself doubted it. Do-gooders there were in plenty who would try to prove all sorts of reasons for their behaviour. A deprived childhood, never having enough money to do the things they wanted to do, behavioural problems. No, on the whole, Agnes was on the side of the woman she had just left. If they were harming other people, causing their death, put them down, fast!

22

When she got back to the flats Major and Mrs Warburton were waiting for her. The Major looked grave and pompous, Mrs Warburton timid and rather embarrassed.

'Mrs Turner, it's about Flat 2, their party last night. Did it keep you awake? It certainly did us.'

Agnes denied hearing any noise at all, which was true.

'Well, it was not the noise so much, but my wife and I saw some of the guests arrive.'

Agnes waited for more and soon got it.

'Well, some of the men were, you know, how do they put it, in drag. You could tell they were men, you know, dressed up as ladies. What will it do to the value of our flats?'

Agnes tried to look suitably shocked and failed. Drugs and husband poisoning were uppermost in her mind at the moment. She did her best.

'Well, Major, why don't you have a word with them, say you were a little shocked to see...'

She paused, her imagination as to what Major Warburton could say running out. Major Warburton visibly quaked at the task as did his wife; their shocked expressions made them look almost ill.

'Oh, he couldn't, we couldn't. I mean, it's so difficult, Mrs Turner, to bring up a subject of that nature – but what will it do to the flats, do you think?'

Agnes picked up Polly and made for the lift.

'I really don't know, Major Warburton. We are lucky to have the flat sold so we mustn't be too picky, must we?'

'Yes, but men dressed as women and such

246

parties, surely someone should object, say something?'

'Well, if you feel strongly, I agree with you, it would be a good idea if you had a word with them.'

She entered the lift and pressed the button for the top floor, leaving the Warburtons still open-mouthed. Agnes felt she had been a bit churlish but she just could not cope with it. She had enough on her plate at the moment. She put Polly down and let herself into the flat. She looked down at the little dog who had had a really enjoyable afternoon in someone else's beautiful garden.

'Polly, this calls for a brandy and ginger ale.'

Polly's tail wagged enthusiastically. She made for her bowl.

'And a really good meal for my dear dog.'

She fed Polly, poured herself a brandy and ginger ale, sat down on the sofa and switched on the news. She sipped the drink with real enjoyment and watched Polly nuzzling her bowl around. Agnes felt perfectly content. Perhaps she was always happiest when she was alone. Perhaps, she thought with her unusual dry humour, being an addict of some sort was rather nice.

The Warburtons, she felt sure, would pursue the matter of Flat 2. They would call a meeting and Miss Horrocks would share their horror and distaste at the thought of men in drag, if that was what the Warburtons had really seen. Agnes felt she must watch out for them as well. She was rather intrigued by 'drag', at least on the television. Some of them looked more handsome as women than they did as men. So what? What did it matter? People were so interested in what other people did. Why didn't they, as teenagers said, 'get a life' and let other people do as their inclinations led them? Did this apply to drugs as well, she wondered? No, drugs killed the innocent while the guilty prospered.

The next day Agnes had callers that certainly surprised her. She had just returned from Polly's long walk which she always enjoyed when there was a ring on her door bell. Not the street door, so she knew it was one of the flat dwellers – probably the Warburtons, she thought. After her encounter with them in the hall she expected them to press again for a meeting to discuss the suitability of the two young men in Flat 2, Louise Le Mesurier's flat.

To her surprise it was not the Warburtons standing outside her door but the two young men themselves. They stood side by side, the one who had been slightly made up when Agnes had met them before not now showing a trace. Both young men looked clean and shining. Neat dark suits, collars and discreet ties. She thought they looked as if they had dressed especially to call on her, but for what? At first she just greeted them and did not ask them in.

'Good afternoon, Mr Bailey and Mr Adams, isn't it?'

Adams made a rather feminine gesture with his hands.

'How clever of you to remember our names, Mrs Turner. I somehow don't think we are flavour of the month with the others, but perhaps it will get better in time?'

Agnes backed away from the door, leaving them room to enter.

'Won't you come in? How can I help you?'

They followed her into the sitting-room and sat down on the settee side by side. Polly wandered in from the kitchen and walked over to them, sniffed their trouser legs, decided they were friends and started a tail-wagging welcome. Both men made a fuss of the dog and when Agnes apologised for Polly's over-enthusiasm, they waved the apology aside. Polly, encouraged, went off and fetched her squeaky toy and brought it back to them.

At last Agnes got Polly to lie down in her basket. This took a little time but it lightened the atmosphere. Agnes noticed that the one called Bailey was carrying a plastic carrier bag. He was obviously the macho side of the relationship and proceeded, after a rather muddled and embarrassed start, to tell their story, interrupted now and again by his companion.

Apparently they had decided to decorate the rooms of the flat, one at a time. They both loved doing the work themselves and had started on the sitting-room. Near the window they had found that the skirting board had been affected by damp and was crumbling and rotten. Instead of replacing the one piece they had taken themselves off to the DIY store and bought plastic skirting boards which were easily fixed and, unless you wished to change the colour, needed no painting.

Agnes was sinking into boredom as they took so long to tell their story until they took out what was in the carrier bag. They had found the contents of the bag in a two-foot long cut piece of the skirting board that lifted off easily, revealing a small cupboard-like hole about eight inches deep and two feet long.

The contents, when unloaded on to Agnes's coffee table, completely demolished any boredom she had been feeling. A plastic bag containing what looked like over a hundred white tablets, another small flat sealed plastic bag in which was a quantity of white powder. Six or seven brand new syringes, still in their sealed transparent packets, and a much larger parcel about as big as a pound bag of sugar containing, Agnes could only guess, cannabis. The contents of the bag lay on the table. The two men sat looking at Agnes expectantly. She had to speak.

'Well, Mr Bailey, Mr Adams, why have you brought this to me?'

'Well, Mrs Turner, you are the only one in the flats who gives us the time of day! We heard a rumour there was to be a meeting regarding our suitability. Perhaps you feel the same, but you've always been pleasant and–'

Agnes stopped the remarks in their tracks, insisting that there would be no such meeting. She was really cross about it, knew the source of the rumours and was quite determined to put a stop to them and the idea of any kind of meeting.

This seemed to relieve the pair and they moved on to the drugs they had found and what to do with them.

'You see, Mrs Turner,' explained Bailey, 'Mr Demain was very good to us, very helpful, and there was no criticism of our lifestyle, if you know what I mean. If we took this lot to the police they'd ask questions about his poor sister and good-ness knows what a can of worms we would open. We don't want that but we do want rid.'

His companion echoed him in a way that

seemed to mirror their relationship perfectly.

'Yes, we do want rid, Mrs Turner, we do want rid.'

Agnes, about to say, 'What can I do with them?' suddenly did not speak the words. She had an idea just how she could handle this. The two men were already gathering up the drugs and syringes and putting them back in the carrier bag, thinking she would say 'No.'

'I can dispose of these for you. Don't worry, I am not going to use them myself,' she said cheekily, 'but I can get them back to the source from which they came. Will you trust me?'

Their faces lit up. They looked at each other and clasped hands. Agnes was glad the Warburtons were not here and the thought made her smile a little.

'To tell the truth, we have had a little brush with the law. Oh, years ago, when we first got together, so we didn't really want to ... you know, don't you?'

Agnes's reply, she felt, made her sound like their mother or at least their maiden aunt.

'Well, I hope you have put all that behind you?'

They both answered her with wide-eyed pleadings and many promises that indeed they had. Agnes could not help thinking they were telling the truth. If they were still using drugs, either of them, they would hardly give up what they had found behind the skirting board in Louise Le Mesurier's flat. They would have kept it for their own use.

They left with many thanks and goodbyes and pats for Polly and an invitation to tea in their flat to Agnes to see what they had done up to now in the redecorating line. Agnes thanked them for the invitation, feeling she might well take advantage of it, though she felt squeamish at seeing Louise's bedroom again, though probably she would not recognise it after their ministrations. Anyway, she felt it would infuriate the Warburtons if they learned that she had been there to tea and knock on the head finally any chance of them calling this beastly meeting.

What could they object to, for goodness sake? The two young men were quiet tenants, made no noise either coming in or going out, no loud music, nothing at all to complain about, except what they themselves had termed their 'lifestyle'. What was it to do with the Warburtons, or anyone else for that matter?

Agnes knew exactly what she was going to do with the contents of the carrier bag. She had a small brown cardboard box she had kept for some reason. It was quite an anonymous box with no name or anything printed on it anywhere. She lined the box with equally anonymous bubble wrap. The drugs, including the larger pack of cannabis and the syringes, fitted in perfectly. Agnes folded the bubble wrap over the top, and put on the well-fitting lid. Brown paper neatly covered the box and she then sealed the parcel on all sides with wide Scotch tape. In thick black biro, she printed the address – Sir George Brennan, Home Leigh, Hill Side, Nr Peacehaven, Sussex.

Agnes did not know the post code so decided she would leave it. She was pretty sure the parcel would arrive safely. She was taking a day trip to London to see Madge Hillier. She would post it there. All she wanted really was to get rid of the drugs safely and who safer than the handler of drugs in bulk – Sir George! It would mystify him, perhaps unnerve him a little. At least he would wonder who knew enough about his activities to send him such a curiously apt package, and from London too! This would confuse him more, Agnes hoped.

As she had packed the drugs in the box Agnes had given her thoughts almost entirely over to Louise Le Mesurier. Never during her brief acquaintance with her did she ever associate her with drug taking. Drinking a little too much wine perhaps, but not drugs. A great many new thoughts had to be shifted round in her mind. Was Andy Weedon her supplier? Then why would he kill her? For the ring maybe? But the idea that he had mistaken Louise for her seemed to be quite blown out of the water. Or was it?

Perhaps Andy had no idea she was an addict with a good store of drugs stashed away. Then who supplied her? Certainly not Sir George Brennan. He had not even shown the slightest interest in the murder in Hove. She doubted he even registered the fact that the woman who was dead was murdered in the block of flats in which Agnes lived. Besides, she would have been much too 'small fry' to interest him drugwise, any more than the children in the schools interested him.

Poor Louise. What unhappiness could have forced her into needing drugs? And what a clever place to hide them, once she had got them. But what Agnes wondered most was who supplied her. Where did she get them?

How had the papers featured it in their headlines the day after she was killed? It seemed such a long time ago now. Agnes remembered the big black print. MYSTERY MURDER OF THE FRENCH WIDOW. That was it! How they would have loved to have been able to add to the gruesome details of the battering, DRUGS FOUND IN

FRENCH WIDOW'S HIDING PLACE.
Well, they didn't know, and as far as Agnes
and apparently the young men in Flat 2 were
concerned, they would never know.

The fact that she took drugs would not
bring her back, only injure the memory of
her more. Some people would say the police
should be told, but why? Agnes knew the
murderer had already served his sentence
for the crime. A death sentence, and his
body was somewhere rotting in the deep
blue sea.

The next day Agnes motored to London.
She posted the neat brown parcel in a post
office in Kensington that she thought would
be red herring enough. Having got rid of the
parcel Agnes felt lighter. The box of drugs
had made her feel guilty and anxious.

She called in to see Madge Hillier in the
Cornwall Clinic. Marcia and her husband
had come from Paris and had stayed two
nights. This had cheered Madge up a lot,
but she was a little depressed by the length
of time the various tests were taking and the
surgeons would not, as yet, tell her quite
what they intended to do about the
recurrence of the small lump.

'I just wish they would make up their
minds and get on with it so that I can get
out of here.'

Agnes brought her books, magazines and
fruit. She stayed as long as she could and

left Madge a good deal comforted and more cheerful.

Agnes guessed the parcel might take a couple of days to arrive at Home Leigh. When it did, she wondered how Sir George would take it, whether he would tell his wife about it. He seemed to tell her most things, and this would be such a puzzle and would probably cause him more anxiety. She would call Elizabeth and ask her to come round and see her flat, have tea with her, but she would wait till the parcel had presumably got there before she telephoned. She smiled as she thought about it.

She came out of the clinic and made her way to the car-park, where there was room for about ten visitors' cars and a special place for the doctors. Two cars up from her own was something she had not noticed on her arrival. A maroon BMW. This in itself was not the surprise. The car was backed into the space, leaving the front visible. On the shelf of the dashboard was a four-inch high plastic bulldog, the same toy or ornament that had been in the car outside Home Leigh when Agnes had arrived to tea with Elizabeth only days ago. The car was not locked, the keys were in the ignition. Was it the same car? Agnes was determined she would check if the BMW had disappeared from Sir George's drive. She could see why. The car could be traced as Andy

Weedon's. This was a brilliant way to dispose of it. Andy Weedon would never be found. His car in the clinic car-park would look as if he had disappeared in London. Andy would eventually be on the Missing Persons register. Maybe his brother would get the car. Maybe it would be used again to hawk drugs around to corrupt, to cause addiction and sometimes even to kill.

Agnes thought of the three men she had met at Home Leigh. Rich men, powerful men. If Sir George died by his wife's hand, someone would take his place, someone only too eager to see him go and profit by it. Depressing.

Agnes drove home through the mild May evening. What made people behave like this? Hunger for power? Money? The only way to cope with them in her mind was to obliterate them. She wondered whether Elizabeth Brennan would give those pills to her husband. Well, she hadn't faltered when a body had been hidden in her house and later disposed of. Agnes could only wait and see, but tomorrow she was determined not to ask Elizabeth to tea at her flat as she had thought, but to suggest calling on her at her house. That would give her a chance to check if the BMW had gone.

23

Thoughts of Pamela and Bella were never a long way from Agnes's mind. What had happened to both of them was all the fault of those three men she had met at Home Leigh. Of course there were others, but she only had contact with these three. Drugs and their supply had to be organised; they had to be brought into the country, manufactured, dispensed, sold and resold. It was a flourishing trade, dangerous, but the enormous rewards made it well worth the risk. The pushers, the little men in the trade, took the same risks, but they could not work, make money, without the big boys, the suppliers.

It was these men who had killed Pamela Roberts and made Bella Goldstein into an addict. Agnes hoped Bella was tackling her addiction now that it was in the open and the girl had the love and support of her parents. Agnes thought that she herself had not been supportive enough, so she determined she would telephone Bella, not only to offer help if she needed it, but to see if anyone had permanently replaced Andy. She telephoned. Mrs Goldstein answered.

'Oh, Mrs Turner, I am so glad you telephoned. Yes, Bella would love to see you, I am sure.'

Agnes was about to ask Mrs Goldstein to give a message to Bella, asking her to tea or to come and see her after school or whatever was convenient to her. But Mrs Goldstein hastily broke in, saying this was not possible and she thought Agnes already knew.

'Bella is in bed, I am afraid, Mrs Turner. She has a leg infection. She scratched it in the garden. She has been in hospital for three days but is now home. We have been so worried about her.'

Agnes was worried too, and wondered whether Bella was really suffering because of a 'scratch in the garden' or because she was back on drugs.

'When would be convenient? I could pop in about four today?'

Bella's mother sounded delighted with this and four o'clock that day was agreed. Agnes could give Polly a nice walk, take some water with her so the little dog could have a drink and a biscuit after her walk, and leave her in the car during her visit to Bella. She hoped she could speak to Bella on her own. She would be more open and probably more truthful than if her mother was there. Anyway she must take her chances with that situation.

When she arrived at the Goldsteins' house

Bella's mother let her in, then pointed up the stairs to Bella's room and took herself back to the kitchen where she was, she said, getting a cup of tea ready for Bella and her guest. This sounded as if she was going to leave Bella and Agnes to chat alone. Agnes made her way up the stairs and knocked on the door Bella's mother had pointed out.

'Oh, hello, Mrs Turner. How nice of you to come. I'm longing to tell you about this beastly leg and things.'

Bella lay, dressed, on the outside of the duvet, her left leg bandaged from ankle to knee. Her bare foot looked red and a trace swollen. She had, she said, only been allowed home if she promised to keep her leg up all the time.

'It's been horrible, Mrs Turner. In hospital I had this drip in my arm with watery-looking stuff and antibiotics in it. When they stopped that I came home.'

Agnes stood up as Bella's mother came in with the tray with teapot, cups and saucers and a plate of biscuits, plain tea biscuits.

'Oh Mum, no Jaffa cakes! I thought you had bought some!'

Mrs Goldstein looked at Agnes, made a little grimace and laughed as she put the tray down near Bella's bed.

'No, I forgot. You will just have to put up with these.'

Agnes noted rather thankfully that there

261

were only two cups and saucers on the tray which meant she would have the chance to ask Bella a few questions, which she certainly could not do if her mother was present. When Mrs Goldstein had left, Agnes poured the tea and sat down, drawing her chair towards the end of Bella's bed so that she could see her face. It would be easier to assess whether she were telling the truth. The questions she wanted answered were important to her. She felt Bella would tell her the truth.

After a little more chat about the hospital and school, Agnes decided to ask the girl how she had managed to injure her leg in the garden. Did she perhaps stumble? Bella played with a biscuit, breaking it up into small pieces but not eating it. She looked up at Agnes then down again at the fragments of biscuit on her plate, her face suddenly flushed.

'It wasn't in the garden, Mrs Turner. I told Mum and Dad that, but I was shooting up. They think I'm clean but I'm not really!'

Agnes felt her suspicions had been right. Did Mr and Mrs Goldstein really understand how difficult it was for their daughter to get off heroin?

'Tell me, Bella, are you having drug counselling?'

Bella shook her head. She looked suddenly sullen and withdrawn.

'Not that's any good. I'm seeing a psychiatrist. He's useless. He keeps saying, "If you really want to give it up, you will, Bella." He's fat and old!'

She mimicked the doctor's voice.

'Well, I suppose that's true, Bella. How did you get it?'

Bella shrugged her shoulders and began to eat her pieces of biscuit as if she was playing for time.

'Andy's brother comes to the school now. He came in Andy's new car just once, then he was in the old blue one.'

She went on, seeming glad to spill it all out to Agnes, someone who knew most of it already. Andy – what he was doing, where he was – seemed the most important question in her mind, and that was a question Agnes had absolutely no intention of answering. She only shook her head at the mention of Andy.

'He must be in London, Mrs Turner, still having treatment at that clinic, mustn't he? I mean, his new car has gone. He would take it and stay in London for the treatment, perhaps?'

Agnes would only nod her head, not committing herself. She was going to see Elizabeth Brennan tomorrow and then she would verify that the maroon BMW was not still parked in the drive at Home Leigh. She was almost certain it would not be and that

263

the car she had seen in the Cornwall Clinic car-park was Andy's. Unless coincidence of all coincidences had happened and two maroon BMWs had a plastic bulldog sitting on their dashboard. Pretty improbable, she thought, but she would not be happy until she had seen the space it had occupied, made sure it had left the drive.

Before leaving Bella, Agnes uncharacteristically gave the girl a quick kiss. She felt Bella had no real support. Not due to unkindness on anyone's part, just through ignorance of the temptations and influences at school and all around her.

Downstairs Bella's mother was in the sitting-room. She came to the door of the room when she heard Agnes's step. She looked bright and tranquil. She invited her into the room. Obviously she wanted a word with her.

'She seems better, doesn't she, Mrs Turner? She's been so poorly. Her leg swelled up alarmingly. She was on a drip, you know. We were worried, but it's better now. Such a nasty thing to happen. I can't think how it did!'

Agnes hardly knew what to say. Bella was under a shrink. She wondered a little about the family GP, how much he figured in the scene. Should she tell Mrs Goldstein that this was no 'garden scratch', that Bella had given herself an abscess injecting herself with heroin? She decided not. There were enough people trying to get Bella to give up using, but not the right ones.

Bella's mother thanked her for coming. She sounded genuine.

'She's so fond of you, Mrs Turner.'

Agnes smiled. Fond, or was it just that she could talk to her?

As she drove away she wondered whether it would all start again when Bella was back at school, with Andy's brother a 'willing supplier' and other pupils, probably friends of Bella's, taking advantage of the change in pushers. What would happen when she was up and about again, going to clubs, raves, parties? Would she still resist taking Ecstasy when her friends were downing a couple and encouraging her to do the same?

Anyway, Agnes did not feel it was her job to look after and counsel a teenager who had family and medical advice available. She was more interested in Louise Le Mesurier. Why the hidden drugs? Had she been an addict too?

The parcel should have arrived at Home Leigh by now. Agnes would be interested to know if Sir George had said anything to his wife, shown her the contents even. After all, he didn't keep anything about his drug dealings from her, or his disposing of bodies either. Tomorrow she had a date with Elizabeth at teatime. Then she might discover the reaction to the parcel and also find out if the BMW had gone to London. If it had, it was a very neat trick.

When Agnes drove through the gates into the large sweeping drive of Home Leigh there was no car in the drive but her own. The maroon BMW was gone. As she parked the Porsche she wondered who had driven the car to London, parked it neatly outside the Cornwall Clinic. Had they returned to Peacehaven in a car driven by someone else, or by train or bus?

So easy and so clever! Anyone who missed Andy Weedon would be deceived into thinking he had disappeared in the area of the clinic where he was receiving treatment for his birthmark, not in Brighton.

Elizabeth was as usual pleased to see Agnes.

A fine misty rain had started as Agnes reached the house and her hostess peered out at the rather grey and overcast sky. It was quite warm but it did not look as if the rain would clear away very quickly.

'What a shame, Agnes! I was going to suggest tea in the garden but I don't think this looks like clearing. The garden is so pretty at the moment.'

The two women went into the sitting-room and sat down.

'George is in London. He will be sorry to

266

miss you, Agnes. He likes you. He doesn't like my friends as a rule. He says they all chatter too much, get on his nerves. Talk about nothing but clothes, make-up and themselves.'

The usual girl came in and placed a tray of tea things on the table in front of Elizabeth. She was just about to pick up the teapot and pour tea when she suddenly stopped, reached into her handbag which was beside her and pulled out a white envelope.

'Do open it and tell me if you can come, Agnes. Then, you need not RSVP me. It will save you the trouble. We do hope you can and will come.'

Agnes removed the card from the envelope. It was an invitation to a party, a ruby wedding party. Elizabeth's and George's.

'We decided to have a "bit of a bash" as the young ones say. We may not reach our golden wedding anniversary.'

Did the meaningful look she gave Agnes confirm her decision to get rid of her husband?

Agnes thanked her for the invitation and accepted.

'Thank you, Elizabeth. A ruby wedding is forty years, isn't it? You are very lucky to have had such a long marriage. So many break up.'

Elizabeth laughed. Her laugh was rather

bitter and rueful, perhaps sarcastic.

'Agnes, you are the easiest person to talk to I have ever met, mainly because you listen and one knows what is said will never go any further. I don't think it's even discretion. I believe it is just because you would rather keep things to yourself. Is that true?'

Agnes thought about what had been said before she answered.

'Yes, I suppose you are right. When I want something to be known, like what I found out about Andy Weedon, I tell whoever I think will be the most useful and effective person, but I usually deal with things myself. I prefer that.'

They finished tea and Elizabeth took the tray out herself. When she came back, she pointed to the french windows. The sun had come out and the garden was sparkling under what was the last of the raindrops.

'Let's take a little stroll, Agnes. It feels quite warm. I want to tell you a story, my story. You have lately become so involved in our lives that I feel it is only fair you should know one or two things.'

Agnes stepped out into the garden. It was warm and the scent of flowers and the wet grass was very pleasant. The two women walked down the grass path between the herbaceous border and the rose bed. The birds sang, the garden was very peaceful.

The first words Elizabeth uttered shattered the peace of the garden for Agnes. She stopped in her tracks frozen.

'You mentioned the French widow. Andy Weedon killed her. I paid him ten thousand pounds to do it. Believe me, in my opinion, it was little enough. I wanted her dead.'

Agnes met Elizabeth's eyes after she had made this confession – although it sounded less like a confession than a self-satisfied statement about a task successfully completed. As she met those eyes, she no longer doubted the fact that Elizabeth was quite capable of killing her husband, her companion and partner of forty years. She no longer doubted Elizabeth's sheer strength of will. If she wished him gone, he would be gone.

But the drugs? After all, Elizabeth had been living on money brought in by drugs for years. Why now, why so suddenly?

'I thought Andy wanted to kill me because of the dog, because I pushed him down the beach steps.'

'Why on earth should he want to kill you, Agnes? You were of no interest to him.'

Elizabeth sounded completely baffled by Agnes's remark. Agnes tried to explain but her companion merely laughed and slipped an affectionate arm through hers.

'Let's go indoors. It's started to drizzle again and it's wet underfoot. I want to explain. We will have a drink, a very small drink. Come on!'

It started to rain in earnest and a sudden flash of lightning lit the sky, followed by a distant rumble of thunder. Agnes was thankful that Mrs Jenvy was with Polly, who hated thunder. Luckily she was doing some ironing for Agnes and she knew her help would not dream of leaving the little dog in a storm.

In the sitting-room, armed with drinks, the two women sat on the settee together. The storm rumbled on outside. Elizabeth leaned back, relaxed, and sipped her drink. Her eyes now had a faraway look, half sad, half resentful. She put her drink down on the table.

'I'll try not to make this boring, Agnes, but, as I said, you seem to have become so involved, and shown such discretion. I want to get it straight, what really happened, years ago, which led up to all this. Deaths, three already, and many more we don't know about, suicides, overdoses – a madness, and it all started like this.'

Evidently the first years of her marriage to George had been uneventful. He had, as far as she knew, been faithful. His business as an engineer had prospered, and helped by his father he eventually owned and ran the firm. George had one fault. He loved to gamble. Horses, greyhounds, the casinos, all were like a magnet to him and there came a time when he seemed only to be happy when taking risks. Elizabeth did not attempt to explain to Agnes how the business had failed, whether it was through her husband's bad management, or the fault of his partner and advisers, or whether, as Agnes now suspected, it was the continual gambling that led to the collapse and eventual liquidation of the small engineering firm. Their house in the suburbs of Nottingham had to be sold and they moved to a rather grotty small apartment in the East End of London.

Here, at this obviously painful part of the story, Elizabeth got up and poured herself another drink, looking enquiringly at Agnes who shook her head. She came and sat down again, this time with her back leaning against the corner and end of the settee so that she was almost facing Agnes as she went on.

They had lived like that for a couple of years, George's father helping out occasionally, but now reluctantly. George was still gambling away any money he could get his hands on and mostly losing. Sometimes he would have a lucky streak. These usually led to a very expensive night out. George would suffer immense regret at how things were going and indulge in a dinner at the Ritz or the Dorchester, putting their finances back to where they were before the lucky streak. 'We must live a little, for goodness sake,' he would say to her. Elizabeth tried to stop this stupidity, but that would make George bad-tempered and moody.

Then everything changed. Just how it happened Elizabeth couldn't remember, except that they were out having dinner at one of the most expensive hotels and George met these two men, Lionel Compston and Gerald Leach. George seemed to be getting on well with them. He started going out for drinks, meeting them in various bars. He made no secret of these meetings and would say, 'Meeting Lionel and Gerald tonight, Elizabeth, expect me when you see me.'

Then the lies started. They owned an engineering firm that was not doing very well. They wanted him to manage it, get it back on its feet, on the right road again.

It was no engineering firm alas.

Elizabeth Brennan got up, walked over to the french window and stood with her back to Agnes. The rain was still falling gently, but the storm had passed and here and there a small patch of blue was showing through the clouds. She came back and sat down again, this time in an armchair.

'As you probably have guessed, Agnes, Lionel and Gerald had no engineering firm. They were drug runners. It seemed to make

George alive again. Money was no longer a worry. It seemed he thrived on the risks he had to take. Going abroad, buying drugs from people who might "shop" him tomorrow, satisfied his gambling instincts. We bought this house. I insisted that it was in my name. As the money rolled in, I made him buy another house in London in my name. I was certain it would all blow up in his face and I wanted to be safe. We settled here. He put on a wonderful front, a councillor, Mayor, magistrate. Through it all I hated him Agnes, hated him. Still do. Money rolled in. I took what I could.'

There was a sudden noise from the hall, a rattle of keys, then the front door banged. George Brennan walked into the room. He smiled when he saw Agnes, a very warm welcoming smile.

'Hello, nice to see you, Agnes. I got back sooner than I thought, Elizabeth, glad to be back too. It's a jungle out there!'

'I'll get you a drink, George, you must be tired.'

Elizabeth got up. George came up to her, kissed her cheek and sat down next to Agnes. Elizabeth put a whisky in front of her husband, and gave Agnes a rueful little smile.

'How about finishing our talk tomorrow, Agnes? I'll meet you for lunch at the Swiss House. They do wonderful salads and I know you are rather a rabbit. Shall we? Or we can have something more substantial, anything you like!'

George broke in after demolishing half his drink in one swallow: 'Don't stop chatting because I've come back. Clothes and make-up and where to get the best facial massage?'

'No, it was nothing like that, George.' Elizabeth looked at Agnes and pulled a face. 'Only come to lunch if you want to be bored again!'

Agnes smiled at her and quite suddenly leaned forward and kissed Elizabeth on the cheek, a gentle butterfly kiss. Elizabeth looked at her and Agnes saw that there were tears in her eyes.

'I haven't been bored and I can't wait to hear the rest. The Swiss House, twelve thirty!'

George got up and went to mix himself another whisky, a generous one as usual. He turned to his wife.

'Why don't you let Hilton do the driving? I'll drive myself to London, then you two can drink as much wine with your lunch as you want to.'

'Thank you, George, that's very kind of you. We won't drink all that much, I expect, but we have got something to chat about, haven't we, Agnes?

Agnes nodded and thanked George as well.

The two women parted at the front door. There was a momentary silence between them.

'I can't wait to hear the rest. Elizabeth, you must have been through so much. I can't imagine what made you...'

She stopped, hurried down the steps and got into her car. She put down the window and waved to Elizabeth who was standing on the steps.

'See you tomorrow, twelve thirty, the Swiss House.'

She drove out, longing to get home. In a way she was dreading the rest of the story she would hear tomorrow, learning why Louise had had to die. She believed she knew, or had guessed, part of the story she would be told.

It would be a late walk for Polly, she thought as she drove home, but no. Mrs Jenvy was still there. She and Polly greeted Agnes with enthusiasm, Polly barking, leaping about, bringing Agnes her squeaky toy.

'I've given Polly a nice long walk. We went on the beach so she had a bath when I brought her back and that took her mind off the thunder – though there wasn't much, was there – and she's had her dinner, Mrs Turner. Haven't you, Polly?'

Agnes wondered how she had ever been so lucky as to have found Mrs Jenvy. She was, as people put it, 'a real treasure'. Her love for animals was so like Agnes's own. Agnes had told her of her many 'rescues' of animals and particularly of Polly's near-strangling. This had given her a real empathy with the dog. Polly loved Mrs Jenvy.

'You are so good to us, Mrs Jenvy. I had not meant to be so long. It was only an invitation to tea, but we got talking. You know how it is!'

Mrs Jenvy assured her it was quite all right. Agnes always paid her by the hour even if she was only sitting with Polly and she was worth every penny. Agnes totted up the hours at the end of each week. Mrs Jenvy usually said, 'Oh, no. That's too much, Mrs Turner,' and Agnes felt she truly meant it, she was no money grabber. But Agnes knew she lived by herself and didn't have a lot of money to keep the wolf from the door.

Mrs Jenvy gone, Polly cuddled, Agnes poured herself the usual evening drink she was beginning to look forward to. Brandy and ginger ale. She took it into the sitting-room, switched on the news on television. She was not at all sure she wanted to think about Elizabeth's story. This afternoon she had heard the beginning but, unfortunately, the end bit had come first. The killing of Louise Le Mesurier. What had led up to that? She must put it out of her mind until the rest of the story was told at lunch tomorrow. Elizabeth would tell the truth, Agnes knew. Perhaps that was a comfort. Andy deserved to die, but Louise?

24

The Swiss House was only a street away from Agnes's flat so she decided to walk there. She stepped out briskly along the wide pavement. Hove was full now. Summer was almost here and the holiday-makers were beginning to throng the streets and the beaches.

Brighton itself was always more crowded than Hove. It boasted more cafés, shops, amusement arcades and the pier. Hove, regarded as more select, was less attractive and had more massive white buildings, once occupied by single families with their attendant servants, nannies, chauffeurs and butlers. Now these big white houses were divided into flats, like Agnes's. Some resented the change – especially the very old.

Although the Swiss House was near to Agnes and a convenient eating place, she seldom went there. It was wickedly expensive, though the food was good. The wine list was reliable and the general atmosphere very upmarket. However, Elizabeth Brennan had made the suggestion and Elizabeth, Agnes felt, could well afford it.

It was a women's lunch place. As Agnes entered and looked around, about three-quarters of the tables were full and not a single man to be seen!

All women, all well and expensively dressed. All, at this time of day, middle-aged.

Agnes went further into the restaurant. Two women passed her, calling out to a friend.

'Ah there you are, darling. Sorry we're late.'

Their perfume wafted back to her as they passed. They greeted their friends already seated at a table with air kisses and more apologies for their late arrival. Agnes suddenly felt very bored, very trapped.

Elizabeth Brennan was already seated at a table on the far side of the large ornate room. A secluded table, which she had probably telephoned that morning to reserve for them.

She greeted Agnes by putting out her hand and grasping Agnes's.

Agnes sat down opposite her.

'I've ordered you a G and T. Is that all right, Agnes? I did remember you don't drink and drive, but I thought just one. It's

278

OK, isn't it?'

Agnes shook her head, and laughed.

'I walked here, so I don't mind a gin and tonic at all, Elizabeth. In fact I shall enjoy it!'

'Oh, you walked here and Hilton drove me. What good luck! We can drink what we like then.'

Elizabeth called the waiter and ordered two double gins and tonic. She instructed the man to bring the small tonics separately so they could add just as much or as little as they wished.

Agnes felt Elizabeth had already had one or two drinks, maybe more. She was not, or did not appear to be, tipsy, but her animated, almost giggly way of talking was not entirely like her, at least not as Agnes knew her.

The drinks arrived, not only with separate small bottles of tonic, but with a small silvery dish divided into two parts. One contained slices of lemon, the other neat squares of ice.

Luxury indeed!

'Mix your own – the way you like it,' Elizabeth said. 'Do you come here often, Agnes dear?'

Agnes shook her head, dropped three ice cubes in her drink and added the lemon before she answered. The tonic fizzed invitingly.

279

'No. I brought a guest here once. Very expensive.'

Elizabeth laughed again, dropping her ice into the gin from rather higher than was necessary. A drop or two plopped over the side of the glass on to the white tablecloth. She sipped the drink.

The wine waiter came to the table with the wine list. Elizabeth took it from him and studied it with some care, obviously knowing her way round a wine list.

'Excuse me, have you ordered food yet, madam?'

They ordered, or rather Agnes ordered by suggesting a small fillet steak, mushroom garnished. Elizabeth agreed with everything. The wine waiter then suggested a red wine which Elizabeth chose.

It was all a little chaotic – perhaps laid-back would be a better word.

At last the red wine arrived. The waiter poured two glasses and retreated from their side. Agnes was longing to ask questions about Louise. But she waited for her companion to begin. She twisted the glass of red wine gently round and round, so gently that the ruby liquid in it hardly stirred.

Then Elizabeth began:

Louise Demain had been living for some time with the man Agnes had met at the party, Lionel. When George joined the

280

'firm', Lionel had found another younger woman and Louise and George became lovers. Initially, as he eventually told Elizabeth, she was just 'a sleeping partner'. She lived in Paris. He often had to go there. Contacts for the purchase of drugs. George spoke fluent Dutch. His mother was a Dutchwoman, and he also spoke a fair bit of French. They found this useful, his new partners.

Then George had grown fond of Louise and she had demanded a more stable relationship. He had bought a flat for her in Paris. He told his wife all this.

'Louise wanted him to divorce me and marry her. Then George found she was being unfaithful to him and ended the affair. The new love was enormously rich and Louise married him! George was devastated for a while then he came back to me, and I took him back. Mad, you think – but maybe not. I'm a fairly ruthless woman, Agnes!'

And there was a ruthless intention.

'We had our silver wedding. I made him buy me Home Leigh, to make the property entirely over to me. Also the London flat. I said it was the only way I would go back to him. Then when I saw her in Brighton, going into that flat in Hove, I thought the affair had started all over again.'

Piece by piece Agnes was beginning to

extract from Elizabeth's long story the events which were relevant to the here and now. The fact that she had known her as Louise Demain showed that she had not been married to Lionel Compston but was his partner or mistress, whatever one wished to call it. That Elizabeth had been to Paris to confront her about her relationship with George explained why she recognised her when she saw her in Brighton emerging from the hairdresser's.

Agnes could understand why she had not demanded a divorce. Demands for alimony would not be simple when George's career and business was 'drug dealer and importer'. No doubt he used some cover-up to explain his income, but that would not be happily disclosed to a searching lawyer. Wrongdoing can have great advantages but disadvantages do appear now and again.

Another piece fell into place for Agnes. When Louise was murdered, Elizabeth Brennan had watched for her husband's reactions. When the news appeared with name and pictures of the now dead woman, George Brennan had not appeared to be terribly concerned, had shown no grief. His remark had been, she moved in dangerous circles, another dealer may have caught up with her or perhaps she got on the wrong side of a desperate junkie.

Surely, Elizabeth must have thought, this

was not the reaction of a man still carrying a torch for his mistress of so long ago. His next remark had gone further to reassure his wife that the old affair had burnt out. Was she wrong?

'I believe she was lucky in her marriage to Le Mesurier. He had a heavily lined wallet – in some thriving property business, I believe.' Again hardly the reaction of a grieving lover, even an ex-lover, one would have thought. But alas something had happened since to make his wife think there had in fact been more between them and lead her to believe that Louise was trying again to link up with George, even if he was not, according to him, trying to link up with her.

'One day when George was away I went into the library, "his room", he always calls it. It is his room too, I never have cause to be in there. I sometimes go in to see if it needs dusting or cleaning in any way. That morning he had left the key in one of the drawers of his desk. He never usually does that, but I usually didn't care.'

Elizabeth paused. She looked partly ashamed of her prying, partly triumphant because of what she thought she had found.

'It was after Louise's death, murder, quite some time, but I imagined she had sent it to George before she died. It was a parcel, wrapped neatly in brown paper, round a cardboard box. Neat, like her. I opened the

283

box, there was a big pack of cannabis.'

Elizabeth named one by one the things Agnes knew only too well were in the parcel, the syringes, the tablets, the cocaine. Agnes's heart began to beat rapidly. Elizabeth went on, her face flushing as she spoke.

'I knew it was from her, the sort of thing she would do, one way of telling him she was clean, off the drugs, would never need the syringes again.'

Agnes simply could not help breaking in at this point, trying to make Elizabeth believe the packet was not from Louise, but she didn't succeed.

'But surely it need not have been from Louise, Elizabeth? Was there no date, no postmark?'

Elizabeth shook her head.

'There was a postmark, but you couldn't read it, nor the date on it, but I'm sure the whole thing had been in the drawer for ages.'

Agnes tried once more by asking her the question she knew must have 'no' for an answer.

'Was there no note, no communication from Louise to your husband? Surely she would have enclosed a letter, a note, some explanation of why...?'

Her companion shook her head. Her expression had become sad now. She signalled to the waiter for more coffee, perhaps realising she had drunk rather a lot but she no longer seemed tipsy or muddled. She waited while the waiter set down a new tray with coffee pot, sugar and cream and collected up the used cups and cream jug. Elizabeth thanked him, then she turned to Agnes and mimicked her words.

'Some explanation of why? Louise was not famous for explanations, Agnes. What she wanted she took, and anyway she was dead. I had seen to that. The fact that George seemed so unmoved by her death comforted and reassured me a little, but not a lot.'

She stirred the new cup of coffee thoughtfully.

'George is good at hiding his feelings, very good. Besides, he had Andy Weedon to deal with. He accused him of stealing from his incoming supplies. Andy couldn't or wouldn't explain where the BMW had come from, or the clinic, how that had been paid for. I think Hilton dealt with him in the end. You saw him in the broom cupboard, that's how you proved yourself a true friend, Agnes, and a discreet one.'

Agnes felt completely dumbfounded. That the parcel she had sent to Sir George should have been assumed by Elizabeth to have come from Louise was indeed something of a mess. Well, Agnes admitted, as Elizabeth summoned the waiter for their bill, she could do nothing about it to enlighten any-

285

body. What she could tell, what she knew, would help no one.

Hilton dropped her at her flat. Elizabeth leaned out of the car window. She took Agnes's hand in hers, gave it a little squeeze, then withdrew it.

'Thank you for listening. Such an endless tale I had to tell, but I feel so much better for telling it. Talking helps.'

The car slid away from the kerb. Agnes watched as it drew away. She felt tired out. She longed to see Polly with her bright brown eyes, her furiously wagging tail, her affection, her optimism, her love of life. She needed no tablets to enhance it. Just a walk in the pleasant green fields, a scamper through the woods, sniffing with zest and enjoyment at the thick carpet of fallen leaves, chasing imaginary rabbits, loving the breezes, and sun and even rain.

As she took her walk with Polly she could not imagine the consequences of sending that box of drugs and gear to Sir George. There had been no note and George had no idea where the parcel had come from. He would know, of course, it was not from Louise. She, he knew, had been dead weeks and weeks before he had received it. It must have mystified him completely. But Agnes wondered, would it contribute to his wife's determination to kill him? She half hoped so. He deserved to die. He had wrecked so many lives. What did it matter if he lost his own?

Someone would take his place, she supposed. The world was full of men and women willing to trade in death, but at least he would be one less. Perhaps, if Elizabeth did kill him, there would be nobody, at least for a time, to supply Andy's brother with his little packets of pills for the schools' very willing buyers. She wondered how his two friends would take it if Elizabeth did do what she was threatening to do.

Agnes felt slightly smothered by the Brennan family and their misdoings and was quite glad to get an invitation to drinks from Flat 2 for the next evening. Having been surrounded by so much formality, it was a pleasure to find these two young men so relaxed. She need not have been worried about being sadly reminded of Louise Le Mesurier by being in the flat. These newcomers had totally changed it. The sitting-room was painted a cheerful yellow and one wall was covered by paintings of huge sunflowers. The coffee table and chairs were steel with grey upholstery and, as Agnes sank into one, she found it surprisingly comfortable. The difference was dramatic.

They asked Agnes to call them Pete and Bob. They insisted on showing her where the drugs had been hidden behind the skirting board. The new plastic addition all round the room looked neat and Agnes voted it a very good idea, though she was not fond of plastic.

'We were glad you took charge of that stuff. We didn't know what to do with it. We're not into drugs at the moment, are we, Pete?'

Agnes was amused at their casual attitude. Was it perhaps less important than she thought? But then she remembered Pamela, robbed of her life. Bella could have maybe lost her leg. No, it was important.

'Well, I hope you don't go back on it,' she said with a certain amount of severity.

Bob shrugged his shoulders and looked at Pete.

'Well, we only used grass, never injected, did we? Most of our friends use smack or uppers. I mean, it's sort of the scene now, isn't it? What can you do? It's the in thing. Another brandy and ginger ale, Agnes?'

Agnes had to laugh, she got what they meant and was amused by the huge wink that Bob gave her when he mentioned alcohol. Booze caused probably as many deaths and more crime than the drug scene. What was one to do? Humans, given the chance, would over-indulge in anything that harmed or even killed them. Smoking, drinking, doping, even eating.

The conversation turned to the other occupants of the flats. Bob and Pete had funny names for all of them.

'They will get used to us, I'm sure. We are so nice, housetrained, quiet, good neighbours, everything!'

'And very modest with it, I'd say!' Pete put in.

Agnes felt more relaxed as they stopped talking about drugs, and she almost managed to forget that in this flat she had witnessed a scene of brutality she would never forget, although with time it would become fainter, more hazy in her memory.

She did not leave until nine and was aware that she had enjoyed the atmosphere that the two men had managed to create. She was quite touched when, as she was leaving, Pete, seeing her to the door, said quietly and seriously, touching her arm, 'We thought this visit, to this flat I mean, would be a bit difficult for you. We know you found her. It must have been awful for you, especially as you knew her as a friend.'

Agnes thanked him appreciating his thoughtfulness.

On her way up to her own flat she made a very firm resolution to herself. She was not going to listen to a word of criticism about the two men she had just left. Their lifestyle was their own affair and if dear Major Warburton or his wife, or Arthur, or anybody else, had anything nasty to say about them, she would tell them what she thought of

289

their prejudices.

Polly greeted her as if she had been away three days instead of three hours. A short walk and a small meal and she was satisfied. Agnes felt her days were certainly full, and perhaps she had not been quite as supportive to poor Bella as she should have been.

Bella had telephoned the previous day and said the leg was better but, 'There will be a great big scar on it, well, as big as a fifty pence piece, Mrs Turner. I'm wondering if I should get a tattoo over it, just a little one. Perhaps a butterfly, or something small like that, perhaps a flower, a rose or a daisy. That's very cool these days. Mum will go ballistic, but I won't tell her.'

Agnes had done her best to put Bella off such an idea but she was not at all sure she had been wholly successful in dissuading her!

As if prompted by telepathy, the girl now rang again. Could she come to tea? Bella never came to see Agnes unless she had some news to tell. Agnes said yes.

Next day when she got back from Polly's walk and came in the back way up the stairs and through the glass and wood doors into her own hallway, Bella was there, standing outside her flat, waiting.

'Two men going out let me in, Mrs Turner. I said I'd come to see you. Is it all

290

right? Oh, hello, Polly, you've got mud on your paws.'

Inside the flat, Agnes gave Bella the job of getting the mud off Polly with an old wet dish cloth. Polly loved this and immediately turned the whole thing into a game, pulling the cloth out of Bella's hands and flying round the kitchen. When calm was restored Agnes made Bella sit down and tell her what was going on about her addiction, the psychiatrist and anything else of interest, including what her parents were doing. Not, she hoped, still going out and leaving her alone too much. Had she been to any clubs or raves? Was she still taking Ecstasy if she was offered it by Andy's brother or anyone at the clubs and parties?

Agnes always felt that Bella was basically a pretty truthful girl, especially to Agnes. Now she demolished a couple of Jaffa cakes before she answered and kept her eyes lowered when she did so. Not, Agnes felt, because she was not telling the truth but because she knew Agnes wouldn't approve.

'Well, one or two Es, Mrs Turner, and there's a new one, a purple lavender colour. It's great! Sam has plenty but I don't take them often, just now and again when I feel a bit tired, you know? No smack or coke, or crack, nothing like that. Bit of grass, but that's not much good if you have been taking the other, you know.'

'No, I don't know, Bella. Do your mother and father know you are still taking drugs?'

Bella took another Jaffa cake and shook her head.

'Well, no, I guess not. I don't tell them or the shrink. What's the use, they don't understand.'

'They understand one of those pills killed Pamela–'

Bella broke in, almost impatiently. 'Yes, but that was different. She was allergic to E or didn't drink enough water. I've taken it for some time, which proves I'm not allergic to it, doesn't it, or I would be dead too, wouldn't I?'

'Well, if you won't stop taking it and are content to take the risk nobody can stop you. If you die, you die, I suppose, but imagine what that would do to your parents, just as it did to Pamela's parents!'

'Yes, that must have been terrible but it won't happen to me, Mrs Turner. Sam won't let me have many anyway and he's put the price up higher than Andy. I don't like him as much as I did Andy, none of us do. Andy would let us have a couple and not pay for them till he came again, but Sam won't do that, he's a real meany.'

Agnes could feel herself losing patience with the girl. At last Bella got up to go and, as she sometimes did, kissed Agnes on the cheek and grinned.

292

'Don't worry about me, Mrs Turner. I'm no good at giving up. As long as I keep off smack I think I will be all right. Thanks for the Jaffa cakes – I love them.' And she was gone, leaving Agnes with a strange feeling that Bella knew herself better than her parents or Agnes or anyone else did. She accepted her own limitations. Perhaps she would be 'all right' as she put it. Perhaps one day the drugs would no longer be necessary to her. Meanwhile, in spite of pleadings from her parents, good advice from her friends and the help or hindrance from her shrink, she would go her own wilful way.

25

Agnes decided to splash out a little on a dress for Elizabeth Brennan's ruby wedding party. She had, as she drove up to London, absolutely no idea what colour she wanted, or what style. She set off, having had a really good look at her body. Her tummy was flat, her ankles slim, her breasts non-existent. She had always been flat-chested. Expensive bras or cheap ones seemed to do very little for her. When she was young it had worried her. But it no longer did.

Her skin, she decided, was not bad for her age – sixties was a dodgy time.

She determinedly drove to a shop in Knightsbridge. She had been there before and found the manageress very helpful and not one of those determined to sell you a dress, suitable or not.

The same woman was there and just as helpful and, after trying on half a dozen, her taste leaned towards a maroon figure-hugging dress with wide shoulder straps. Wide enough to cover a good part of the shoulders, not to look too bare. Agnes turned this way and that. She liked it! Surely shiny material made her skin look younger, less sallow?

'Ruby,' she said, doubtfully.

The saleswoman turned her head to look at her, her eyebrows raised, her lips pursed, questioningly.

'Madam doesn't like the colour, or is it the style?'

Agnes shook her head and explained that she felt she could not be the one wearing a ruby dress for someone else's ruby wedding celebration. Perhaps Elizabeth would choose ruby, or a colour near it? No, she could just imagine her not being pleased. Agnes started to search round again and at last apologised and left the shop. Agnes hated to shop alone, especially when she had no idea, absolutely no idea of what she was looking for.

She decided to have a light lunch, then go and see Madge. Probably she would decide to wear a dress from her wardrobe that the Brennans had not seen. She lunched in Goodge Street. Not because she liked the restaurant particularly but because it had its own car-park. Parking in London was always a headache.

After lunch, she collected her car and drove to the Cornwall Clinic. Agnes asked the receptionist to ring Madge's room to make sure she had not got visitors already. The girl shook her head and said Madge was free, so Agnes made her way along to her room. She knocked and entered.

Madge gave a little scream of pleasure when she saw Agnes.

She looked better, more relaxed, a much better colour.

'I didn't let you know I was coming, I was afraid you might have visitors here already.'

'No.' Madge shook her head. 'Nobody today, Agnes.'

Agnes could see she had had a hair-do with a little tint. A manicure too.

'I've had some rather good news, Agnes. Very good news. My chest X-ray is clear. The little lump under my arm, the biopsy is non-malignant after all. Thank goodness for that! I'm so very relieved, Agnes. I'll still have to have the little lump out but they say I can have it removed under local anaesthetic. I'm a bit sick of general anaesthetics, I find them a bit frightening. I know it's silly.'

'Soon you will be able to come and stay with me.'

Agnes was genuinely pleased and looked forward to having her in Hove and looking after her.

Now, for the BMW. As she had parked to go in and see Madge, she had noted that it was not in the same parking space she had seen it the last time she had visited. There was an empty space where the car had been parked. Agnes knew there was another staff parking space behind the clinic. She walked round to the back of the clinic and there it was!

A few leaves had lodged on the bonnet and in the screen wipers. The car, though new, had rather a neglected look. Agnes tried the door handles. The car was locked and all the windows were closed. She peered inside. Nothing. Only the plastic bulldog gazing out with black eyes at nothing. Why had Andy chosen that hideous ornament for such a smart and expensive car? Perhaps he liked bulldogs and thought it was nice.

Agnes drove home, as usual through heavy traffic. Mrs Jenvy was with Polly and would probably have given her a good walk. Some people were so good, so reliable, so helpful and kind. Why were the others, many others, so careless of hurting, ruining lives, not caring a fig who died or who survived? Having thanked Mrs Jenvy and said good-bye, Agnes switched on her answering machine.

Agnes had hoped that her recent conversation with Bella would be enough for the moment. She sincerely wanted to help the girl kick her habit but felt that any addict who wanted to get clean had to really want it themselves. Whether Bella was telling the truth about exactly what she was using she was beginning to doubt. The frantic telephone call on the answering machine rather added to her suspicions. She listened, turned the message back and listened again. Certainly Bella was upset.

'Sam told me, Mrs Turner. The police have found his car, you know, the lovely new one. It's been parked in London for weeks. I don't know how long. Sam says they telephoned him from London, asked him what he thought ... you know, where his brother could be all this time, leaving his car. They traced where he had bought it and got in touch with Gunnells, the agents for BMW Isn't it awful? Sam says they wouldn't say any more to him, only asked him about his brother's "state of mind". I think he's dead, Mrs Turner, I think he's dead!'

The tape stopped, to Agnes's relief. That was why the car had been moved round to the back of the clinic. Soon, if it wasn't collected, it would be impounded – was that the word? If Andy did not turn up to collect the car – and it wasn't likely that he would! – they would merely list him under Missing Persons. Well, he would be hard to find indeed! Agnes wondered whether Bella was really concerned about what had happened to Andy Weedon, why he had disappeared, or whether her main concern was that she was finding his brother Sam a harder nut to crack. Agnes felt she couldn't just ignore the girl in the state she was in but she also felt she had taken quite enough of the responsibility already.

She rang Bella's number, hoping to get her mother, and luckily it was Mrs Goldstein who answered the telephone.

'Oh, Mrs Turner, how nice to hear from you. I have been so busy worrying about Bella, I simply have not known which way to turn. She's stealing things from the house, selling them to get drugs. We won't give her money now but it's no use, no use at all.'

Like mother like daughter, Agnes thought, as Mrs Goldstein burst into tears and could hardly speak. She eventually managed to continue with difficulty, taking deep breaths and sobbing like her daughter.

'What can we do, Mrs Turner? We send her to the psychiatrist such a nice man. She doesn't go, lies about going.'

Agnes felt her irritation growing apace.

'What do you mean, send her? Don't you go with Bella? You surely don't trust her to go on her own?'

'Yes, we send her there by taxi, tell the man where to go, see her in and everything, but she doesn't turn up. He's not very pleased about missed appointments either, the doctor I mean.'

Agnes felt like speaking her mind, telling Mrs Goldstein exactly what she thought of her methods for helping her daughter break this terrible habit, but she refrained. What was the use? They had no idea.

'Well, Mrs Goldstein, your daughter is going through a very bad time. She will resist all your efforts of help. You must go to the psychiatrist with her, talk to him each time, see she attends – take her yourself!'

There was a pause while Bella's mother was obviously taking this advice on board and not finding it palatable.

'I'll try, Mrs Turner, but I'm a very committed person, you know. Committees and things, social functions.'

'Well then, I'm so sorry, Mrs Goldstein. Unless you can see, can understand how much more important your daughter's drug taking is than your social commitments, I am afraid I don't know what to say.'

Agnes put the receiver back gently, resisting the longing to bang it down hard. If it rang again immediately, she would not answer it. It didn't. Agnes felt sorry for Bella. She was perhaps old enough at sixteen to control her addiction, but the teens were a tricky enough time, without anything else to harass you. Agnes remembered her own teens in the convent. The nuns appeared never to have been teenagers. She thought how little support she had received in growing up, how the added problem of drugs would have been impossible to cope with. Thoughts of her own past had always influenced Agnes and given her empathy with her teenage patients when she had been a nurse. However, she felt she could not do any more now.

Agnes wondered if Elizabeth had heard anything about the car. Would the brother be allowed to use the car while Andy was registered as a missing person? She decided to telephone Elizabeth and ask her to coffee. She felt the less Sir George and his wife appeared to know about Andy Weedon or his BMW, the better. But someone – the police perhaps – was bound to connect Andy and Sir George eventually. Hilton, perhaps, had been the go-between. She must warn Elizabeth.

26

Two days passed and Agnes looked in the local paper to see if Andy Weedon's name appeared, or any reference to an abandoned car. An abandoned BMW, brand new, would command more interest than a clapped-out Mini!

Elizabeth was coming to coffee and Agnes had made some butterfly cakes topped with cream and strawberry jam. She was rather proud of them. She had not done much cake-making in recent years and these looked so light and fluffy no one, she hoped, could resist them. Her guest arrived at a quarter to eleven, obviously driven by Hilton. Agnes guessed this because she noticed Elizabeth made no reference to parking difficulties, which she surely would have. Parking was one of the big difficulties for any guests arriving at the flats. Luckily in the block where Agnes lived the occupants didn't appear to do much entertaining, so the difficulty seldom arose.

Elizabeth was impressed by Agnes's flat, insisting on seeing all over it.

'I love the view, and it's quite big enough for you, isn't it?'

Agnes shrugged her shoulders and laughed a little.

'It can hardly be compared with your lovely house, Elizabeth.'

Her guest looked at her with wide eyes, her mouth drawn down at the corners.

'Agnes, that house is a big nonsense. Have you seen the library? It's like the backdrop to a play.'

'Well, perhaps it is a shade overdone, but at least it's very beautifully overdone, Elizabeth. Lush-looking, and your garden is an absolute joy, you know it is!'

Agnes went to the kitchen and wheeled in the trolley.

'Butterfly cakes. I haven't seen those for ages and ages.'

'And I made them myself. What about that, Elizabeth, so you will just have to have one or you'll disappoint me.'

'Indeed I will, and how clever of you to make them.'

She had two cakes with her coffee and enjoyed them. She had her coffee in the window because she liked the view and liked, rather to Agnes's surprise, to see the cars and people going by. The sea too, and the glimpses across the sea. Fishermen, and a family opposite who suddenly started to have a row and tell the kids off, none too quietly.

'Oh, it's so interesting and lively, Agnes.

You can see nothing from our house. Yes, the garden's lovely, I know, but it's rather lonely just looking at flowers.'

Her next remark was rather upsetting to Agnes.

'When George is gone I shall sell Home Leigh straight away and get something nearer the town.'

Agnes felt she had to put in her next remark, but she knew the woman beside her had already made up her mind about what she intended to do, and do it she would.

'Sir George may not want to leave Home Leigh, Elizabeth. He seems so fond of it, it's like his stage – as you said, his backdrop.'

Her companion looked at her, her eyes slightly hooded, her gaze intense and rather deadly. At that moment Agnes thought she looked as if she was capable of doing anything.

'You don't really believe what you are saying, Agnes, do you? You know I will do what I say. Don't think about it, if you would rather not. He was still keen on her. That parcel was proof, though I never found the note.'

Agnes switched the subject to Andy Weedon, but suddenly felt unsure of exactly how far Elizabeth would go if one crossed her. Let her hear from the police or the paper where the car had been found. As usual the wise thing to do was to keep knowledge to yourself. Anything given away could be used against you. Silence was better.

'Oh, Andy. He seems to have faded completely out of the picture, doesn't he, or been washed up perhaps? His car has turned up though. We use the same garage. They are agents for BMW. The police have been asking these questions about the car, not Andy.'

As she watched her guest prepare to leave, open her bag and take out her mobile telephone and call Hilton, take out her lipstick and small mirror and repair her lips, Agnes thought with a little shiver, This is a very tough lady. Sir George hasn't much of a chance, but he probably deserves it. Agnes tried to think of Pamela.

'We must lunch again next week, Agnes. Would you like that? I so enjoyed it. I've told George he must get another chauffeur. I need Hilton. He makes visiting and shopping so much easier. The only thing is, he may want to stay with George. He's loyal to George.'

She suddenly looked at Agnes with a really mischievous smile. She traced a tiny little pattern on the shiny side of her handbag, then looked up at Agnes again.

'You needn't worry about George until after the ruby wedding, dear. I wouldn't want to celebrate it on my own would I now? You can see that, I'm sure.'

She walked across the hall towards the lift. Agnes went to follow her, but she turned and shook her head.

'I can manage the lift, Agnes dear. Don't forget our lunch date next week and I know you won't forget our ruby wedding. I'm looking forward to it so much.'

The lift doors swished open at the touch of the button and closed again after her, swish.

Agnes went back into the flat. She didn't feel like lunch. She sat down, the coffee cups and tray still on the table. Polly brought her ball and let it fall from her mouth at Agnes's feet. She bent down and picked it up and threw it across the room. Polly tore after it, sliding on the polished floor, taking the mats with her. Agnes thought of the three pills, the white pills, the replacement pills. She didn't even know if they would work.

'Oh Polly, Polly!' she said.

She wished she could rub out, take back what she had said about the three pills. She had as good as said that three amphetamines might well be fatal to a man who already had heart trouble. Why hadn't she just said she had no idea or she was rather out of date about these new drugs? Anything, rather than the remarks she had made, which she believed had strengthened

Elizabeth's confidence. Well, if she did it, she did it. Agnes could deny she had said anything, insist that Lady Brennan had not mentioned her plans to her at all and that if she had, she would have gone to the police.

Rubbish, Agnes thought. She wouldn't do anything like that. When had she ever relied on the police for anything? She would do what she always did. Wait, and say nothing to anybody. She got ready for Polly's walk. That would calm her down. Almost each time she met Elizabeth Brennan the meeting left her weary, worried. She could not really cut off the friendship with Elizabeth; basically she knew it was because she was slightly afraid of her. There was a ruthlessness about her that only showed now and again. Agnes also wondered just how much Elizabeth was and had in the past been involved in her husband's drug smuggling, whether she had ever taken any active part. She had spoken of her husband's 'vile trade' many times, but did that mean anything? Would she, if George did die, renounce all involvement with the 'vile trade'? Or would she go on working with those two men Agnes had met at the party? She had seemed to be on very good terms with them. They had treated her as one of the team, as it were. She might even try to involve Agnes in it. Agnes had learned a lot about their business, how they conducted it.

She had seen the corpse of Andy Weedon and kept quiet about it. Was Elizabeth laying a trap for her?

Agnes told herself she was being over-imaginative. It was silly to build up non-existent worries like this. She came back from her walk, partially satisfied that her forebodings were unreal, but nevertheless, when Polly was fed and watered, she poured herself a rather larger than usual brandy. She rebuked herself as she poured it, realising she was getting to look forward to this drink a bit too much.

27

The next day Agnes began to feel a little less stressed by her thoughts of the Brennans and how the whole thing would end. She felt that even knowing them was like sitting on a time bomb. She determined to take her mind off her problems by trying the Brighton shops for a dress. With great success, she found one. Pale grey georgette with tiny sprigs of black, the skirt and top separate but blending beautifully together.

'Madam has just the figure for it, just the figure.'

The young girl serving her sounded as if

she really meant what she said. Agnes carried the dress home and tried it on again in front of her long mirror. It was lovely, a good fit as the girl had said, and the dove grey colour would do nothing to detract from the star of the show, Lady Elizabeth Brennan!

After trying it on and hanging it up in her wardrobe ready for the great day, Agnes checked her answering machine and got a very upset Mrs Goldstein. Bella had been at a friend's party, it had been raided by the police and Bella had been found with heroin in her pocket. She had been arrested and her parents informed and told to join their daughter.

'She calls it "busted", Mrs Turner, and seems to take it so lightly. Her father is devastated. It's really making him ill. I don't know what to do.'

The message ended and Agnes put the receiver down. She did not bother to get back to Bella's mother. The parents seemed to Agnes so inadequate, so spineless, about it all. If it were my daughter ... she thought, but then stopped. If it were her daughter, sixteen years old, on the heavy stuff, what would she do? She didn't know. She had no advice to offer so for the moment she left it, but she felt guilty doing so. She had no idea what the penalty would be for Bella. She was a 'first offender', Agnes believed. Maybe that would help. But, heroin. That would incur a harsher penalty than Ecstasy or cannabis, she was sure. Poor silly Bella! Would she tell where she got it?

Surely there were other people, relatives or friends, they could appeal to? Perhaps they were too ashamed. Jewish families could be very close and proud of their children and their good name. Perhaps that was the reason. Agnes decided to call back later after all, but she would not know what on earth to say.

When she did eventually ring, Mr Goldstein answered the phone.

'Mrs Turner, my wife telephoned you. It's nice of you to ring. Bella is very fond of you. There was a man who came to the party. Bella seemed to know him. How a strange man got into the house I don't know. I suppose one of the teenagers let him in. Bella said–'

Agnes tried to cut the conversation short by asking what was happening to his daughter.

'She was arrested and ... sorry, there's someone at the door, Mrs Turner, I must go.'

He sounded completely distracted. Agnes put the phone down. She had really learned nothing. Was Bella being held in custody, did they allow bail in such circumstances? Agnes had no idea and she felt suddenly that she didn't want to know. She was getting utterly sick of the so-called drug culture.

She went back into the bedroom and took out her new outfit. She shook it and made the skirt shimmer. It was lined with a pale grey lining and the small slits at the sides of the patterned skirt revealed the lining as the skirt moved. She was very pleased with it. The top even made her look as if she had a little more bosom. She pushed Bella out of her mind.

Elizabeth did not forget her remark about lunch. They met during the next week, three days before the ruby wedding. She appeared in good spirits.

'Let's go to a salad bar, Agnes, do you mind? I'm a tiny bit worried about my ruby wedding. New dress, it's a trace tight here, I think, so...' She indicated her tummy area with her hands. 'So, I've been dieting a bit, just to make sure.'

Agnes smiled and they took themselves to a quite famous salad restaurant where rotund ladies ate their salad-only lunch. Then, Agnes suspected, went out and bought cream cakes to take home for their tea.

But of course, not always. Some were genuine and were trying on doctors' orders to cut down their weight.

'Can we have a salad dressing, waiter?'

Elizabeth asked the young man who put their salad in front of them with something of a flourish.

'Certainly, madam. We have a low calorie dressing.'

This was fetched and put on to the salad.

Elizabeth did not speak for a few moments, then looked up at Agnes.

'Do you mind if I ask you something, Agnes?'

Agnes shook her head and wondered what kind of question Elizabeth wanted to ask her. She looked serious.

'When you came to see George about Andy Weedon and his drug pushing outside schools and asked him to do something about it, had you seen him before?'

Agnes looked as mystified as she felt at the question.

'No, Elizabeth, I had never seen your husband before, but why ever are you asking me such a thing?'

Elizabeth poked her salad about her plate – she did not appear to be enjoying it very much. She looked up.

'Agnes, I believe George visited Louise at your flats and I thought perhaps you might have seen him.'

Agnes shook her head. She realised how important this was to Elizabeth and she tried to reassure her.

'Elizabeth, I rarely see people who call at

the flats. I walk Polly twice a day, but I nearly always use the stairs and the back door. I almost never see guests of the other flats coming in the front door or the back.'

Elizabeth shrugged her shoulders and started to eat her salad and sip her glass of white wine.

'What you are really saying is that George could have visited Louise without you ever seeing her or coming into contact with him?'

Agnes leant back in her chair and looked searchingly at Elizabeth. Could she be right? Had George been there? He could certainly have visited several times without her knowing, or meeting him coming in or out.

'Elizabeth, don't think such things. You said yourself George was almost unmoved when he heard of Louise's death. Surely if they were still seeing each other, having an affair, it would have been impossible for him to so completely hide his feelings from you?'

Her companion shook her head and stabbed her fork quite anxiously into a tomato. It burst and the contents flew off the plate on to the white tablecloth.

'Oh no, Agnes. You don't know George. He can hide his feelings absolutely when he wants to, believe me – and anyway Andy lost his life, didn't he?'

'Yes, but I thought that was because your

husband discovered he was putting money into his own coffers by stealing drugs and using the money for himself.'

Agnes began to see a little light.

'You think he killed him because he knew he had killed Louise, Elizabeth, don't you?'

Elizabeth Brennan nodded, picked up her wine glass, downed it and signalled for the waiter. He came over and refilled her glass. The new wine caught the sunlight and reflected it on to the cloth in a bright yellow circle, a golden ring.

'Yes I do, or at least I suspect it. If George knew I was responsible ... well, he is completely unforgiving. He would say nothing but sooner or later he would react, I know him.'

Agnes shivered a little, Elizabeth seemed to see her husband as a terrifying figure, waiting his time to exact vengeance and meanwhile showing no emotion other than what he wished to show. Controlled passion. Maybe, she thought, he could hear of people dying in a very indirect way by his hand and not appear to show any sorrow or regret. Whether he felt any regret, Agnes doubted. If he did surely he would stop what he was doing, renounce the drug trade and try to make good the harm he was doing by importing drugs.

The two women parted outside the restaurant. As Agnes walked to her car she saw Hilton drive up and double park, and Elizabeth got in. She waved to Agnes as they passed her.

It had been a strange lunch. The next time they would meet would be at the ruby wedding party.

Before they had left the restaurant Elizabeth had made a suggestion to Agnes that she thought was kind, but she was not at all sure she wanted to accept it. She had been invited to stay the night at Home Leigh after the party. Then she could rest, get up late if she wanted to the next morning. It would be more restful, Elizabeth said, and she added that George had been enthusiastic about the idea.

'Do stay! You'll be the only one staying the night, Agnes and we would both like you to.'

Agnes had at last agreed. She was sure Mrs Jenvy would not mind staying over in her flat and Polly would not be put out by the arrangement at all. It would be nice, if the party went on late, not to have to turn out and drive home in the dark. Also, at any time after midnight, if the party went on that long, and Agnes was pretty sure it would do so, she would prefer not to have to park her car and unlock the front door of the flats. There were so many lager louts about and other dangerous people.

It would be nicer to go home the next morning after the party.

George and Elizabeth were a quaint mixture. On one side kind and considerate and on the other drug dealers and killers.

Elizabeth had said no more about changing George's pills for some she hoped would be lethal and Agnes was very glad she hadn't. Perhaps, after all, the idea had petered out, gone out of Elizabeth's mind, at least for the moment. Agnes hoped so. This hope, however, was not at all reinforced by her friend's questions about George's visiting Louise. If she thought, and obviously she did, that George had gone back to his erstwhile lover, then his chances of living were minimised!

Agnes felt the tingle of excitement she loved to feel. Not knowing quite where you are in a situation was the breath of life to her. Boredom brought on depression and depression was the feeling that Agnes most dreaded.

Once, long ago, it had forced her into a mental home and anything, anything, she felt was better than letting that happen again. She remembered it with horror and always tried to avoid boredom and the feeling she often had of being totally alone in the world, which in fact she was.

She concentrated now on the Brennans' ruby wedding anniversary party. Mrs Jenvy agreed to stay overnight in the flat and look after all Polly's needs.

315

It would be a change to be spoilt, as she was sure she would be, while staying at Home Leigh.

28

On the morning of the great day Agnes had a telephone call from Elizabeth. She sounded in very good spirits and not at all worried by the chaos that must have been going on around her. Agnes could imagine it from the medley of background noises.

'Agnes dear, Hilton will call for you at six o'clock if that is acceptable. Then we shall have time to install you in your room before the show starts!'

Agnes was really touched by her thoughtfulness.

'How kind of you, Elizabeth, but I can drive myself there. I am sure you will be needing Hilton around.'

Elizabeth was adamant and swept aside Agnes's protestations.

'No, the parking here will be pretty dodgy. We have got permission from the police for some extra parking places outside for our friends who overspill the drive, but it won't be easy and Hilton will solve the problem for you.'

Agnes thanked Elizabeth. She felt that with Hilton, and a room arranged at Home Leigh, she was really being treated as a very privileged guest indeed and was grateful for it.

She packed a small overnight case. Mrs Jenvy was to come at four thirty and take Polly for her walk. When she got back and Polly had had her main meal of the day, it would be almost time for Hilton to call for her. Wonderful when she thought of it all.

Why was she apprehensive about this visit?

Agnes was quite impatient with herself for not being able to shake off the feeling. She put it down to Elizabeth's threats about her husband. But Elizabeth had said she would not do anything about that until after this celebration.

Would she do it at all? Agnes seriously hoped not. This party, however, was just a party and Agnes knew she had no reason to feel any apprehension of trouble. Firstly, she told herself, it was just a rather super anniversary party. She was going to enjoy it, and 'Don't think of anything else.' Though she said this to herself, and said it quite often, the feeling of foreboding would not entirely go away. Indeed, as the time for Hilton's arrival approached, it became a little stronger.

'Have a lovely party, Mrs Turner. Enjoy yourself. It sounds wonderful and it will be

317

so nice staying the night there.'

Hilton arrived on the dot of six. He was always punctual.

Agnes said goodbye to Mrs Jenvy and Polly and wished suddenly she was not going.

As she got down to the front door, opened it and saw Hilton, standing like a real chauffeur with the door of the car opened all ready for her and a welcoming smile on his face, she felt a little better and told herself to relax, for goodness sake. She thanked Hilton as he closed the door after her and received only a 'Madam' in reply. Hilton was turning into the complete chauffeur, probably under Elizabeth's expert tuition. He drove smoothly to Home Leigh and drew up outside the door. Agnes got out, went up the steps to the house door which was wide open. All the lights in the house were on. The usual maid came up to Agnes, and took her very small overnight bag from her.

'Will you come this way, Mrs Turner? I'll show you your room. We've put you in the guest room for the night.'

'Thank you.'

Agnes followed her up the stairs. The guest room was obviously prepared for her, flowers on the dressing-table and in the window, the bed turned down, towels by the bed on the dressing-table. A bowl of fruit on the bedside locker. Everything.

Agnes looked in the long mirror and smoothed down her dress over her hips. She was just as pleased with the dress now as when she had bought it. She wondered though when she should go down and join the party. Would someone call for her or should she simply just go down when she heard a good few people arrive? Suddenly Agnes felt, for her, a very unusual feeling, shyness. She wished she had someone with her so they could go down those stairs together – not necessarily a man, but a girl-friend or woman friend.

She need not have worried. Only about two cars had driven into the drive when there was a knock on her door. When she opened it, there was George Brennan. He smiled at her.

'Thought you'd be thinking it was a bit of an ordeal to come and join the mob downstairs, Agnes. Thought I'd come up and fetch you. Not many people turned up at the shindig yet, good time to come down for a quick swiftie, eh?'

'How very kind of you. Yes, I was rather dreading it, coming down those stairs on my own. Thank you.' She closed the door behind her.

They walked clown the stairs. Guests were pouring through the front door now. They made their way towards the back garden and the large marquee where people were already assembling.

The marquee was erected at the end of the garden so that the guests could walk down the beautifully cut and edged lawn beside the herbaceous border which had chosen, with the help of the two gardeners, to be in its best possible colour and bloom. The perfume from some of the flowers was quite perfect in the summery evening and the guests could be heard murmuring their appreciation. Agnes heard someone say that it was like a painting by Monet.

There were dozens of guests now, walking down the grass path and entering the marquee.

'Oh, how spectacular!' Agnes said as she left Sir George to join Elizabeth at the entrance and greet their guests. Spectacular was right.

The sun shining on the canvas of the great tented marquee gave the whole place a golden glow. Along the walls were draped swathes of ruby coloured nylon, looking like silk, pinned at the top with big flat bows like huge butterflies. On one long table covered with a white tablecloth were innumerable glasses of all types. Champagne tulip glasses, cut glass whisky glasses, wine glasses, smaller sherry glasses and engraved goblets. In the middle of all of these sparkling glasses stood a huge silver punch bowl, from which a wine steward was serving a pink punch with a silver ladle. There were all kinds of bottles, every kind of drink, alcoholic and soft.

Chairs and small tables were in plenty. So many of the guests were older, some really old, walking with sticks. Agnes supposed them to be members of the Council. Some were younger, businessmen perhaps? They all looked prosperous and their wives were well dressed and in many cases well jewelled. There was a curiously old-fashioned look to the crowd as it moved about on the decked floor of the marquee exchanging air kisses, hand clasps and handshakes. There were a few young couples but they looked out of place and appeared slightly overawed by the arrangements.

Agnes accepted a glass of the pink punch and wandered away, sipping at the drink and trying to look as if she was enjoying herself, which she wasn't. Indeed, the talk and chatter and laughter around her was deafening and she was wishing that she was at home in her own flat, looking at television with Polly's warm little body snuggled up against her on the settee. Or maybe reading a very interesting autobiography she had got at the moment from the local library. She tried to pull her mind away from thoughts of home. She was here, and she would have to stay until tomorrow morning, so that was that.

Suddenly Elizabeth appeared out of the crowd.

'Agnes dear, are you all right? I sent George to fetch you here. It's rather shy-making when you don't know many people at a party. I was worried about you.'

Agnes reassured her hostess that she was having a great time and complimented her on the decorated marquee. She remarked on Elizabeth's dress which was stunning, she said, and then added that there was not a trace of tummy showing. 'Flat as flat' Agnes said and asked Elizabeth did she think it was their salad lunch that had done the trick. The dress, as Agnes had half suspected, was ruby red, long-skirted and long-sleeved. Elizabeth laughed at Agnes's reference to their lunch.

'No, it's not that, Agnes, because it seemed much the same after it. It's because I'm very carefully holding my tummy in when I am walking about, makes you breathless!'

Elizabeth, doing her best to be a good hostess then brought to the table where Agnes was sitting a husband and wife, Mr and Mrs Watts, who bore a surprising resemblance to Major and Mrs Warburton. Agnes, after Elizabeth's departure to 'mingle' as she put it, had to put up with a very boring hour of conversation mainly of reminiscences and praise for Sir George Brennan. Mr Watts had apparently sat on the Council with the great man and though they were both retired now, he still played a monthly game of golf with him. Mr Watts made it sound as if this was indeed a great favour bestowed on him by the ex-Mayor and much admired Sir George Brennan. Their praise was extravagant.

'Nothing was too much trouble for him, no Council business too taxing or too trivial. Always punctual, always at all the meetings. A lesson to us all, he was.'

His wife said little except to corroborate her husband's words in a rather timid and breathless way: 'Oh, yes, certainly he was a lesson to everyone.'

Eventually Agnes could stand no more and got up, saying firmly that she must mingle. She was glad to lose them in the growing crowd and put her glass of punch down on another table. She was caught in this act by a man coming up to her. She remembered him at once – it was Lionel. She was quite pleased to see him, anything or anybody was better than the Watts. She rather guiltily finished placing the glass of pink punch on the nearby table and grimaced.

'I picked a glass of punch. My fault, but I don't like it,' she said half smiling and half making a little grimace.

'I was going to say, you're not drinking that muck, are you? Hold on, I'll get you a glass of champagne.'

He disappeared in the direction of the drinks area but was soon back with two tulip glasses of sparkling champagne.

'Good stuff, this. I got it for old George at thirty-five pounds a bottle instead of about forty-five. Still, he's a good mate and often does me favours.'

Agnes looked at him with interest. This was the man who had been Louise Le Mesurier's lover and who had left her for a younger woman. That was some years ago. Maybe Lionel had deteriorated a bit since then, maybe he had once been attractive. Now he was rather overweight, red-faced and with a large patch of scalp showing where the hair was receding. George Brennan was certainly the more attractive of the two men. He had kept his figure. He was not red in the face and had a full and well-kept growth of wavy white hair. George, Agnes felt, was a vain man and this had probably gone a long way to making him watch that he did not get too fat, though Agnes had to admit she had not seen him holding back very much on the booze.

'Is there going to be anything to eat, Lionel?'

Agnes was beginning to feel hungry. Lionel laughed.

'Wait about two minutes and all will be revealed.'

Almost as he said the words a curtain was pulled back along the far side of the marquee and, as Lionel had said, all was certainly revealed. A huge buffet of magnificent proportions. Two tables of goodies, in fact everything was so beautifully arranged and prepared it reminded Agnes of her trip with her dear Bill to Las Vegas and their one dinner in Caesar's Palace. No champagne fountain, but that appeared to be the only thing that was missing. Chicken, ham, sliced cold lamb, beef, venison, very appetisingly displayed. Pineapples, ready cut, flanked by ripe plums and all manner of exotic fruits and vegetables. White hearts of lettuce nestled against sliced avocado. Melons, small and delicate, filled with lemon mousse. Large slices of red watermelons. Pears, apples, polished and shiny. Oranges, sliced lemons and limes. The foods were all arranged in colourful and geometric patterns. As the curtains pulled back revealing the food, six or seven hired hands carried in pedestals of flower arrangements. Agnes had thought, as she looked around the marquee, that it was strange there were no flowers. Now they came in and were placed in prominent positions.

As this happened, suddenly the whole marquee was illuminated. By now dusk was gathering outside. A great chandelier with plastic, one presumed not glass, drops, all different colours, had been cleverly connected to the house electrically and now began to revolve slowly like a huge strobe lamp, throwing its colours, ruby, green, gold and blue all over the sides and roof.

Everyone started to clap and the servers moved behind the buffet. It was certainly, as Lionel said to Agnes as they queued up, 'Some party!'

When they had filled up their plates with the delicious cold meats and salads, rather to Agnes's surprise, Lionel followed her back to a table for two and smiled as they put their plates and cutlery down.

'I'll go and get a couple of glasses of white wine for us to have with this. I know one of the good ones.'

'Because you got it for him yourself?'

Agnes laughed as she teased him. She felt pleased he had decided to sit with her. He was an easy companion, drug smuggler or not. He was back within a short time and put the two glasses of white wine beside their plates of food. He tasted it and shook his head a little.

'Bit of an edge to it for this food, but next time I'll try and find a nice cold Samos, rather more a country wine than this. I got that for George as well – in fact I got all of it.'

'You know your wines by the sound of it, Lionel.'

He nodded, 'Yes. I was brought up in Italy and was drinking wine and water when I was six with my Dad asking me what kind of vino it was, where from etc.'

Quite suddenly he brought Louise Le Mesurier into the conversation. He seemed to hesitate and stumbled a little as he tried to mention her name, tried to do it casually.

'Louise Le Mesurier was killed in your block of flats, wasn't she? Not very nice for you – you knew her a bit, didn't you?'

'Yes I did, a little bit, and so did you, I believe?'

Agnes found this turn of the conversation rather embarrassing and was not pleased the subject had been brought up.

'Yes, I dumped her for someone else, younger. I think I always regretted it. Then she and George fell for each other and that was that. Did you get on well with her, Agnes?'

Agnes also hesitated before she could bring herself to reply.

'Yes, I did. We only went out to a dress show and a couple of lunches, but yes, I liked her. I found her body.'

'Yes, I'm sorry I brought it up, bad-mannered of me at a show like this. George was gutted over her death, wouldn't show it, of course. Elizabeth thought the affair was over, but it wasn't. He put on a good show of it meaning nothing to him, but he was gutted.'

Agnes shook her head. She wished the subject of the French widow had not arisen, but she had to say one more thing before she stopped Lionel talking about it.

'Don't be too sure that Elizabeth believed the affair was over. She was suspicious and did not trust George.'

'Really? I thought he had managed at last to convince her.'

Agnes shook her head again and frowned at him.

'I would rather not talk about this, please. Louise was just beginning to become my friend and Sir George and Elizabeth are certainly my friends now. I would rather not talk about their personal lives.'

Lionel looked at her for a few seconds without saying a word. Then he put out a hand and covered hers.

'Quite right. It was in bad taste to even mention it. Sorry I did, Agnes, but I was just curious.'

He got up, collected the two empty wine glasses.

'I'll go look for some Samos. I know there is some, because I got it for him. Must add that bit!'

He moved away towards the wine table. Agnes wished she had not mentioned suspicions. If Elizabeth did this terrible thing to her husband Lionel might now suspect her of doing something to cause George's heart attack.

Lionel came back with the wine and they continued their meal. Not another word was said about the affairs of George and Elizabeth. Lionel was an entertaining conversationalist. The chatter around them, which had been partially silenced by the arrival of the food, began to grow increasingly animated. Some guests went up for more food, and the serving plates became more and more depleted.

'Strawberries and cream with a sprinkling of sugar?'

Agnes said yes and Lionel fetched two portions. The Samos went perfectly with their lovely taste.

'I know the music will start in a minute.' Agnes's companion gave her a little mischievous smile. 'I bet, knowing George, it will be something from *The King and I* or a Julie Andrews number. You'll see, Agnes, you'll see!'

He was quite right. As Julie Andrews burst into song, he burst into laughter.

'Don't tell me, you got him all the records or all the tapes!'

Agnes had not felt so relaxed and at ease since dear Bill her husband had died so tragically.

'Come on, Agnes, we've got to dance.'

They joined others on the carefully prepared floor. The dancing was sedate, old-fashioned. No reason for any Ecstasy or crack here, Agnes thought. But then again, how many of them were on sleeping pills, anti-depressants and goodness knows what? As a nurse Agnes knew how many people were dependent on tranquillisers. What was the difference, she wondered as she danced with Lionel? What was the difference? Perhaps the drugs were more dangerous in the hands of the young, more exciting. That was why these drugs went in and out of fashion.

Lionel looked down at her as they danced.

'Very serious face, Agnes. Are you thinking what I imagine? About the things we supply?'

Agnes nodded and her face remained serious.

'It's up to people, Agnes. They can take it or leave it. You have obviously decided to leave it. But some don't and that is their problem, and not mine.'

'What about children, Lionel, who do it for fun?'

He shrugged his shoulders and his mouth was grim.

'Up to the parents, Agnes. Up to the parents. If they looked after their kids better, it wouldn't affect them.'

In spite of his kindness to her this evening Agnes could sense the sheer ruthlessness of the man she was so near as they danced. Had Louise fallen in love with this ruthlessness? It was in George too and in his wife Elizabeth. They would set the bait and the people would get hooked. Well, that was entirely their affair. They would kill to get themselves out of trouble and anyone who encroached on their territory would be dealt with. It was almost impossible to believe that she was spending such a pleasant and agreeable evening with such a man. But in fact she was almost sorry that the party had to end.

Now it was dark, Agnes was glad she was staying the night and did not have to face the journey home. She felt tired but rather happy and pleased with herself and she knew the reason was because of Lionel's attention and laughter.

How could she expose anyone else? She knew what he and George and Elizabeth did to make their lives rich and prosperous. Yet she had spent a happy evening in their house and with one of their team!

29

The anniversary party went on and on. At about ten o'clock a few of the less hardy souls thanked their hosts and said 'Goodbye' and limped out. Some said, almost apologetically, that they didn't stay out late, or that their husbands or themselves didn't like driving in the dark, or any excuse rather than that they were getting too old for dancing and were tired out.

The dancing went on and Agnes, because she was staying the night, was rather a captive member of the party. Lionel, with many apologies, had been called away. She tried to stifle her many threatened yawns and decided on no more dancing, although she had several would-be partners. She sat herself down at a table for two, the other chair vacant, having fetched herself a lemonade and lime.

At about eleven thirty, two smaller food trolleys appeared with soup cups of cold consommé, sitting in saucers of flaked ice, and tiny but delicious-looking ham and lettuce sandwiches. In spite of the feast a few hours ago, the new offerings were greeted with enthusiasm, especially the cold soup.

Agnes was certainly going to pass on this when suddenly Sir George appeared at her table carrying two consommés. Though Agnes politely refused, he set one bowl, clinking in its ice bedding, in front of her and the other in front of the opposite chair and sat down with rather a tired thump. He did not attempt to eat the consommé.

'Agnes, I'm sorry but I have not been able to have a chat with you the whole evening.'

He looked round at the few dancers, barely any now, and the few eaters and gave a huge yawn.

'We thought serving this would indicate the party was over and I think it's working, don't you?'

Agnes nodded and tried to be as non-committal as she possibly could. Out of courtesy she spooned up a little soup.

'It's been a lovely party, George, and so beautifully organised. The marquee was such a delightful surprise when you came into it. Everybody was exclaiming. And that clever way of doing the buffet!'

He looked pleased and pushed his consommé to one side, leaning back tiredly in his uncomfortable chair.

'I'm going to get a whisky. Can I get you a drink, Agnes? Other than that?'

He looked enquiringly at the glass of lemonade and lime in front of Agnes. She shook her head and thanked him. He got up and as he went towards the other side of the marquee Agnes noticed he weaved a little. She guessed quite a few more whiskies and champagne had preceded the one he was fetching now. She could see too that the barmen were cleaning up, packing the glasses away. She noticed George pouring his own drink and the whisky, when he brought it back to the table, looked dark, dark amber. If there was any soda or water in it, it was just a dash.

As he walked back to the table two of the remaining guests, husband and wife, grey-haired, had embraced him. The woman kissed him, the man patted him on the back and shook his hand. They, Agnes noticed, as they left the marquee, were weaving more than slightly. She hoped neither of them would be driving home, but she felt too tired to do anything about it.

Though Sir George was not walking very steadily at least he was already home and not having to drive anywhere.

'Let's go indoors and finish our drinks in comfort. They can get on with cleaning up and take that damn chandelier down. Have you ever seen anything so awful?'

Agnes was completely at a loss as to how to reply to this. She had a feeling that the offending chandelier might have been the choice of Elizabeth. If it wasn't Sir George's, who else could have chosen it but his wife?

He was staring morosely into his whisky and did not seem to notice that Agnes had not replied at all.

'Louise would never have chosen that garish thing. Her taste was perfect, always, always perfect.'

He took another swig of his whisky and got up.

'Let's go in, comfortable in there, better.'

He started out and wavered a little. Agnes put out a hand to steady him. She was wishing she was anywhere but here at this moment. She looked round for Elizabeth. She was nowhere to be seen. George passed the long bar table, now almost cleared, and held out his glass to the barman. He took the glass from the rather shaky hand, looked at Agnes, a meaningful look as if to say 'He's had enough already', but poured some more whisky into the glass and added a good measure of soda water from an open bottle on the table. While he was pouring it, Sir George put his hand over the top of the glass. Some of the soda water splashed on to his hand. The barman again looked at Agnes and shrugged his shoulders as if to say 'I did my best to make it a bit weaker', which obviously was his intention.

'Don't drown the bloody whisky, for God's sake.'

George scowled irritably at the barman.

They went into the sitting-room and

Agnes was as glad herself as her companion appeared to be to sit down in a comfortable chair and be relieved of listening to the dance music.

'You see, Louise was perfect. The only perfect woman I ever met. She was gentle, quiet, not bossy.'

He waved the glass in the air and some of the contents spilled on to his trousers. He brushed it off.

'You met. You knew her, Agnes, didn't you say?'

Agnes shook her head. She was longing to take her shoes off, go to bed. She felt deadly tired and trapped.

'Yes, I did, but not very well. We only went to a dress show and lunch together, George.'

He gave a long, long sigh, drank the rest of the whisky and put the glass safely on a side table.

'She killed her. Thinks I don't know but she did. Elizabeth. Well, got Andy to kill her. I know, I know, I know!'

He leaned back in the chair, closed his eyes and began to snore. Agnes relaxed back too, but at that moment Elizabeth came into the room. She sat down as thankfully as Agnes and her husband had done.

'I've had a time of it. Marie Howes had a shocking migraine. She was vomiting and had a really frightening headache and couldn't see properly.'

Agnes was immediately sympathetic and understanding. Elizabeth really looked tired and stressed out.

'The party was a great success though, wasn't it?'

'The food was wonderful, and the marquee! I have never seen such beautiful decorations. Don't you feel very pleased with it all, Elizabeth?'

Elizabeth smiled wanly and pushed her hair back and smoothed her forehead as if her head ached.

'Yes, I suppose so. It was too big though, too many people. We shall know better at our golden, won't we, George?'

George sat up. Maybe it was the sound of her voice.

'Yes, you're right, Elizabeth. It was too bloody big, that's true.'

'No need for that language in front of Agnes, if you don't mind, George. No need at all.'

Her husband apologised. Agnes excused him at once. Indeed, she was aware how he was feeling. She felt utterly worn out with the party herself.

'We are all tired and if you will excuse me I think I will go to bed in my lovely bedroom. Thank you for putting the flowers there and making it so nice.'

Elizabeth got up and asked her if she

would like a hot drink or some milk when she was ready and told her there were biscuits and fruit by the bed if she should feel like them.

As Agnes mounted the stairs to the bedroom she was very aware again of how she wished she were at home in her own flat, in her own bedroom, in her own bed with her own things around her and Polly cuddled up beside her, warm and uncomplicated.

'I'm getting old and set in my ways,' she said aloud to her reflection in the mirror of the dressing-able as she started to clean off her make-up. After a shower, she was just getting into bed when there was a light tap on the door.

It was Elizabeth. She came into the room carrying a steaming hot drink of some sort.

'Forgive me, Agnes. I know you said you didn't want anything and don't please think I am getting senile, but I think a hot drink does help you sleep. I've made you some Horlicks.'

She placed the steaming cup on the bedside table, gave Agnes a quick kiss and left, closing the bedroom door behind her very gently.

Agnes got into bed and drank the hot drink. She had not tasted Horlicks for ages and the milky taste was very pleasant. She finished the cupful then cuddled down in the unfamiliar bed. Then, whether it was tiredness or the hot drink, she sank, almost at once, into a comfortable dreamless sleep.

30

When Agnes opened her eyes it was morning. She could see the sun was shining round the edges of the drawn curtains, still making the room dark by their thickness. She stretched luxuriously. Agnes was not a sound sleeper. Usually she woke up during the night once or twice, although she dropped off again pretty quickly, but this night she had slept, as it were, round the clock. She was just beginning, rather sleepily, to wonder what time it was, when there was a tap on her door. She called, 'Come in', and the maid came in carrying a tray with teapot, milk jug, cup and saucer and sugar basin. Pink flowers on each matching piece of china. It would be pink for the pink bedroom. Agnes could not help a small grin. When the Brennans did a thing, they did go slightly over the top in their efforts to do it properly.

'What time is it, Maria? Late, I am sure.'

'Lady Brennan said to let you sleep in, Mrs Turner. It's just quarter past nine. Shall

I pull the curtains?'

Agnes was appalled. She could not remember 'sleeping in', as Maria had put it, before in her whole life.

'I must get up at once. What will they think of me?'

The girl smiled. She put the tray down and swung the top of the rather ornate bedside locker nearer to Agnes.

'Lady Brennan and Sir George have got a Do Not Disturb card on their door, though he was up and dressed quite early. Well, about eight o'clock. He came down to the kitchen and had tea with me.'

Agnes sank back on her pillows reassured by the news of Elizabeth still being in bed and enjoyed the luxury of early morning tea from the pink rosebud cup. After she had finished the tea she got up, had a quick shower and dressed. She was not over-worried about the lateness of the morning. Mrs Jenvy was staying till lunchtime with Polly and Agnes had left her a cold lunch all ready in the refrigerator.

She packed her small overnight bag, looked round the room to make sure she had left nothing behind, put a five pound note in the envelope she had brought with her, wrote 'Thank you, Maria' on it and put the note on the little rosy tea tray. Then she went downstairs into the sitting-room. Sir George was sitting, upright and tense-looking, in a charming Hepplewhite chair near the french window. He was gazing down the garden. All signs of the marquee had gone. The gardener was busy raking the lawn where it had stood. Agnes was amazed that she had slept through what must have been a considerable amount of noise. Sir George noted her surprise and reacted to it.

'They were very good. They worked all night, that was in the contract, they were very good.'

He looked at his watch and nodded. He looked pale and pinched and older. He rubbed his forehead.

'Is Elizabeth still sleeping, Sir George? It's ten past ten. Shall I go up and...?'

He got up and steadied himself by putting his hand on the arm of a chair. Agnes wondered if it was still last night's alcohol that was affecting him, or had he taken more?

'Are you all right? You look a little pale and...'

He waved her hand away, held out to help steady him.

'Yes, Elizabeth is still sleeping. We will go upstairs.'

He went up the stairway very slowly, holding firmly on to the bannister rail. Agnes followed him. Her heart was beating fast, and she felt very faint, yet she didn't know why. Had he discovered his wife's plan to kill him, had he looked too closely at the tablets? They arrived at the closed door. He opened the door and they both entered the room.

Agnes had not been in this room before. The thick curtains were still drawn, and the sunlight filtering round the edges did not let in much light. The far bed was rumpled and unmade. The duvet was pulled well up to Elizabeth's chin. She was lying on her right side with her hand under her face, her eyes closed. George crossed the room and drew back the curtains. The sunlight flooded the room, lighting Elizabeth's face.

George Brennan went closer to the bed where his wife lay. He drew down the duvet away from her neck and shoulders. The frilly shoulder straps of her nightdress were still in place. Around her neck were purple and red bruise marks. Agnes looked in horror. Her nursing experience told her that without any doubt Elizabeth was dead and, though Agnes was no pathologist, that she had been strangled.

She looked up at George. He was looking down at his wife then his gaze shifted to Agnes, expressionless.

'You did this to her, you did, Sir George!'

He nodded but did not speak. He carefully replaced the duvet, tucked it up where it had been when Agnes entered the room. Elizabeth looked again as if she were asleep, pale but asleep, peaceful.

'She had Louise killed, Agnes. I never loved anyone all my long life as I did Louise and she had her battered to death, her poor sweet head battered.'

He moved suddenly away from the dead woman to the locker beside his own bed. It took Agnes a moment to realise what she was seeing on the bedside table. Then she took it in. There, arranged in a neat row, lay one orange pill, one yellow, three white, all similar in size and shape. He picked up the orange pill. There was a glass of water half full. It was all so neatly set out. No one else could have done it but the dead woman in the bed so close to them.

Agnes went round towards him but he waved her back as he had downstairs when she had put out her hand to try to help him.

'Elizabeth always did this, laid them out in a row. Glass of water, everything. She always did it, it's for my heart and blood pressure.'

He swallowed the orange pill and picked up the yellow one, took a drink of water and looked across at Agnes.

'Don't take any more, that will do for now.'

He looked at her and laughed and picked up the three white pills.

'Don't you think I know what these three are, Agnes? She wanted rid of me and I wanted rid of her when I found out what she

343

had done to Louise.'

He suddenly threw the three pills into his mouth, finished the water, banged the glass down and walked across the room to the door. At the door he turned and faced Agnes, almost smiling.

'I hope these work and kill me. If they don't I'm in a lot of trouble, aren't I?'

Agnes stood frozen by Elizabeth's bed. She thought if she moved she would fall. She watched him. He went out into the hall and then turned back and spoke once more to her.

'Call someone, an ambulance or something, for both of us, will you, Agnes? And thank you.'

Agnes heard him cross the hall, heard him reach the top of the stairs. Then she heard him cry out.

'Oh, my God!'

She ran to the door and caught just a glimpse of him holding his chest, then saw him fall, straight forward down the stairs to the bottom.

Agnes went downstairs past George's body to the telephone in the sitting-room. When she had succeeded in stilling the shaking of her hands a little, she picked up the receiver. She looked out of the glass doors into the garden before she dialled. The border of flowers was just as beautiful as ever. It must have rained in the early morning because a lovely smell of fresh cut grass was drifting through the open door. The gardener was trimming the edges of the lawn.

'Will you send an ambulance, please, to the home of Sir George and Lady Brennan. Home Leigh, Peacehaven. Yes, there has been an accident.'

Agnes put the receiver gently back in place and walked forward to get a wider view of the radiant flowers and feel the peace of the unknowing garden.

She imagined, as she stood there, saying in court, 'No, I can hardly say I knew them all that well.'

She also thought the ambulance was taking a long time to come – but then, she went on to think it really didn't matter how long it took.

The publishers hope that this book has given you enjoyable reading. Large Print Books are especially designed to be as easy to see and hold as possible. If you wish a complete list of our books please ask at your local library or write directly to:

Magna Large Print Books
Magna House, Long Preston,
Skipton, North Yorkshire.
BD23 4ND

This Large Print Book, for people
who cannot read normal print,
is published under the auspices of

THE ULVERSCROFT FOUNDATION

Other MAGNA Titles
In Large Print

LYN ANDREWS
Angels Of Mercy

HELEN CANNAM
Spy For Cromwell

EMMA DARCY
The Velvet Tiger

SUE DYSON
Fairfield Rose

J. M. GREGSON
To Kill A Wife

MEG HUTCHINSON
A Promise Given

TIM WILSON
A Singing Grave

RICHARD WOODMAN
The Cruise Of The Commissioner